W9-CCI-258

TELL ME SOMETHING REAL

TELL ME SOMETHING REAL

CALLA DEVLIN

atheneum

NEW YORK LONDON TORONTO
SYDNEY NEW DELHI

An imprint of Simon & Schuster Children's Publishing Division
1230 Avenue of the Americas, New York, New York 10020

The text for this book was set in Chaparral Pro.
Manufactured in the United States of America
First Edition
10 9 8 7 6 5 4 3 2 1
Library of Congress Cataloging-in-Publication Data
Names: Devlin, Calla, author.
Title: Tell me something real / Calla Devlin.
Description: First edition. | New York : Atheneum Books for Young Readers, [2016] | Summary: "The three Babcock sisters must travel to a Mexican clinic across the border so their mother, ill with leukemia, can receive alternative treatments. The sisters' world is about to shatter under the weight of an incomprehensible betrayal . . . an illness far more insidious than cancer that poisons their home"—Provided by publisher.
Identifiers: LCCN 2015039224
ISBN 978-1-4814-6115-3
ISBN 978-1-4814-6117-7 (eBook)
Subjects: | CYAC: Sisters—Fiction. | Mothers and daughters—Fiction. | Leukemia—Fiction. | Betrayal—Fiction. | Family secrets—Fiction.
Classification: LCC PZ7.1.D488 Te 2016 | DDC [Fic]—dc23
LC record available at http://lccn.loc.gov/2015039224

For my sister, Robyn

PART ONE: *Symptoms*

One

Neighbors call us brats, unruly yelling monsters who pick fights with their children, litter their lawns, and scream at night when we should be asleep. We hear "Where is your mother?" daily, a question as boring as bedtime prayers. Adrienne, my older sister with the filthy mouth, always yells back, "She's dying, so why don't you shut the hell up?"

Adrienne is beautiful; her strawberry-blond hair and yellow sundress disguise her poisonous tongue. A cream puff with tacks inside. As we walk to the car, a tidy row of deceptively innocent-looking girls, I trail behind like an afterthought. I want to be a mixture of my sisters, gathering fragments and putting them together to create a mismatched whole. Unapologetic like Adrienne. Gentle like Marie.

Adrienne takes after our mother, inheriting her cornflower-blue eyes, high cheekbones, and full lips. She rides shotgun. Marie and I cram in the back, where I watch Mom's hair whip around her face in the rearview mirror. She commits her gaze to the road. I want her to glance up and blow me one of her rare and elusive air kisses. I rest my head against the window and evaluate the sky. Dark clouds cluster together as if they are scared to be alone.

San Diego is a strange mix of border town and resort. As we drive through the neighborhoods, I can identify the rich from the poor with ease. The run-down houses with cracked stucco blur into larger, freshly painted versions of themselves. Some streets are tree lined; others are dusty and filled with potholes. American flags wave at the major intersections, a constant reminder of the bicentennial and recent end of the Vietnam War. Fire hydrants have lost their bright yellow color in exchange for a more festive red, white, and blue. It's 1976—the most significant year of the twentieth century. Fireworks trump the moon walk.

I love the car, the simple act of being in motion. Marie climbs over the emergency brake and turns on the radio. Sparing us from her beloved disco, Adrienne takes requests for stations, and we sing along to Neil Diamond and the Carpenters. I pretend that we're taking a road trip. A vacation to the Grand Canyon or Lake Michigan or Mount Rushmore. I sing loudly.

"I love your voice, Vanessa," Mom says.

Adrienne agrees. "You have a goddamn angel voice."

The highway curves against the ocean, the shore so close that the salt water stings our eyes. Mom tells us that if we look hard enough, we might see dolphins beyond the breaks. Marie and I stare for what feels like hours, dying to see the arched gray backs emerge for a brief moment before disappearing into the surf. Adrienne says that she's more interested in the debris floating in the waves: logs, seaweed, a broken surfboard. She wants to see sharks and teeth.

We pull up to wait in line for the border crossing. Adrienne blasts the radio until guards glare at us. She stares right back, smiling as she runs her tongue over her teeth. She is seventeen and defiant, confident now that she's going to be a senior. Mom looks at the guards and then at Adrienne before turning down the music. Being blond makes the crossing effortless. A guard waves us right through. We're halfway there.

Mom says Tijuana looks like a city that's been bombed. In the streets filled with pedestrians, our pace slows. We pass refrigerator boxes that house families. Children younger than me, younger than Marie, who is nine, run after the car, begging.

"Be grateful," Mom says.

Marie leans against the window, needy, the youngest. "When are we going to eat?" she asks. She wants a bottle of Coke and a burrito.

Mom answers, "When we're out of Tijuana, honey."

My father told me that Mom's symptoms began when she was nineteen. They were students at UCLA. She studied nursing, and he studied architecture. My mother had a tumor. A small, ugly bump on the back of her neck. Dad said it was the only ugly thing about her. She explained that it was cancer and had it removed. Except for the faded scar, they almost forgot about it, until five months ago, when she told Dad about the leukemia. Now cancer possesses us; we are its hostages. We occupy a world of illness. Rooms filled with closed curtains, a kitchen sink overflowing with dirty dishes. We are ungrateful. We don't appreciate the present or the past. We want more, and each unmet need germinates into a nagging resentment, multiplying like infected cells.

Laetrile is cyanide. Its origins seem harmless: apricot pits. It should be nutritional, like a vitamin or dietary supplement. A few years ago, a bigwig doctor declared it the miracle cure. Others call it poison. Thousands of people diagnosed with cancer—mostly blood cancers—go to Mexico for Laetrile treatment, staying in the clinics for days or weeks or months. It is illegal in the United States.

At first, we visited the Mexican clinic weekly, staying a night at a time. We learned a handful of phrases: "*por favor*" and "*gracias*" and "*donde esta el baño?*" Bilingual in medical terminology, Mom manages communication, freeing us from doctors and details. We like the children at the clinic because they are as loud as us. They don't appear full of fear. They don't pity us for having a sick mother. Their parents don't banish us from their houses because Adrienne utters phrases like "shit-faced rat fucker." Later I realize how easy it is to simplify people when you don't share a common language. When you can't ask questions and understand answers.

At the clinic, Mom has found a community among the patients. She improves her already excellent Spanish. There, nurses take care of her while we lounge in the courtyard looking out at the ocean as though on holiday.

I don't want to believe Mom is as sick as the others. When we first came to the clinic, she looked so much better than the other patients. She had color in her cheeks and enough energy to shop in Ensenada. Now she doesn't feel well enough to ride her bike; she stopped visiting with friends; she threw out her makeup. Mom is sick, but her illness is abstract. My parents are strained with each other, always tired and preoccupied with something larger than our family—the grief of living each day as though it could be the last.

Once we pass Tijuana's crowded streets and finally arrive at the clinic, Mom disappears upstairs. We sling our backpacks over our shoulders and cut through the kitchen into the courtyard, pausing so Adrienne can sneak cold bottles of Coke from the fridge.

"We won't be here long," she says. "It's just a blood-work day. An hour, tops." She stretches her long legs on one of the chaise lounges and pulls out her arsenal of fashion magazines, pining for peasant blouses, wrap dresses, and jumpsuits. Like her idol, Stevie Nicks, she wraps her hair back with a scarf.

As I read one of my Agatha Christie mysteries, the riparian tree casts shadows across my body, a temporary tattoo of leaves. I try to concentrate on the book, on the perils of the Orient Express, but the breeze flutters the pages, disturbing my already poor concentration. I never understand what happens to Mom upstairs, where they insert needle after needle into her arm, taking out blood and pumping in medicine. A war rages inside her, white blood cells against furious red, crowds cheering for life or death. A spectator sport too complicated to follow.

Marie can't sit still, too busy with her virgin saints, torched maidens engulfed by flames, that have obsessed her since Mom's diagnosis. We aren't Catholic, not even churchgoers. Until the diagnosis, we only spoke of God in profane terms.

Copying Saint Lucy, a waif of a girl who carried her gouged-out eyes on a plate, Marie walks with her eyes closed, stumbling over calla lilies and gardenia bushes.

"Park it, Marie. I'm sick of this," Adrienne says.

"Sick of what?" Marie pops open her eyes and blinks in the sun.

"All of your bumping around. Come here." Adrienne pats the vacant chair next to hers. "I have something for you." She spills out the remaining contents of her backpack.

"What do you have?"

Adrienne hands her a plastic box. "It's a Make-Your-Own-Rosary kit." She taps the box with her finger. "See the beads?" She kisses Marie's cheek. "Now sit down."

Marie organizes the beads by color, rattling off their

meaning: violet for penance, green for hope, red for love, and white for purity. She leaves the black beads in the box.

I point to the sky. "Here's the storm."

"You should do the weather on TV." Adrienne smirks. "It's like you're psychic."

I shoot her an I-told-you-so look when rain splatters her magazine. We can't pack up fast enough. I hold my hand out to Marie. "Come on, you can play with that inside."

In the lobby, we gawk at some newcomers, all so pale I can't tell which one is the patient. An older woman, at least twenty years older than Mom, tries to catch my eye. I look away, disinviting greetings and questions. If we aren't careful, they'll join us on the couches and ask us about treatment and prognosis statistics, disregarding our ages, our obvious lack of medical degrees.

Mom returns twenty minutes later, almost normal looking, holding a brown paper bag. She pulls out four folded dresses, all made of the same crisp white cotton, like sheets. Each is embroidered with a different colored thread. One is decorated with birds. Another roses. She hands them to me. "Lupe made these for us."

I run my hand over the cool fabric. "Can I go say thanks?" I ask.

She tucks my hair behind my ear. "You're so thoughtful, sweetheart. But she's too busy. Let's go."

We leave the clinic grounds and drive up the coast. I close my eyes and listen to the rain pound the windows, harder and harder. The clouds are so dark, afternoon is indistinguishable from midnight. By the time we cross into San Diego, I can barely see across the street. Lightning creeps down from the sky to claim a giant sycamore tree. The storm snatches each branch of wood, and the entire time I fear it will take us.

Adrienne switches off the radio so we can concentrate on the road. I calm myself by mimicking the piano, tapping the notes of a Beethoven sonata on my thighs. I yearn to touch hard ivory keys rather than insubstantial flesh.

Mom hunches over the steering wheel. When she reaches for the gearshift, her hand trembles. I tap Adrienne's shoulder and mouth, *"Do something."*

"Pull over, Mom. I can drive."

"You've never driven in a mudslide. I'm fine," Mom says. "Remember, I grew up with hurricanes. This is just a thunderstorm."

Water slips under the wheels, and we swerve from one side of the lane to the other.

"Come on, Mom. Let me do it," Adrienne says. "You're not strong enough."

After she pulls over and turns off the car, everything is quiet except for the steady wrath of rain. I make out another fallen tree and worry about dangling power lines. Mom rests her forehead against the steering wheel, taking in deep, shaky breaths.

I ask her if she is okay. Mom meets my eyes in the

rearview mirror. "I wish none of this was happening. Let's switch seats, Adrienne."

Marie snuggles close to me. As soon as they open the doors, I feel the whoosh of wind and wet.

"Holy shit!" Adrienne yells once she sits safely behind the steering wheel. She turns the key and the car's headlights make the road look grainy, like an old silent movie. Mom seems even worse in the light.

Adrienne pushes in the clutch and taps the gas. We lunge forward and then snap back into place. Mom squeezes her eyes closed. "The wheels are stuck in the mud. Marie, climb up front and do as I say. Come on, girls. We need to push."

"There's no way you can," I say.

"Just do it."

Her face hardens. End of discussion.

By the time we reach the rear of the car, we're soaked through. Mom places her hands palms-down on the trunk. It is cold to the touch. Cars whiz by, and in that moment I understand why Mom's hands tremble. We're only a yard off the asphalt, and all I can think about is colliding with a hydroplaning semi. I watch Mom's mouth move, but I can't hear her over the traffic and thunder. Our feet sink into the mud, our shoes ruined. Adrienne lines up her palms next to mine.

"Push *now*!" Mom hollers. As I do, I feel every muscle in my body. The car doesn't budge. We try again. My feet sink deeper into the mud. We push with all our might, two more times before a colossal Buick pulls up next to us.

A pink-faced man climbs out of the car. His wife smiles through the closed window, and I get the sense that this act of kindness is her idea.

"Let me give you an extra set of hands." He holds them up for us to appreciate, and I do, especially as I register his height.

With his added strength, the car rocks forward and I slam my weight into the metal, pushing until we heave all four wheels onto the pavement. Adrienne's hair looks like Niagara Falls, the water cascades down with such force. Mom's crumpled dress clings to her legs.

"We can't thank you enough," Mom says. Instead of looking at our Good Samaritan, she keeps eyeing me.

We slog back to our seats. Slowly, we join the other cars on the road and make our way home. Our block is completely dark.

Even Mom dashes to the front door. She holds out her hand for the keys, then struggles with the lock until the door blows open.

"Take off your shoes," Mom says. "I don't want to see a hint of mud on my carpet."

I nod and take Marie's hand. "Help me get the candles." We rummage through the buffet's drawers until I feel a box of matches, a bag of assorted tea lights, and tapers, plus flashlights.

"Here," I say as I place a flashlight into her hand.

"Look at me." Marie turns on the light beneath her chin, grinning like a jack-o'-lantern.

When I strike a match, the scent of sulfur fills my nose. Mom looks like she just had an infusion: pale and weak. Her favorite pink dress is destroyed, a smear of dirt and motor oil streaked across it like a beauty pageant sash. Mud graces her forehead and chin. She eyes each of us with an unreadable expression.

"How come I look like the last soldier in the Vietnam jungle and you three look beautiful? Just like you were swimming in the ocean."

Dirt discolors my fingernails. I smell like a wet dog. "What do you mean?"

"You can't understand. You're just girls. I was your age once. People said I looked like Catherine Deneuve. Vanessa, change your clothes. That shirt is sheer and I can see your nipples. That pervert couldn't stop staring when he helped with the car. He'd rather have a child than a grown woman. Disgusting."

My hands fly to my chest. Before I can respond, she retreats to her room. I wonder when she'll come out—if she'll come out.

Adrienne takes the bag of candles from my hand. "Don't worry about it. I can barely see your tiny boobies. She feels like shit, that's all. Get changed and make sure Marie's in some dry clothes, will you? I'll make us something to eat."

Marie stands in her room, already in her Virgin-Mary-blue nightgown, and makes shadow puppets on the wall.

"Watch me," she says as her hands flutter like a butterfly and snap like a crocodile. "Will you do some?"

"In a minute," I say, and follow the beam of my flashlight to the bathroom. Mom is right—even in the dark, my sodden shirt looks translucent. I've been wandering around the house like an amateur nudist. I peer into the mirror, searching for a hint of Mom and Adrienne's beauty, finding nothing. Our resemblance is a transitory one. We share gestures and smiles, quick movements that can't be pinned down. I turn on the hot water, and the steam creeps up the mirror until my reflection disappears. It takes forever to feel clean. I scrub the mud off my hands and run the washcloth up and down my skin, trying to erase the renegade specks of dirt.

Rain pummels the windows, and I wonder if a typhoon has ever descended upon Southern California. My flashlight illuminates Mom, wrapped in a towel, on her bed. "You want anything?" I ask.

She turns toward me. "I feel like I've been buried in a mudslide."

Mom shakes her head when I offer to run a bath. I can't reach her when she is this far away, so deep inside herself.

"Dad should be home soon."

Relief softens her eyes. "Thank heavens. I'm going to rest a little while longer." She rolls onto her side. Her shoulder blades protrude like fragile wings.

I find Marie in her room. She sits cross-legged with a

colorful book in her lap. "Want me to show you my new favorite?"

"Yeah." I plop onto the floor next to her as she turns an oversize page.

"Saint Margaret was very beautiful. She glowed. If she walked in the dark, she lit up the streets like a human flashlight. And the best part . . ." Marie claps her hands enthusiastically, her cheeks bright. "She got eaten by a dragon. He gobbled her up—he was really the devil—but she was magic and made him split in half so she could come out. You're Saint Cecilia. She could play any instrument she picked up, and she had a beautiful voice. Angels followed her everywhere. But they put her in a hot bath and cut off her head. Sorry." She thumbs through the book and then flattens it so hard that the spine cracks. "And Adrienne's this one, Saint Cristina the Astonishing. She could fly. Can you believe that name? I'd like to be astonishing."

I don't ask how Cristina died, knowing all the girls suffered horrifying fates. I reach over and tuck Marie's hair behind her ears. She needs a haircut. "Want me to braid your hair like hers?" I point to the Margaret painting.

Marie nods and resumes her reading. I hug her close. Marie still has a girl's body, and her small stature only emphasizes her youth. She takes after Dad, with the same warm eyes, round face, and high forehead. Plumper than Adrienne and me, Marie's body consists of small circles, baby-faced with round cobalt eyes. She quit her soccer team when Mom and Dad told us about the diagnosis, and now she looks even softer than before. I part her mermaid hair, weaving piece after golden piece until it falls down her back, a long fishtail.

The front door opens with a bang, and I hear the familiar thump of Dad's heavy briefcase as it hits the floor—the telltale sign he'll be sketching building designs after dinner. Marie hops up and pulls me down the hall, hollering, "Daddy! Daddy!"

"Iris! You and the kids okay? Can you believe this weather? Ash Street is flooded. No one knew what to do when the traffic signals went out. It took me ten minutes to go three blocks."

Envy pays a brief visit as I watch Dad lift Marie off the ground. Adrienne lined the tabletops with candles, something straight from a movie set. Even Mom's wedding candelabra is aflame.

Dad takes a deep breath when Mom walks in wearing one of Lupe's hand-embroidered dresses. Roses climb the length of her torso, and she's pulled her hair into a loose bun. "You look very pretty in the candlelight," he says.

"Thank you, darling."

Depositing Marie on the ground, he walks over and kisses her cheek. "I'm glad you got home safe and sound."

"Barely, right, girls?"

"Yeah," I say. The little hairs on the back of my neck rise to attention. "It was rough."

Mom smiles at Dad. "Now that you're home, I can put the day behind me."

"Thanks to the rain. If the power hadn't gone out, I'd still be at the office. Richard thinks we're going to miss the deadline. What's the plan for dinner?"

"I made sandwiches," Adrienne says. "Salad too."

"It's a picnic, and a fancy one," Dad says. "Let's eat."

I join Adrienne in the kitchen. "Nice look," she says. I've changed into sweats and an oversize black T-shirt covered with dancing piano keys, a favorite from music camp. "I definitely can't see your boobies in that."

I pass out sandwiches, and Adrienne chatters away as she scoops fruit onto Marie's plate. Mom recounts the drive home, comparing it to her hometown storms back in Charleston. "You would have been proud of the girls," she says to Dad. "They were very brave. And strong. You should have seen us pushing the car."

The lights flicker on and the phone rings, announcing the return of electricity. Dad answers and runs his hand through his hair. "I know the power's back, but I can't reach the freeway with the flooded roads."

I hear the sound of an insistent voice come through the line. Dad regards us with a concerned expression. Mom tenses in her seat, staring at him with a desperate look.

"I brought the plans home and they'll be done by the morning. We'll have time to run through the presentation, Richard. I assure you." He turns his back to us. "I'm well aware that I can't work on the model at home. I'll come in early. Name the time."

"Who won?" Adrienne asks when he hangs up the phone.

I watch Mom watch Dad. This isn't the first time we've witnessed one of his negotiations. His boss usually wins, reminding Dad of deadlines and bonuses, of how the work can only be done at the office with the entire team present. The firm depends on him—as if we don't. Sometimes I want to grab the phone and remind his perpetually sweaty boss about Mom and cancer and needles and the clinic. It shouldn't take a flash flood for Dad to stay home.

"Me," he says. "I'm home until five in the morning. God, forgive me, I completely forgot—what'd the doctor say about your tests?"

Mom closes her eyes and takes in a deep breath. Even the candles still in anticipation.

"Iris," he says, "what is it? What's wrong?"

I watch the color drain from her cheeks. She opens her mouth to speak, but closes it again. She looks at each of us, and when her eyes meet mine, I hold on, knowing something is about to change, something irreversible. Our tear ducts race, our eyes filling.

She looks down at the table. "I'm terminal."

I swear the blood in my veins pauses. I hear it churn, the blood working its way from my heart to my fingertips. I feel my heartbeat where my palms bruised from pushing the car.

Adrienne drops her fork, but it is Marie who speaks first.

"You're going to die." I marvel at the surety of her tone, not at all questioning. I have seven years on her, but lack her certainty.

I can't look at Mom—or any of them. My eyes wander around the room in search of a safe place to rest, somewhere quiet, but the rain continues to pound and I watch water seep through a windowpane.

Two

Paper litters the floor like confetti, crinkling with my every step. I've had the same locker combination all year, but now, on the last day of school, I struggle with the combination:

10 09 37: Mom's birthday

01 14 76: Diagnosis Day

11 25 76: Thanksgiving, six months after her terminal prognosis, the last month she'll likely be alive.

I'll be a motherless junior.

In my memory, the day of the storm feels both compressed and drawn out. I don't remember the next morning or going to school. I don't remember climbing in and out of the car. I can't tell you what played on the radio. The only thing I remember is the expression on Mom's face and the stark realization that in a matter of months, a yet-to-be-determined number, she will leave us for good.

Jasmine, my best friend since sixth grade, cruises by, pausing long enough for me to notice. Before the diagnosis, we had a rhythm of sleepovers, beach days, and evening phone calls. I told her everything—until the diagnosis. I became more consumed with Mom's sleep and eating habits. I lost track of conversations about boys and crushes. I stopped answering the phone. My friends tried, asking questions and offering to help. They gazed at me with such suffocating pity that I couldn't be alone with them. Adrienne and I fled campus for lunch, driving through McDonald's, dividing chores over Happy Meals. We returned late, tossing our crumpled burger wrappers out the car window and ducking into classes long after the bell rang—not once punished with a tardy slip. Jasmine persisted through months of my monosyllabic answers to her kind questions. But patience has an expiration date, and she moved out of our locker. No one took her place. It didn't take long before they all avoided me.

My fingers twirl the lock, this time the right combination. I press so hard that the numbers emboss my skin, briefly obscuring my fingerprints. I empty the contents of my locker into the trash before heading to the music room.

Surrounded by concentric circles of music stands and chairs, my orchestra teacher boxes up sheet music. The chalkboard urges us to practice, the word written in her spidery cursive.

Mrs. Albright raises her head and smiles. "I've been waiting for you." She passes me a thick folder before brushing silver hair from her face. "I'm giving you twice as much as anyone else."

I glance at the grand piano, levitating on the stage like one of Marie's saints. Freshman year, I didn't like the separation from the winds and strings. It made me feel fake, like some sort of imposter who bullshitted my way up there. I couldn't look down at the seniors who played with ease. The flautists terrified me the most, the girls who puffed air into flutes, cheeks as full as squirrels, yet still looked beautiful. The cheerleaders' instrument of choice.

Now, though, I welcome the distance and bulk of the instrument. I think of my little spinet tucked away in a dining room corner, the only place Mom would allow. After my middle school music teacher pronounced me gifted, she urged my parents to invest in a piano. Dad drew up sketches that required rearranging the living room, entertaining the possibility of removing a wall. He'd forgotten about his promise to Mom and their original design of the room: sunken, a clear separation between family and adult space.

Mrs. Albright isn't the swooning type. While she acknowledges my skill, she says it's worthless unless I work. The piano chose me and I am in its debt. When I told her about Mom, she doubled my workload, saying, "I know grief. We'll play through it together."

Chopin. Beethoven. Bach. Mozart. Haydn. She spares me Satie, whose notes sound like tears.

I shroud my piano in blankets, topped off with an Amish quilt, to muffle the sound. It's the only way to practice without waking Mom.

I flip through the pages, a year's worth of pieces. "I can't get through all of this."

Mrs. Albright squeezes my hand and I meet her eyes. I want her to be family. A grandmother. An aunt. Someone bound by blood or vows. "You just have to play. This might be too much. It might not be enough. Promise me you'll keep up with it. Conservatory work is rigorous."

For the first time since I hit puberty, I'll miss summer music camp in LA—trapped at the clinic instead. I can't imagine getting into one of the conservatories, playing for hours a day, leaving home for the luxury of music, replacing regular high school with a performing arts education. Mrs. Albright and I spent hours filling out applications and recording cassettes, but in the end, only three schools invited me to audition after I applied last fall—before the diagnosis. Back then, my only hurdle was getting in. There are so many obstacles now, but that doesn't change my dream of going. I want to spend my days at the piano, hours on end, losing myself in the notes. I didn't think I could want anything so much. Until Mom.

"I don't know how much I'll be home," I say. "We're in Mexico so much. There isn't a piano there. Honestly, with how things are with my mom, I don't know if I can even go. I haven't even told my parents."

"Would it better if I have the schools send the acceptance letters here? We won't hear for a couple more months."

I'm filled with relief that I won't have to worry about

telling Mom and Dad now. Or Adrienne. The last thing I want is for her to intercept my mail. "Yes, that would be better."

Mrs. Albright gives me a tender smile. "But you need to practice whenever you're able. Agreed?"

I promise with my whole body, eyes squeezed shut, hands clutching the music, head nodding.

"Good," she says. "Turn over the folder."

Louise Albright

555-3722

269 Mariposa Street

"In case you run out of music."

I want to hug her, but something about her, maybe her perfect posture, prevents me from doing so.

"Play every day," she says.

In the hall, Adrienne and Zach lean against the cinder-block wall near the door. Tall and lanky, Zach bends his head as he listens to Adrienne. She shakes her head. He speaks. She shakes her head again. Poor Zach.

"Hey, Vanessa, tell her I can come with you."

"For the millionth time, no. Babcocks only. It's tradition." Adrienne flashes a smile, half-playful, half-dangerous.

His eyes meet mine and I shrug an apology.

"We've got to get Marie," she says as she reaches for her art supplies. "See you soon."

I turn away when she gives him an enthusiastic kiss good-bye.

Half of the parking lot waits at the exit, bumper to bumper, so close they resemble boxcars hitched to a steam engine.

Adrienne tosses her stuff into the backseat. Mom hasn't driven the car since the storm. I'm promoted to shotgun.

I lean my head out the window. "Marie's going to freak out if we're not there," I say.

She backs out of the space and drives in the opposite direction of the honking line. "These fools don't spend half their time driving through TJ."

Our wheels crush a patch of marigolds as Adrienne barrels over the sidewalk, off the curb, and into the street. Seamless and daring. She raises her middle finger at the school. "See you later, motherfuckers."

Chaos hasn't consumed Torrey Pines Elementary. Parents sit behind steering wheels, anxious and smiling. A small gaggle of mothers, wearing a uniform of pastel clam-digger pants and jelly sandals, huddle near the entrance. Probably moms of kindergartners, a club to which Mom once belonged. I don't remember running through the doors and into her arms. I can't imagine a time when she was strong enough to lift me.

Marie walks out alone. She wears a butter-yellow shirt with a drawing of one of her saints, horrible portraits sketched with an amateurish but sincere hand. Bloody-eyed

Lucy. Flame-licked Joan. Marie only wears pastels because she believes God prefers pale colors. Adrienne likes to tell her that God is a smoking pile of horseshit and maybe she should wear the color red once in a while. Marie sticks to baby blue, sherbet orange, and carnation pink.

The kindergarten moms call her name. One strokes her hair. Our tragedy has blazed through the gossip mill.

She beams as soon as she sees us, excited as when she scores a goal at a soccer game. "Come on, come on, come on!" she says. "I've been waiting all day!"

Adrienne doesn't rely on her south-of-the-border driving technique to get us to Luigi's. They sit us at a small table in the back, not our usual family-size one in the front. I stare at the empty chair.

"We should get something for Mom," Marie says.

Adrienne shakes her head. "She won't eat it."

Marie frowns. "But she always comes with us."

I tug Marie's braid and focus on the menu, even though we always order the same thing. Personal pan pizzas, pepperoni for us and veggie deluxe for Mom and Dad. "We're already bringing one home for Dad," I say. "Might as well get Mom a cheese just in case."

Adrienne cocks an eyebrow. "Couldn't hurt."

The waitress offers the parlor's annual graduation day fanfare: lemonade decorated with those little paper cocktail umbrellas, and pepperoni smiley-face pizzas. Marie savors her ice-cream sundae, eating so slow that the ice cream melts before she finishes. She raises the metal bowl to her mouth and slurps the last few drops. Mom, with her South Carolina manners, never would have let her get away with that, but I laugh at Marie's messy face as I wipe her clean.

Dad beat us home and we find them both sitting at the kitchen table. Mom cradles a cup of steaming tea. Maybe it's the warmth, but she has more color in her cheeks than usual. She smiles when Marie presents her with the pizza.

Dad sets a speed-eating record, polishing off his meal in under ten bites. My stomach clenches as I watch Mom sample a slice, marveling as she eats the whole piece except the crust. She catches me staring.

"It's a good day, Vanessa. How does it feel to be an upperclassman?"

"You mean, how does it feel to be a senior?" Adrienne asks. "Amazing."

Dad relaxes into his chair. Yesterday, his boss flew to Vermont for his son's college graduation. Gone for an entire week, which means we have Dad home for breakfasts and dinners, and he can take Mom to the clinic. I can play the piano as much as I want.

"Are you sure you don't want to come?" he asks me. We celebrate matriculation almost as enthusiastically as graduation, and Marie's gift is a visit to Mission San Luis Rey, a historic museum glorifying the conquering and converting of local tribes, completely disregarding genocide. I hate the idea of going. While I know Marie will love the gilded ceilings, she is more interested in the gift shop. She collects saint prayer cards with the fervor of a baseball fan.

I shake my head and ignore Adrienne's glare. She knows I'd rather eat glass than go to the beach and watch her make out with Zach. I've never been to one of their infamous bonfire parties, and I have no intention of starting now.

"Looks like it's just you and me," Mom says, smiling.

She's pulled her hair back into a ponytail, and even though I spend my days looking at both of them, I still find it startling how much Adrienne is a carbon copy of Mom. Over the past month, Mom looks like she's aged about ten years. They warned us about that at the clinic, how the more aggressive treatment will erode her like the walls of San Clemente Canyon.

She swears she will keep fighting. She'll continue with the Laetrile until her body can't endure the treatment any longer. Sometimes I open my dictionary and read the definition of "terminal" as a reminder. Miracle drug or not, Laetrile won't save Mom. She says so herself. When we point this out to Dad, he tells us that hope gives her strength, gives us all more time, more days, maybe weeks, maybe even months. He looks like he's aged ten years too. I didn't know you could watch someone's hair turn gray. His full head of hair has lightened from sandy blond, the gray almost looking sun bleached.

Mom picks the cheese off a second piece of pizza. "What time is Zach picking you up?" she asks Adrienne.

"In an hour."

"Let's play a game. Why don't you get Parcheesi?"

We crowd around the kitchen table taking turns playing the Royal Game of India. Marie teams up with Dad and we all let Mom win. She knows we're doing it, and with each roll of the dice, she looks happier reaching this small victory. It's like we're carrying her over the finish line.

After Adrienne, Dad, and Marie leave, I rinse the dishes. Dad came home with a dishwasher the week we found out about the leukemia. In my mind, I link the machine to Mom's decline, another failed attempt to treat her illness. I only remember seeing her use the dishwasher once, loading it for the inaugural wash.

"Do you want to rest, Mom?" This is a record: two hours straight without needing to lie down.

"I'm okay. I have some energy. Do you wish you had gone with your father instead of babysitting me?"

"I'm not babysitting you," I say.

"Want to play another round of Parcheesi?"

Suddenly, I want to do anything but sit in the kitchen. Last year, it would have been inconceivable to scatter in different directions. Mom and Dad would have planned something special, like dinner on a boat—anything to mark the beginning of summer. Last year we went to the Hotel del Coronado and listened to music, a dozen men playing trumpets and clarinets. Dad loves big band jazz, and he'd persuaded all of us to dance. I flinch at the memory.

"If that's what you want," I say.

"You look disappointed."

I shrug. I want to go to Swensen's for ice cream or see a movie: *Bad News Bears* or *Freaky Friday*. Even *Jaws* for the sixth time—it's still playing at the second-run theater. What I really want to see is *Taxi Driver*, but I know she won't take me to anything R-rated. I'm old enough for cancer, but too young for sex and blood.

"Why don't we go to a movie?"

"I'm sorry, but I don't want to overdo it."

I look at the silverware scattered at the bottom of the sink, like silver fish flailing in a shallow pool. Maybe I should have gone with Dad. I want to be with Mom, but in this moment, I want to be out of the house, with or without her. Nothing sounds better than the cool, quiet movie theater.

"The theater isn't far. I've been practicing. I could drive with my permit."

"I said I don't feel well enough, Vanessa." Her voice sounds thin.

I can't turn around and look at her. "I meant I could drive myself."

"That's out of the question."

"Why? It's the last day of school. I want to do something fun."

She coughs and I listen as she sips her tea. "You should have gone with one of your sisters. I'm sorry I'm not any fun."

"You used to be." The words fly out, and while I know

they hurt—they hurt me—I can't bring myself to stop. "Why can't you go? All you have to do is sit there. That's all you'd do here."

"Look at me," she says.

I feel equal parts embarrassed and angry. I collect a handful of silverware and shove it into the dishwasher. The forks clank in protest.

"You're acting like a child."

I turn to face her. "That's because technically I *am* a child."

I meet her eyes, which contain every possible emotion. I expect to see frustration and annoyance, but I see so much more. She looks almost angry, and that makes her look almost strong.

"I don't understand why you can't see a movie," I say. "I don't get it."

"We can watch TV. We have popcorn."

I wipe my cheeks dry. "I want to go out."

"Get your bike, then."

"I hate your cancer!" My voice rises an octave with each word. I turn back around. This will be our last summer together, the last time she'll be here when we come home from the last day of school. Just one instance in a long series of last occasions: last Fourth of July, last daylight savings, last birthdays.

Mom is the only person who can be quieter than me.

"I really hate it." I throw a spoon into the dishwasher, but it hits the floor. I throw another one and then slam the dishwasher shut.

She absorbs my tantrum. A minute passes before she leaves the kitchen without a word.

I drove her to her room, probably for the rest of the day, now ruined.

I'm alone with my chores, I think, as I wipe down the counter and kitchen table, sweeping the crumbs into the palm of my hand. I leave Mom's mug of tea, still warm.

An empty box from the clinic, once filled with vitamins and medication, blocks the entrance to the family room. I kick it aside, a little too hard. Consumed by the final weeks of school, we haven't bothered to pick up after ourselves. Art supplies, a torn Twister mat, books, magazines, and at least two dozen records cover the family room floor. She is sick. She doesn't feel well. She can't help it, I remind myself as I slide the records into their assigned places, following Dad's instructions: alphabetical order by the name of the band. Even with the albums and books returned to shelves, the room looks nothing like it once did, back when Mom organized piles of clutter. Now, water stains cover the end tables, overlapping concentric circles distorting the wood, which I cover with a fan of old *Seventeen* magazines.

I look up when she clears her throat. Mom hugs her pillow, and car keys dangle from her hand.

"I'd better drive," she says. "You haven't had enough practice."

"I thought you didn't feel well enough," I say.

"I'll manage. I can nap in the theater if I need to."

I'm being selfish. A baby. Already, she looks paler than just five minutes ago. "I'm sorry, Mom."

"It's the last day of school. You're right—we should celebrate."

She joins me in the family room, lowering herself onto the couch as though the soft cushion will somehow hurt. "You're missing a lot because of me. I know you're disappointed about music camp." She runs her hand through my tangled hair, liberating knots. "I know how hard you work. I know what you do for me. I forget to thank you, sweetie."

I rest my head in her lap. "We don't have to go."

"But I want to. You're right, a movie shouldn't be too taxing."

I wrap my arms around her, wanting to be as close as possible, anything to keep her next to me. I want to stop thinking of today, or any day, as being numbered, a cruel countdown.

"I don't care what we see," I say.

"Good, because I have it planned out. Now, please help me up."

We drive for twenty minutes, away from the border, leaving San Diego and heading toward the northern part of the county. Brush replaces grass as we follow the ocean. Her fingers circle the steering wheel, and her wedding ring glints in the sunlight. When we finally pull into the parking lot, she says, "Let's save *Bad News Bears* for Marie. How does *Carrie* sound?"

She knows I've been dying to see it, any horror movie where chaos and murder cancel class.

We sit in the middle of the crowded theater. I realize that I haven't seen a movie in months, since before Christmas, maybe Thanksgiving. Struggling to focus on the plot, I think more about the sound of her breathing. I drink a Coke as Mom sips a small 7-Up. I watch her more than the screen. She sits engrossed with the blood-soaked prom scene, raising the straw to her lips, swallowing slowly. All of her movements are delicate. I wonder if she'll fall asleep, but the pillow remains in her lap.

Last year, this would have been unremarkable. On a whim, usually when Dad was out of town, Mom would drive us to school, only to turn around midway and take us on a day trip to feed giraffes at the Wild Animal Park, ride roller coasters at Magic Mountain, or pick apples in Julian. Random and spontaneous and completely unexpected.

We emerge from the theater, squinting in the bright sunlight. I'd forgotten it was still daytime. Mom drapes an arm around my shoulders, tucking her pillow under the other, and looks at me. "One more surprise," she says.

We drive with the radio turned up. Mom sings along, her voice quiet compared to the jangly guitar of a Beatles song. At one point, she reaches for my hand. I look at our overlapping fingers, how mine are longer than hers. Soon, I will be taller, all of my limbs longer than my mother's, if she lives that long.

I don't ask where we're going.

I gaze out the window at the long stretch of beach, flanked by an endless concrete sea wall and strip malls. An ugly cousin compared to the hills near our house, perched above the ocean, covered with Torrey pines, their twisted branches distorted by decades of wind. Mom slows when we reach the modest pier, a shaky wooden structure that I expect to fall apart like pick-up sticks, planks tumbling into the cresting waves. She parks in front of the concession stand.

"You pick," she says. Clam strips or soft serve ice cream, our guilty pleasures. They serve the best ones here. Dad, Adrienne, and Marie insist that clams taste like deep-fried fingers. When running errands, just the two of us, Mom and I stop here. Like the movies, I haven't been in months.

"Can you eat more?" I ask, skeptical after the pizza.

"I just want a bite. Come on, you love it as much as I do."

When Mom is happy, her Southern drawl emerges, elongating vowels, her words blending together. The voice of bedtime stories and lullabies—almost forgotten.

I order one of each from the man who has staffed the counter my entire life, regardless of the weather or height of the waves. Fishermen, he says, are always hungry.

Mom accepts the cone, and I blow on the crispy clams, too hot to touch. She turns down the music. "Wait for me, Vanessa," she says. "I'm trying. I'm scared too. Wait for me to feel better."

"You're not going to get better," I say.

She doesn't look away. "I'm not giving up, Nessie. We'll have more days like this."

She nicknamed me Nessie when I was a baby, and used it until I came to her as a teary-eyed second-grader and begged her to stop. Adrienne had told me that my pet name was shared with the Loch Ness Monster, a name for nightmares and beasts. Mom couldn't convince me otherwise, and she never said it again, not until now.

"Just wait for me."

Three

The boy stands in the shadow of a bougainvillea climbing the arch of the courtyard entrance. The sun diffuses through paper-thin leaves and casts a ruby hue on his Hawaiian print shirt and long, below-the-knee surfer shorts. It's as though he stands in the center of a pink spotlight. He looks healthy, sunburned, and rosy cheeked like me. It isn't until he steps through the entryway—away from the protection of the flowers—that I recognize he is one of them.

In the clear light, he is sick and gray-skinned, with half-moon shadows the color of bruised plums under his eyes. He is one of the leukemia kids, his chemo buzz cut growing out like the jarheads sprung free from Camp Pendleton. He looks tall and older than me.

Now that it's summer, the sick kids avoid the outdoors. They wither in the heat. So we litter the courtyard with nail polish bottles, back issues of *Seventeen* and *Tiger Beat*, and beach towels. We don't bother picking up.

The sick guy leans against the wall as if waiting for a bus. He tries to act casual. He may have been cute before the cancer, but his patches of hair and zombie skin ruin him. I stretch my legs on the picnic bench and apply Coppertone to my bare shoulders.

"You're not allowed out here, sick-o," Adrienne says. "Off limits. You're trespassing. Go back inside and let the nurses take care of you."

He ignores her and glances around the courtyard. His eyes meet mine, but I look away and screw the cap back on the suntan lotion. My nose fills with the scent of creamy coconut.

"What's the big deal if I hang out here?" he asks.

"You get the hospital. We get the courtyard. *Comprende?*" Adrienne says.

Guadalupe hollers from an upstairs window. "*Mijas*, come up to visit your *mamasita*. She's ready for you."

I stand and wipe dust off my clothes. I'm wearing my new shorts, the ones with the seam arching rainbow-style across my butt. All I want to do is stroll down Tijuana's streets so I can turn heads and let my ears ring with whistles. Adrienne is teaching me how to walk like her, the girl everyone wants.

"You better be gone when we get back," Adrienne says to him.

The three of us assemble a line, falling into rank according to age. Adrienne leads the way. Guadalupe cruises down the hall toward the one open door and waves us through. My mother rests with her back against several pillows, propped up with her eyes closed.

"Iris," Guadalupe says. "Iris, your girls are here."

My mother blinks three times, reminding me of one of my favorite shows, *I Dream of Jeannie*. She manages a hint of a smile and waves hello. "*Gracias*, Lupe," she says. "What have you girls done today?"

"Same as every fucking day," Adrienne says.

"Language, Adrienne. Please at least try. Sit down, girls. I need to talk to you."

Marie occupies the foot of Mom's bed, and Adrienne and I plop down on the vacant one. Adrienne continues to flip through her magazine. Marie, tired from the heat and still young enough for an afternoon nap, yawns and stretches out on the mattress.

"I talked to your father a little while ago," Mom says.

That gets Adrienne's attention, and she tosses the magazine to the floor. "About what?"

"Given that the FDA's banned Laetrile in the States, a lot of people are coming to Mexico to treat their cancer. Most aren't as lucky as we are, living in San Diego so close to the border. The clinic is getting calls from people all over the country. What do you think of having people stay with us? Not a lot, but on occasion? We'd be a safe house."

"Not in my bed," Adrienne says.

"You'd have to share rooms," Mom says.

"Why?" Adrienne narrows her eyes. "It's bad enough we have to hang out here all the time. Now you want to bring them home with us? I can't believe Dad said yes to this."

"Please stop," Mom says before coughing. Her cough grows louder as it progresses.

"Now look what you've done." I climb off the bed to get water. I hand a plastic cup to Mom, who drinks, takes several deep breaths, drinks some more, and returns the cup to me.

"This is important," Mom says. "Even if you can't see it, we're very lucky. There's a family who needs help right now. A teenage boy and his mom need a place to stay."

"Must be that guy outside," Adrienne says to me.

"You met Caleb?" Mom asks. "He's seventeen. Dark hair. Lymphoma."

"We saw him," I say. "How long do they have stay with us?"

"Maybe a month or two. Then he'll be back at the hospital so the doctor can monitor his cells. They might have to adjust therapies. We'll talk if he needs more time by the start of school. Vanessa, you and Adrienne can share a room."

"But you're sick," Adrienne's voice sounds sharp. "We can barely take care of you. How can we take care of *more* sick people?"

"It would be nice to feel like I'm doing something for other people. Everyone at the clinic has been so good to us. When I met Barb, I wanted to help. She'll take care of Caleb, and she promised to help with the house. I don't want you girls to have to do everything. It should be easier with them there. Not harder. Your father agreed. Okay?"

We all nod but Adrienne, who mutters something about the goddamned Von Trapp family meeting the Brady Bunch. Adrienne and Marie curl up next to each other on the spare gurney, napping. I agree with Adrienne—I can't believe we are going to have to share our house, especially with someone as sick as Mom. This boy needs to understand how hard this is going to be for us. That Mom is really sick. *Dying* sick. He can have a room or two, but that's it. I slip out the door and make my way back to the courtyard.

He sits on the picnic table, pale skin baking in the heat. I want to walk over confidently like I've seen Adrienne do a hundred times. But all I can do is comb my hair with my fingers and slide a coat of bubblegum Bonne Bell on my lips. Caleb turns and looks my way.

"So, are we roomies now?" he asks.

"You knew who we were?"

"It's hard to miss three blond girls in Mexico."

"You should have said something, like, introduced yourself."

He doesn't apologize. We're feral, but at least we have manners.

"You want to check out the beach?" He starts walking out of the courtyard.

It's less than a quarter of a mile to the ocean, an easy distance if you don't have cancer. It is off limits, forbidden territory. Patients and their families are discouraged from straying from the clinic grounds. They warn us of armed robberies, kidnappings, unpredictable riptides, and hazardous currents. But Caleb keeps walking without looking back to see if I've made up my mind. I glance around the empty courtyard. It's hot, that unbearable late afternoon hot. I follow.

I catch up with him and we walk down the dirt road to the beach.

"How long have you been coming here?" he asks.

"Don't you know everything about us, *roomie*?"

"Not really. Just what your mom told mine."

"A few months," I say.

"Your mom's not any better?" He sounds tense.

"Worse."

"Where's your dad?"

I shrug and repeat what Mom always says when we ask her the same question. "Someone's got to pay the hospital bills. He comes when he can, but his boss is a jerk."

"At least he stuck around. Mine bailed right after I got diagnosed."

Before I can respond, Caleb draws in his breath. We stand a few yards from the water.

"You okay?" I look him over, top to bottom. He seems fine. A little pink, but that's all.

He nods. "The last couple of months have been really hard. Nothing's worse than chemo. I used to surf and play water polo. You know, before. The best thing about Laetrile is moving closer to the beach."

When I look at him, I see a mixture of sickness and strength. Something about him makes me want to leave this place, to escape the clinic even just for a little while. Maybe Adrienne is wrong. Maybe it could be okay having them around. I nod. "Let's go this way." I point north toward Rosarito.

We walk with our feet in the water. We talk about school and how no one understands what it's like to be uprooted by illness. I tell him how I breezed through my final exams with the certainty of passing, of my teachers grading me with pity.

"Until you got sick, did you know anyone with cancer?" I ask.

He gazes at the ocean; the water swells beyond the waves. "My grandma. That's it. Until I started chemo, I thought I was the only kid with cancer in Seattle. But now I see it everywhere."

"You look good," I say. "Considering."

"You sound like my mother."

Mortified, I stare at my feet. He looks a lot better than Mom. That's all I meant, but this proves I'm completely incapable of having a normal exchange with anyone my own age, cancer or not. I feel stupid and start asking inane questions that adults always ask me. "What grade are you in?"

He stops and sizes me up. No one has looked at me like

that in months, not since Mom and Dad met with the principal and explained our family crisis and increasing absences. I'm not prepared—to answer his question or for the way he makes my heart pound twice as hard. We embark on a staring match. Indisputably, he used to be good-looking. Probably popular.

When I followed him to the beach, he seemed determined to walk away from everything, maybe even his illness. Now he stands statue-still, radiating calm like a steady breath.

He wipes sweat off his forehead with the back of his hand, bruised from an IV. "Why don't you ask me something real?"

I kick a washed-up piece of seaweed, slimy on my foot. "Like what?"

"Something that means something. Do you know how many times someone has asked me what grade I'm in or what's wrong with me? Everyone from the phlebotomist to the grocery store clerk." He gives me a weak smile, and his words sound more like a plea than anger. "Like, what's your favorite book? Answer that one."

I squint in the sun, nervous about his dare. Sheet music doesn't count. "Agatha Christie, I guess. I like them all. *And Then There Were None* is a good one. Maybe her best. She's easy."

"Easy? Your favorite author is easy? Your sister, the older one, seems more like the fluff type. Not you."

I look away with a scowl. "You don't know anything

about her," I say. "Besides, taking care of my mom doesn't leave much time for serious reading." I don't defend myself by summarizing *To Kill a Mockingbird* or reciting lines from *A Midsummer Night's Dream*. "There's a collection of poems."

"Does it have a title?"

We stand in the same spot, on the packed sand where, when the tide comes in, as it is beginning to do now, crabs will emerge. Our presence scares away the pelicans. Seagulls caw overhead. When I look at him, I see he is interested in what I have to say. Genuinely interested. He isn't mocking me.

"*Leaves of Grass*."

"See," he says. "That's what I meant by *real*."

"Your turn." I don't look away from him. With anyone else, I would have. Except for Adrienne and Marie.

His face changes when he smiles, truly smiles, even if it's fleeting. Without hesitation, Caleb says, "*On the Road*. Kerouac. His poems are amazing too. I'll read you some while we're *roomies*."

Never heard of him. I walk past Caleb and brush his hand with mine. An almost accident. "Come on, let's keep going."

It takes him a minute to catch up. I remind myself to slow down, that he is sick. His confidence makes me forget. I listen to our feet slap the sand, which fills the spaces between my toes. It doesn't take much for the ocean to claim you. I don't want to turn around and head back to the clinic. I don't regret coming with him, but I learned from Mom that each word is a risk. It takes a certain amount of courage to converse, especially when one of the primary topics of conversation is terminal illness. I tell him about Whitman's poems, Dad's asshole boss, and about Mom. That is enough for now, unless he is the courageous one. As we walk, I glance over my shoulder, looking at the clinic, now small in the distance.

"To answer your original question, I don't think I have a grade anymore. If I hadn't gotten sick, I'd be starting my senior year. But I missed most of last year, so I guess I'm back to being a junior. If I go back. Nothing freaks people out like sitting next to the walking dead in calculus. They acted like I was contagious."

"Your friends?"

"Not really. Well, some of them. Mostly the people I saw every day but didn't really know. And my friends couldn't handle it, especially when my hair started falling out. They tried for a while, but things got weird. They couldn't just hang out with me and talk. You know, like how we're talking now. It was like I had to pretend that I wasn't sick to make them feel okay. Then I got too sick to hang out with anyone."

"Same with us."

"How come your Mom still has her hair?" he asks.

I stop. "What do you mean?"

"After chemo."

"She didn't do chemo," I say. "We came straight here."

He frowns and runs a hand over his patchy crew cut, confused, but doesn't respond.

As the sun drops from its heights, we wander until we spot a cluster of fishermen huddled over the day's catch, and Caleb says he's getting hungry. He looks pale except for big red blotches spreading across his skin like a rash. Sweat runs down his face, and I realize he probably won't tell me when he needs to take a break. I look at Caleb and then at the group of fishermen. His breathing changes, his exhalations grow louder. I touch his arm and he grabs my hand. There is no way he'll be able to walk back.

"I'll be right back," I say.

As soon as I let go of him, he drops to the sand.

I rush over to the men and in my limited Spanish ask them if they have some water and if they'd drive us back to the hospital. One man, the oldest, sprints to his truck. Another man lifts a bottle of soda from the sand and hands it to me. It's warm, but I run to Caleb and instruct him to drink it. While he drains the bottle, I try to act calm, talking with the fishermen as they pack up their catch of crab and snapper. My stomach turns at the smell. I'm too scared for Caleb's health and whatever punishment awaits me at the clinic. Mom won't approve of my walking a dying boy closer to death.

"Hey, these guys are going to drive us back, okay? Do you want me to help you up? Their truck is right over there." I point to the road.

Caleb nods and reaches for my hand. His palm is hot and sweaty and I try to pull him to his feet, but my hand slides from his and I teeter backward. The man who gave me the Coke and another fisherman walk over and lift Caleb from the ground.

We ride in the back with the rods and bait. Caleb leans against the side of the truck with his eyes closed. I inch toward him, my clothes catching on the tackle. I hear my shorts rip, and my skin burns where hooks dig deep into my legs. It's a quick drive, and when we pull up to the clinic, Caleb's doctor runs out and helps him out of the truck. Guadalupe rushes over to Caleb and checks his pulse. Satisfied, she scolds me first in Spanish and then again in English for not telling anyone where we went. I disappeared with a patient and she was frantic. Our mothers, she says, are furious.

I look past her as Caleb disappears through the door.

Guadalupe scoops my chin in her palm.

I shake free. "He'll be fine. Maybe he just needs some water."

"*Mija*, you've got to be careful with the sick ones. They're not like you."

I hang my head as she rushes back inside. I sit on the stairs to inspect my legs, which are covered in sand and torn by tackle and reek of dead fish. Trickles of blood run down my skin, escaping from the many scratches and punctures. At first, I cry for my cuts and shredded clothes, and then for Caleb. I sit until the sun disappears and the Mexican sky brings out its enormous mantle of stars. I'm not sure how long I'm outside before he offers me a plate of tamales. He looks better, just plain lymphoma sick.

"I never should've let you walk like that. I wasn't thinking of how sick you are. I mean, you're dying. Sorry, I guess I'm not supposed to say that."

His skin is pink in some places and a horrible white in others. I keep looking at the unevenness of his color to remind me that he is ill, like Lupe said.

He sits down and hands me a fork. "I just got dehydrated, and you should know that I'm not dying."

"I'm sorry I said that. Really."

He coughs into his hand and, just like Mom, makes this terrible hacking sound. "I'm not dying. *Really.*"

"Then why are you here? You're sick. Obviously."

"This isn't a last-ditch thing for me. My mom just wants to cover all of the bases. She's not satisfied with remission. She wants me cured."

"You're in remission?" I stare into his eyes, startled by how beautiful they are, green and as big as teacups.

"They think so. I just need to finish this course of treatment. I risked my mom's wrath to bring you those tamales, so you'd better eat them."

"You ate already?"

"Soup and a saline drip."

I look away and raise a bite to my mouth. He is the first person besides my sisters and the nurses who truly understands. I don't have to explain a thing. Maybe it's because of my healthy white blood cell count and lack of parental supervision, but this boy seems different. Or maybe it's me who is different. I can talk to him. I can break the rules. I can be a little bit like Adrienne. I sneak a glance at his profile, and for the first time, I feel with my body instead of my brain. I take another bite even though I know the rumbling inside my middle isn't coming from my stomach.

I practically jump when he taps my arm.

"Thanks for being my tour guide."

Four

At the clinic, we come and go as we please. Unless Mom is sleeping, we're permitted to visit, sitting by her side as the Laetrile drips into her veins. We scavenge the kitchen. We sunbathe in the courtyard. I'd broken the rules by walking on the beach, but overall, rules are few and far between. We are captive to Mom's leukemia, quarantined in Mexico, but we have the freedom to pass the time as we please.

I never venture to the pediatric floor, avoiding children hooked up to needles and fluids. The morning after our walk, though, I wake wanting to see Caleb. Maybe it's guilt. I need to see that he's well. I want to prove Lupe wrong—that he isn't like the other sick kids. He actually has a chance to survive.

As soon as I climb the stairs to Caleb's floor, a stout nurse, far older than Lupe, shoos me away. I wait an hour and try again, but there she is, darting in and out of rooms. I wonder which is his.

Adrienne sees right through me. She doesn't believe my made-up excuses to go inside: that I'm checking on Mom or using the bathroom or wanting a snack immediately after breakfast. After my second failed attempt to check on Caleb, I walk into the courtyard to her smirk.

"Love at first sight?" she says.

Adrienne laughs when I tell her to shut up. Marie sits with a book in a shaded corner, hiding from the sun, which rose with furious intensity. I want to escape the heat and the nurses. I want to feel like I felt yesterday, when Caleb stood still and had his eyes on nothing but me.

"Are you just going to stand there?" Adrienne asks, squinting at me. She's immune to the fireball in the sky. Adrienne's skin radiates pink for an hour, then turns to honey. She's Alectrona, the Greek sun goddess. Adrienne raises her arms, as if she's summoning solar powers. She makes a simple stretch look divine.

I plop down on an empty chaise. My mind flashes to yesterday, to the beach, to welcoming the waves on my feet. To Caleb. Yes, I want to make sure he's feeling better and that I didn't somehow end his remission with our prison break to the beach. But I also want to walk next to him.

I'm in orchestra—not band. The piano requires the most space, a true centerpiece. I like it that way. I've never understood the giddiness of band, of marching alongside someone, playing the same melodies. With the piano, I don't need anyone else—the music is mine, the orchestra a mere accompaniment. Yesterday, though, I started to understand the appeal of being in unison.

"Don't be such a coward," Adrienne says. "Just go up and act like you know what you're doing. Walk like you belong there and no one will stop you. It works all the time at school."

"I don't even know what room he's in," I say.

She raises her eyebrow at me. "You can figure it out. Go now, because you're driving me nuts just moping here."

"I'm not moping." I sound petulant, which doesn't help my case.

I'm on the receiving end of her dramatic eye roll. She picks up her magazine. A dismissal.

"Fine," I huff.

I reach the pediatric floor in time to see the nurse disappear into a room. I peek through the open doors. A redheaded boy, a little older than Marie, dozes. An older girl sits on her bed, with slumped shoulders. She glances up and meets my eyes. I've never seen her before. The girl could be an apparition with her pale skin and dark hair, such startling contrast in color. She looks like she's never been outside, never seen the sun. I freeze midstep. It feels wrong to leave her here. I should go into her room and ask her name. She turns away before I find the courage to do so.

"You slumming?" Caleb asks.

He must have been watching me and the girl from his room across the hall. A smile fills his face, and I know that's what I woke up wanting: to see him smile again. To be on the receiving end.

He sits up, and I'm overcome with the urge to touch his face, to put my finger on the cleft in his chin. I sit a safe distance away and tuck my hands into the pockets of my jeans. Suddenly, I don't trust myself. My boldness is a surprise.

"How did you sleep?" I ask.

He smiles at me again and I dig my hands deeper into my pockets.

"You snuck up here to see how I slept?"

I nod, smiling back at him. He's contagious in all the right ways. "I guess so."

"I slept, but mostly I'm bored shitless. I want to take another walk."

"I know," I say. "I'd love to go to the beach again."

He shakes his head. "The beach would be nice, but I meant I want to take another walk with you."

I'm brazen and chickenshit at the same time. I want to join him on the hospital bed and closely examine the freckles on the backs of his hands. I'd like to feel his skin on mine in the same way I can't resist warming my palm over a candle's flame. I don't feel like myself, yet I've never felt more like myself.

Who the hell is this boy?

"Me too," I say. I look him squarely in the eye and allow myself to be seen.

Yesterday, I thought he would be a nuisance, nothing

but one more thing to manage. A burden. Now, I wonder about the color of his pajamas and if he sleeps with his shirt on or off.

Adrienne is going to give me endless grief.

He leans into the cushions, and then all I can think of is Mom. The same bed and the same pillows. My eyes search for an IV, but Caleb is tube-free. A relief. I focus on his face and try to see him—not his illness.

I hear footsteps, heavy and purposeful, most definitely belonging to the nurse.

I stand before she walks into the room. "I have to go, Caleb."

He leans forward. "Hey, promise me we'll take a lot of walks when we're roomies."

"I promise," I say.

She enters with a scowl. Before she can speak, I slip out of the room.

Caleb's mom has a commanding presence, warm and authoritative at the same time. Her cropped hair emphasizes her deep green eyes and cheekbones as prominent as cliffs over the sea. She wears a long skirt and peasant blouse, which look incongruous, like Roman columns on a modern building. It's easy to picture her as a military general, a sea captain, someone taking charge in perilous situations.

Barb fills my arms with a box of clothes. Our house seems to shrink considerably as the Dunnes move in. We haul in books, dishes, towels, and toiletries. An entire crate of vitamins.

I guide Caleb to my room. He looks around, and I'm suddenly shy of my lavender quilt and "Hang in There" kitten poster. However, I'm proud of Adrienne's hand-me-down copies of junior English novels: *The Great Gatsby*, *A Separate Peace*, *The Adventures of Huckleberry Finn*, *The Crucible*, and *My Antonia*. Nothing fluffy. I returned *Leaves of Grass* to the library when school ended for the summer.

He places his skateboard wheels-up on my bed and sits down while everyone carries boxes into the house. With Caleb its occupant, my room becomes foreign territory. Barb stands outside the front door, inspecting contents and directing. When we finish unloading their massive Suburban, I pick up a stack of Caleb's T-shirts and place them in the dresser. I'm not being polite; I want to see his things rest in my drawers, hang in my closet. I haven't felt this possessive since I had dolls.

I reach into his suitcase and pull out his shorts and jeans, sloppily folded. I smooth them out and fold them again, aligning the hems. Caleb concentrates on a box and tosses a clear produce bag onto the floor. I spot his toothbrush and want to run my fingertip along the bristles simply because it's been inside his mouth. The toothpaste pushes against the bag, poking a hole through it. I finish folding the stack of clothes and fill the rest of the drawer.

In her room, Adrienne blares "You Sexy Thing" by Hot

Chocolate, just one song in a series of taunts: "Boogie Fever," "(Shake, Shake, Shake) Shake Your Booty," and "That's the Way (I Like It)," which she sings as she dances down the hall. My punishment for falling for one of the sickies.

I glance at the now-empty suitcase and zip it closed. Caleb places a stack of books on the bedside table, obscuring the view of my alarm clock. I scan the titles: a token math textbook among books about the Beat Generation, poetry by Lawrence Ferlinghetti and Allen Ginsberg. He throws his pillow onto the bed and kicks the box aside, the hollow cardboard buckling with emptiness.

I don't know what to say. All of my *real* thoughts are inappropriate. Since leaving him at the clinic, I've spent my time remembering the brief moments when his skin touched mine. After our beach excursion, I kept sneaking into the pediatric wing, where we talked in his room until the stout nurse evicted me. He read bits of Kerouac poems, lines about Buddha and meditation and jazz—all things I never considered, and honestly, that bore me a little. I tried to listen but ended up concentrating on inconspicuous parts of his body, parts likely overlooked by anyone else: the curve of his big toe, the rough skin of his elbow, the mole beneath his left earlobe. A scavenger hunt.

"Here," he says, cradling a shoebox. "I wanted to show you these." He sits on the floor, cross-legged. Our knees bump, but he doesn't move away. He spills the contents onto the carpet—dozens of slides and a few photos. I pick up a slide and raise it to the light. A miniature Caleb smiles back at me with a wide grin. He must have been nine or ten, around Marie's age. Healthy looking, almost frenetic, like he'd been doing jumping jacks. He stands on a porch bundled in a hat, scarf, and mittens.

"Let me see it," he says. He leans toward me to identify the image. "That was a crazy ice storm. They closed all the schools. I was so psyched. Almost everything was closed. My folks didn't go to work; the power was on and off, same with the phones. It lasted for days. Did anything like that ever happen to you?"

Rain, wind, the threat of mudslides. My clothes soaked through. *I'm terminal.* I blink away the memory.

"It doesn't get that cold here." I sift through the slides, plucking a handful of faded Polaroids and Technicolor snapshots from the bottom of the pile. He describes other storm photos and I gaze at the images of a younger, healthier Caleb, of his beaming smile and broad little-boy face. So this is how he looked before lymphoma turned his blood deadly. His family had cooked on a camp stove and roasted marshmallows in the fireplace. The storm turned their home into a campground. Barb, with a sheet of long, straight, dark hair, looked easy and relaxed, less in charge.

"Why'd you bring these with you?"

"My mom thinks it helps to bring part of home with us. She says it's something to keep me fighting. She's too scared to believe we already won."

"Do you have any brothers or sisters?"

He shakes his head. "Nope, just me."

I envy his position as an only child, a person all his own, contained and complete. Adrienne and Marie glow at such high wattage. I'm the soft light compared to their ultraviolet. Unlike me, he isn't one of three, a constant comparison, the middle child flanked by far more intriguing sisters.

"You don't talk about your dad much," I say. "He's not in the pictures."

"He took them. There's not much to say now that he's gone. My mom says there's nothing keeping us in Seattle anymore. She thinks the sun is good for me. She's thinking of moving us here."

"Staying for good?" I pull at my powder-blue shag carpet. He could stay, maybe in one of those Easter candy–colored bungalows in Pacific Beach or Del Mar. A little house right on the ocean. Sand instead of a front lawn. He could be permanent, remaining long after summer, after New Year's when the calendar flips to 1977. After Mom.

He gives me that look, like the one on the beach that slows down my heart rate and allows me to take a deep breath. His intense eyes sparkle as he smiles with his lips closed, a serious smile, almost gentle in its power. Cancer strips everything away—hair, energy, laughter—and the only thing left is your true self, diminished but pure. That's what I learned at the clinic.

Caleb is pure. Honest and curious and calm, but more

than that. Lymphoma wipes out high school bullshit. As I meet his eyes, my awkwardness slips away. How could anyone sit so still? Perfect posture with a ramrod straight spine, the kind my ballet teacher demanded, back when I thought I'd rather dance to music than create it. I see his resilience and healing. His determination to outrun this thing, but maybe that's because he's in remission.

He nods his head. "Yeah. Probably."

Marie peeks in.

"What's up?" I ask.

"Mom's not feeling so good and I need to take care of her and you have to help Barb in the kitchen."

I feel a twinge of guilt. She should be outside kicking her neglected soccer ball, not in Mom's room—my job. At least Mom reads to her, the two of them nestled under the quilt, turning pages from the thick stack of library books.

"Where's Adrienne?"

"The store."

"Again?" I ask. She just went.

"Mom wants yogurt. She says it's the only thing she can eat. We're out."

"I'm okay," Caleb says. "I kind of need to rest anyway." He lifts himself from the floor and sits on the bed.

I notice how he holds onto one of the slides and wonder which one he clings to, which memory.

"See you in a while." I close the door behind me.

Marie disappears into Mom's room. I watch as Mom

stretches out her arms and wraps them around Marie. Barb has opened all of the curtains, cracking windows, reminding us of sunlight and breezes. I can't remember the last time I walked down the hallway with the curtains open. I pause at one of our family photos taken at Sea World a couple of years ago. Dad must have shot it. The three of us stood in front of Mom, holding shells in our hands, oysters with pearls inside. We had spent the morning with killer whales, dolphins, and pearl divers, who retrieved the shells at the bottom of a large tank. Upon prying open the oysters' jaws, Mom and Adrienne's pearls were perfect iridescent spheres, while mine was black. Of all of us, I'm the only one with brown eyes, inherited from Dad's French Canadian mom. I remember looking at the pearl and instead of appreciating the rare gem, I was overcome with a desire to throw it back at the diver. I didn't care that she dove to the bottom of the tank, all the while wearing a mermaid costume and holding her breath, to dig through the sand just to give me that shell. It felt like a dirty trick. I drew the short straw.

The picture was taken upon the opening of Marie's shell, which contained twin pearls. Someone banged a drum and a group of employees hooted and clapped, the ritual when discovering twins. Dad captured the moment: Marie grinning with delight, Adrienne too distracted by her own treasure to bother looking up, Mom offering Dad a healthy smile, and me standing off to the side. In the hallway full of light, I lean toward the photo, so close that my breath fogs the frame.

I want to see Mom before the cancer, but the glare is too bright and all I see is my own reflection in the glass.

Barb bellows my name, and I find her in the kitchen with her arms full of natural foods cookbooks. She declares she'll leave our meals to fate and beckons me near.

"Close your eyes. I'm going to flip the pages of this cookbook and I want you to put your finger on a page, like this." She guides my hand. "Let's start with *Vegetarian Italian Cooking*," she says. "And then we'll move to *Soups for Good Health*."

My finger selects a main course of tofu lasagna accompanied by a thick Hungarian mushroom soup. "I haven't had that before."

"Very nourishing. We'll make a salad, too." Barb continues to unpack the rest of her cooking supplies. Vitamins of every variety line the counters. "We're all going to eat the vegetarian anti-cancer diet." She holds up two pill bottles, the labels in Spanish. "Why is your mother taking both of these?"

I scrutinize the labels, but don't know what the bottles contain. "I'm not sure."

"This is a very dangerous combination. It doesn't make any sense. Our doctor said these are never to be combined."

"Maybe that's because he's a pediatrician? Mom's a nurse and she says that cancer is like a fingerprint. You know, different for each person."

A strange expression crosses Barb's face. "Doubtful." She pulls groceries from the refrigerator. "Dear one, what's your family's schedule?"

It's summer, so we don't have a schedule. When we aren't at the clinic, Dad brings home dinner and then works all night, sometimes in the dining room, and other times in his study. Mom stays in bed for days at a time. Adrienne and I handle meals and make grocery lists.

"What do you mean? Like school?"

She laughs. "No, what time do you all get up and eat your meals? Do you have an early dinner or a later one? What time do you kids go to bed?"

"Whenever. It depends on how my mom's feeling and when my dad's home."

"That explains a lot."

"What do you mean?"

"I have the sense that life is a little too chaotic. I'm going to put you on our schedule and see if that helps." She places a wet carrot in my hand. "Peel this for me?"

I spend the next half hour listening to Barb's intricate theories of nutrition's relationship to cancer, causing me to worry about the fate of our pizza nights. I quarter mushrooms and chop spinach and endure her lecture on the exact amount of sleep a body needs to function.

Once my final bowl brims with peeled and sliced vegetables, Barb frees me from kitchen duty. I practically run to my room, where I find Caleb not resting in bed, but inspecting my desk. He picks up a sheet of music I keep in the top drawer. "I hear you're a prodigy."

"Hardly," I say with an edge to my voice. Another drawer

hangs open, exposing pens and a notebook. Thank God I don't keep a diary. I can't help but glare.

"Sorry, I was snooping. I couldn't help it."

He hands me the music. Bach. Not a favorite. Somehow, a relief.

"Please don't do that again," I say. Maybe I'll make a list of rules and post them on the wall. *Touch me but don't touch my stuff.* I place the music back in the drawer. I want to be the one who tells him about me, not anyone or anything else.

"Really, Vanessa, I'm sorry. I shouldn't have." He walks to the bed and sits down. I remain at my desk, feeling embarrassed and territorial. He smiles at me, trying to change the mood, giving me enough space to let the moment pass.

I'm peeved with him, but there's something more. That piece was on my audition tape, and suddenly I'm filled with anxiety. I want to run to the phone and ask Mrs. Albright if she's received any letters from the conservatories. But then I remember that it's June. School has only been out for two weeks. We won't hear from the conservatories until early August. Two months of torture. I promised myself I wouldn't obsess about my applications, count down the days until I'm accepted or rejected. It's not like I can go anyway.

I meet Caleb's sheepish eyes. "I like how I feel when I play. No matter how many people are in the room, it's just me and the piano. It makes me feel like I count. With my mom sick, sometimes it's hard—" I stop, not wanting to sound selfish and not wanting to hurt my mother or offend Caleb.

"She told my mom that you were getting recruited by conservatories." He looks at me sideways.

"It doesn't make a difference. That was before my mom got so sick." Mrs. Albright will receive the letters in just two months . . . but the conservatories are an impossible dream. Nothing more.

He grows quiet for a moment. "I think I know what you mean about playing. That's how I feel when I'm on my board." He flings the skateboard to the floor and places his feet so one is in front of the other, the forward leg bent at the knee. "Like this, it's just the board and me. Nothing else. No disease."

I point to the photos and slides, which he's returned to the shoebox. "What do you miss the most? You know, when you look at those old pictures and think about everything before."

"Before getting sick?"

"Yeah."

He stares at his sneakers. "It's messed up because he left, but I miss my dad more than anything." He rubs his scalp. "Even my hair."

The thought of losing Dad is as inconceivable as Mom's leukemia. I close my eyes and wish I could take back my question. "I'm sorry."

"What about you?"

I miss my healthy Mom, the mom in the photo, the one who smiled and led us through the amusement park, the last one wanting to leave. The mom from the movies and the pier, only cancer-free. "I want her to get better."

We sit on the bed until Barb shouts that dinner is ready.

We haven't had company since Mom got diagnosed, so imagine my surprise when I see the dinner table decorated with place mats, *cloth* napkins, and candles—not as many as the day of the storm, but a few.

Mom emerges from her room, looking a little better, but not much. She's coated her chapped lips with a soft pink lipstick, a shade I've never seen before, and she gives us all a tight smile, which I recognize immediately. She's pushing herself too hard. She's trying her best to be normal, but she'll pay for it later with nausea and fatigue. I remind myself to give her some medicine right after dinner. Maybe a sleeping pill, too. I watch her rally. She takes a deep breath, samples the hippie food, and returns her fork to the plate. She doesn't take another bite. I want to hijack a car and buy her clam strips, even if it just gives her the memory of something she loves. As if she reads my mind, she gives me a knowing smile.

While the rest of us eat, Mom quizzes Barb about different natural health treatments. As she explains her own poor appetite, Mom asks what food helps which symptoms. They go on and on until Adrienne and Marie clear the table and wash the dishes. They keep out a plate for Dad, who is stuck at work again.

Caleb and I escape to the family room to watch *Wonder Woman*. Halfway through the show, he puts his hand on mine. I hold my breath, not wanting anything to move. I've held hands with boys before. I've been kissed, even underwater at the public pool. I've had crushes, both requited and not. I may be a wallflower compared to Adrienne, with her devoted cult following, but I know that boys see something in me. Some boys—not the ones like Zach. Mine are in Model U.N. or band or orchestra.

None of them gave me vertigo or tremors or heightened nerve sensitivity, though. Not a single one made me feel like I wasn't so alone.

Caleb squeezes my hand. I look up and find his eyes on me—not the crime-fighting supermodel—and he smiles. There isn't anything bashful about him. Without thinking, I inch closer, just enough that our shoulders touch. I'm so distracted by the heat of his palm on my skin, I can't tell you how the program ended.

Later, after I feed Mom her pills and we have all gone to bed, I whisper to Adrienne about Caleb holding my hand.

"Jesus Christ, Vanessa, you're sixteen years old with a live-in boyfriend. Now you really have something to brag about when you start school."

Five

The house is quiet, but not in the captive way it once was. Small sounds of life fill the rooms, reassuring sounds, sounds of string beans snapping, iced tea pouring, and breezes swaying kitchen curtains. The sounds of the living.

Over the course of two weeks, Barb has renovated our day-to-day lives. With her in charge, we wake to a warm breakfast, orange juice, and herbal tea. She bans coffee, much to Dad and Adrienne's dismay, but they keep the complaints to themselves and frequently sneak in steaming Styrofoam cups.

Dad built our house on a hill, with a solid foundation and good bones, filled with strong weight-bearing walls that would survive a major earthquake. Barb, with her equally solid frame, adds a layer of bedrock. By planting her feet on the floor, she strengthens the whole structure, even if she nags us a little too much, earning her the nickname Bossy Barb. After a late-night conversation with Barb, Dad insisted on meeting with the president of his firm, going over Richard's head. He came home victorious. Mr. President granted him family leave, plus weeks of the vacation time he accrued over the years but barely ever used. He just has to finish one project, the university arts and letters hall, which shouldn't take more than a month. Maybe two.

In the meantime, he devotes his attention to Mom and Marie, who need him most. Marie enrolls in soccer camp and vacation bible school. As soon as Dad changes from his suit into shorts, they practice, running the length of the yard until he comes in sweaty. It isn't until then that he can sit still, reach for Mom's hand, and talk about the week's medical schedule. He remains out of breath.

Adrienne escapes to the beach with Zach. After breakfast, she packs her backpack with her magazines and sketch pad and bolts out the front door. She refuses to allow Zach to pick her up at the house, stopping him at the bottom of the hill, where she climbs into his pickup. She comes home full of stories about how they spend their days at the beach, hanging out at one of the cafés where the staff treats them like adults, serving them free coffee refills. But her giddiness wanes quickly when she asks about Mom, disappearing altogether amid talk of Mom's appetite and energy and mood. Barb relieves us of our responsibilities as nurses, cooks, and housecleaners. We're almost kids again. An impossibility, but we try anyway. It is worth it when Mom smiles at our daily reports of swimming, soccer, and skateboarding. The luxury of boring details.

I'm content to stay at home with Caleb, playing cards on the front porch and taking skateboard lessons. The incline of the driveway functions as the beginner's slope as I learn to balance my body on the board. I circle the driveway until I do it ten times in a row without falling. Mastering that initial skill, turning the board without crashing, takes an entire week, and Caleb instructs me on distance, on how to ride beyond the driveway, beyond a block.

A couple of weeks ago, it was inconceivable to spend hours outside, to do anything that didn't require caring for Mom or Marie. However fragile Caleb may be, he's not my responsibility. Caleb is teaching me the difference between desire and obligation.

He looks so much better, barely like the boy who nearly fainted on the beach. Swirls of dark curls sprout on his scalp, and I have to resist the urge to trace the tendrils of growing hair. He doesn't have tons of energy, but he has enough to keep him out of bed until eight or nine at night. After dinner, we lounge in my room, door open due to Barb's strict rules, and play one of our clinic waiting-for-Mom board games. I lose over and over again because of the close proximity of his legs against mine. I catch him looking at me as I assess the Yahtzee dice or weigh the cost of the crown jewels of Monopoly: Boardwalk and Park Place. I glance up in time to catch him, and instead of bashfully looking away, he meets my eyes.

"You don't have to let me win," he says.

"I'm not *letting* you win."

He taps my naked toe with his own. "You don't have to be so nice."

Without thinking, I laugh and repeat something Mom often says: "Adrienne's the pretty one, I'm the nice and quiet one, and Marie's the baby."

He places the dice on the Monopoly board and stares at me a little too seriously. I can't read him, which happens sometimes when he isn't feeling well but refuses to tell me so. "What?" I ask. "Are you okay?"

"Why would you say that? It's totally messed up."

I straighten the neat piles of bills, smoothing out creases, taking my job as banker way too seriously. "It's nothing. Just something stupid that we say."

"It's bullshit."

I want him to look away, at his thick stack of properties or line of hotels. At the wall. At anything but me.

"I mean it," he says. "First, it's not true, and second, who says something like that?"

I don't know what to say. They're just facts in our family, as clear as the fact that Dad is an architect and I'm a pianist and Mom is sick. Small and identifying details. Nothing more. Nothing to debate or get upset about.

"Vanessa?"

My eyes remain on the board. "It's nothing," I say. "Don't make a big deal about it."

"Adrienne looks like she could breathe fire. You *are* nice

and you're quiet in a good way. You actually listen to people. I've never met anyone who listens like you do."

"Can we please keep playing?" I ask.

"Yeah, in a minute. Did you hear me?"

I nod. Of course I want him to say these things about me, but not this way, not in comparison to my sisters, not in response to something utterly and completely stupid that slipped out of my mouth. "I just want to play, though."

He exhales, and I can't tell if he is annoyed with me. "Can I say one more thing?"

"Sure," I say.

"You're the beautiful one."

I close my eyes, just for a second, and snatch the dice, tossing them with conviction. Double ones.

He leans close. "Aren't you going to say anything?"

I'm about to land on Reading Railroad, one of my favorites. "Snake eyes," I say.

"I mean it," he says.

I tear my eyes from the game, mustering enough courage to look at him, to see exactly how much he means it. I wasn't fishing for compliments or putting myself down. I was just talking. Babcock conversation. Nothing more. But when our eyes meet, I understand that he knows I'm not playing games. He sees *me*. It's clear by his smile and the way he looks into my face, surprising and foreign and, although I didn't know it until that second, necessary. He nudges my foot, tapping until I smile. I force myself to not look away.

Mom is a different person with Barb around, as though our houseguest possesses supernatural healing powers. After a couple of weeks with the Dunnes, Mom now rises with the rest of us, and although she looks pale and weak—sometimes not getting dressed for a couple of days—she sits in the kitchen with Barb for hours at a time. Barb seems to steady Mom's moods, too. She takes better care of Mom than we ever could, and Mom hasn't snapped at us once since Barb and Caleb arrived. They talk exclusively of cancer, detailing various ailments, their language consisting of phrases like "cell's reproductive cycles" and "white blood count." Their conversations are constant, and they have a feverish energy between them, as though their discussions might lead to a cure. Barb says she's fascinated with Mom's leukemia, and Mom absorbs the remark like a flower does the sun.

We settle into a new rhythm crossing the border; with Barb behind the wheel, our excursions are speedy and efficient. She manages the short trips to see doctors and receive test results, as well as the overnights when Mom and Caleb rest as Laetrile drips into their veins. We go for tests and infusions and to build up the arsenals of vitamins and supplements. Sometimes I stay at home with my sisters, just the three of us again, free to take Mom's car anywhere. Other times, Barb takes Mom alone. Her treatment is more frequent and rigorous. We don't speak of her prognosis. Barb believes positivity is essential to recovery. We don't dare remind her that there is nothing positive about terminal cancer.

When I attend summer music camp, time becomes arbitrary and meaningless. We practice together in the sunlight and roast marshmallows in the dark. It feels the same with Caleb. I have to check the clock and the calendar to remember the time and date. Hours blend into days. I don't need anything but the piano—not that I've been practicing enough—and him, and he's easier to touch. He helps me focus on the moment, not the future. He helps me forget that the conservatories are just a dream. With Barb managing the house, I'm more aware than ever how much work is needed to take care of Mom. Leaving is out of the question, no matter how much I long to concentrate on music.

Caleb is more than a distraction. When he holds my hand, he reminds me that I have fingerprints and nerves have endings. A gesture, a touch, can be as important as words.

This morning I look at the calendar: Thursday. When Barb gets ready to drive Mom to the clinic for another infusion, we all pretend the rigorous treatment isn't linked to her declining health. They plan to stay the night, returning before breakfast to beat rush hour and border traffic. The rest of us stay home, and they promise to call to say good night. Adrienne leaves with Zach, and Dad drives Marie to camp. My only duty is to tuck her cleats into her backpack.

I watch as Dad backs the car out of the garage, marveling at how just weeks ago, such a day was inconceivable. We'd be at the clinic for the rest of the week. The kitchen would've had the sharp smell of a full trash can. The refrigerator empty. Dad would be scrambling to leave work, pick up a pizza, and come home before eight.

Stacks of newspapers cover my neglected piano. Despite my promise to Mrs. Albright, I've barely played, stealing time when I can. My fingers long for the keys, but Caleb is sleeping and I can't risk waking him. When I pace through the house, all I find is a clean kitchen and a refrigerator teeming with leftovers. I have nothing to do. I pass Caleb's room—my room—to get a book. When I press my ear against his closed door, I don't hear a thing. I wait there for a minute, wishing I had bionic superpower ears that would allow me to listen to his heart as he sleeps.

A towering oak tree shades the front porch. In our pre-leukemia life, Jasmine and I often stretched out on a blanket there and tackled homework. I can't remember the girl I was back then, much less the stuff I used to care about—now completely irrelevant. I don't want to think about Jasmine and what it will be like when school starts. I haul out a kitchen chair so I won't have to sit on a lonely blanket, a reminder of how things used to be. My feet rest on the railing and I open another Agatha Christie novel. I need the comfort of knowing the mystery will be solved, the criminal caught, and peace restored.

Three chapters later, Caleb pads out barefoot and sleepy-eyed. He looks good except for the bruises on his arms, Laetrile track marks.

"You okay?"

He yawns and nods. "Hungry. I see you're reading more fluff."

I shake off the criticism. "Did anyone ever tell you that you're a little judgmental?"

"You're the first."

"You're a snob," I say as I close my book. "Agatha Christie is an international best seller. Have you even read her?"

He shakes his head. "I'd rather spend my time talking to you about anything other than Agatha Christie." He stretches, raising his arms above his head and touching the top of the door frame. His T-shirt rises, showing off an exposed inch of his belly. I almost reach out to touch him. Instead, I stand. "Come on. Your mom made a bunch of food."

He laughs. "I'd kill for a burger and fries." He drops his arms from the door and turns the knob back and forth in a restless way, like he wants to move his body for the simple sake of moving. He has energy—extra, even.

"I can make you a quesadilla," I offer.

"You mean I could have a tofu-free meal?"

"Yes. Extra cheesy and full of fat."

As he follows me into the kitchen, he snatches a satsuma from the overflowing fruit bowl and liberates it from its peel. "That would be awesome. Real food. I mean, my mom does all this for me, but—"

"You need something really unhealthy to feel human?"

"Exactly. Have a slice of this orange."

He separates a piece for me and puts it in the center of my palm. We look at each other, frozen in place, just staring. His eyes hold every possible color, green with flecks of gold and aqua blue. My healthy blood pumps through my veins, filling my heart so much that I think I'll go into cardiac arrest. How could the body redirect everything to one organ? That's how I feel—blood abandons my lungs, my kidneys, my liver—everything else that keeps me standing upright, here, in front of him. Bones and skin and that giant bundle of muscle, my heart, the only thing that matters, and I want to reach into my chest and hand it to him, as he handed me the orange. He makes it all worth it. Not Mom's cancer, obviously, but the resulting collateral damage: losing Jasmine and my friends. Walking down the halls alone. Not having anyone to call when Adrienne is out with Zach. It's like I spent sophomore year trying to take a deep breath, and I couldn't, not really, until he walked into the clinic's courtyard.

"You should eat that," he finally says as he pops the remainder of the fruit into his mouth.

My taste buds fail me. All I feel is his finger tracing my hand. "Let me cook." Remarkably, my voice box still functions.

I watch him eat one quesadilla, then another, along with two more oranges.

"You're better."

He nods. "Yeah. I feel good today. What do you want to do?"

Nothing that would change this day, his good, energetic, pink-cheeked day. This is the best he's looked, so much better than when I first laid eyes on him three weeks ago. "We don't have a car to steal."

"Let me take a shower and think of a plan."

Caleb in the shower. I turn away so he won't see me blush. "I'll clean up."

"I'll be fast."

"Okay," I say.

The bathroom is at the other end of the house. He won't be able to hear me. I have just enough time to run through Beethoven's Piano Sonata No. 31 in A-flat Major, one of Mrs. Albright's more difficult pieces. I scoop up the newspaper and sit down on the piano bench, a homecoming. My fingers sweep the keys. I try to focus on the music. The piano anchors me in place, but my mind rises and falls with the piece, levitating through the music.

"You're so good. When do you practice?"

I drop my hands into my lap. "I haven't been. Not enough, anyway."

Water drips from his skin. He didn't take the time to dry off. He dressed hurriedly and I finger the hem of his T-shirt, which is inside out.

"Keep going," he says. He pulls my hand off his shirt and moves it back onto the keys. "Come on. I want to hear."

I left the front door open, and a breeze rustles the sheet music. I close my eyes and concentrate on the notes. I don't start over, back to the beginning. I pick up where I left off and play with everything I have, pouring myself into the music, to the crescendo, and finally the end. He puts his hands on my shoulders and mine remain on the keys. I feel his breath on the back of my neck. The piano and Caleb, both at once.

I turn around. He pulls me up and kisses me. The kiss I've been waiting for since our doomed walk on the beach when I almost killed him. This is the kiss that I wanted when he moved in, when I go to sleep, and when I wake up. This is exactly how I imagined, the closeness of his body, the way he holds the back of my head in his palm.

He will be fine. Just look at him, I tell myself, a promise. This is what remission looks like, the inching back to life, skin looking like skin again, not like parchment, yellowed and thin. I kiss the place where his cheek meets his throat, tickled by his stubble, and whisper, "You're not dying."

"Told you so."

He pulls me closer and I get my wish: not just the kiss, but the sound of his heart.

"Will you play more?"

"Later." I lead him back to the porch and we sit on the steps.

He nudges his knees against mine. His skin is still warm from the shower. "Come on," he says. "Play more. It's just me here."

"Maybe in a while, okay?"

"You're really good, Vanessa," he says. "I mean it. I've never heard someone play music like that except on a record or on the radio. No wonder you're getting recruited."

I look at my bare feet, at my chipped cherry-red nail polish. "I love orchestra, but it's a lot of traveling on weekends and events at night. My teacher wants me to do it, but I can't bail on Adrienne like that."

"Yeah, but how can you bail on something you've worked so hard for? And you're really good." He looks at me, waiting for me to keep going.

"It's not about being good, though. Playing was the only time I could breathe at school, so I played whenever I could. Mrs. Albright knew that the only way I was getting through this was by playing. She gave me harder and harder pieces and I just blew through them. She says I need to think about my future, like transferring. But there's no way, right? I mean, how can I do that, ask for that, when we have to take care of my mom?"

"You don't have to explain," he says.

I nod and rest my head against his shoulder. When I open my eyes, tears spill down my cheeks. "I had science last period. My favorite class after music. I'd walk into class and my teacher, he's really cool, would tell me to go see Mrs. Albright. He'd nod his head and tell me to go. That's it. They always knew when I needed to play. You know, on the hard days. It was hard to be away at the clinic, and it was hard coming back."

"Going back to your old life," Caleb says. "Reentry sucks. Nothing's the same, but everyone wants you to be the same. Even when I looked like this." He rubs his scalp, but he doesn't look like a chemo victim anymore. He is just a boy, maybe too skinny, with weird hair. "It's ridiculous," he says. "You'll never be the same. No matter what."

I nod. "Exactly. Now I don't have much time to play."

"Why don't you play in front of us?"

"I don't want the noise to bother anyone." I don't tell him that it scares the hell out of me, to be closely observed by people I know. I need the cover of a dimly lit auditorium.

"You have to play every day," he says.

"There are more important things now. It doesn't feel right to spend all my time practicing when your mom is taking care of the house. No one should be taking care of me." I hang my head. "I'm not sick. You're the one who had to go back to school and have everyone stare at you, even when you were doing chemo. I can't imagine how you felt."

He doesn't let go of my hand. My veins pound and my wrist tingles. He presses his finger harder, digging deeper into my life line and heart line, making our fates permanent, intertwined. I feel his illness, his slow recovery, how it must have felt when his dad left.

He takes a deep breath and lets it out slow, relaxing his fingers. "I stopped going. I couldn't take it anymore. I quit water polo. The coach waited for me to tell him. He wasn't going to kick me off the team. Kick someone when they're down. When I saw another guy wearing my number, I went home and told my mom I wasn't going back to school. She tried to homeschool me, but I wouldn't read. Then I was too sick to even try. No one made me go back, even when they told me I was in remission."

He squeezes my hand. "I know we're different. Your mom's the one who's sick—not you. I'm not dying, but I'm not cured."

I nod, knowing he doesn't want to say the obvious: Mom is dying, and she doesn't have a chance of going into remission.

"You're not the one who has cancer," he says. "But people still stare at you, right? It's not your body, but you still have to live through it. You just know you're going to live."

I kiss him softly, first on his cheek because that's closest, and then I turn his head and meet his lips. "You're not dying, remember?"

"I remember," he says.

"Prove it."

He cups my chin and kisses me until I forget about everything else, even the piano.

Six

Adrienne's bed is empty, a pile of rumpled blankets and sheets. I close my eyes as soon as I open them, remembering Caleb: his touch and taste and the way I exchanged the air in my lungs for his. The steady beat of his heart calming mine, racing rabbit-fast in my chest.

My toes curl at the memory of his hand on the small of my back. He was still warm from the shower. His shirt, a little damp, clung to his skin. He is everything I imagined and still a mystery. I embarrass myself with a ridiculous smile that won't go away.

I think I knew, back on the beach just three weeks ago, that he would change me somehow. And when I walked into his hospital room the next day, watching him sit up and smile at me. The way he looked at me, the way he looked *into* me, isn't that different from the way he kissed me. Like I was the only thought in his head. Like I was the only one he wanted to touch.

I want more of him. I want all of him. He is asleep in the next room, in my bed, and I want to crawl in next to Caleb so I can hear the strength of his heart in his chest. I close my eyes and hope his heart is beating stronger because of me.

Piano becomes a public affair. After Caleb made the error of mentioning my playing, Barb clocks my time on the piano bench. She goes as far as suggesting I play during dinner like a jazz pianist in a bar, the sort who uses a fish bowl as a tip jar.

I refuse.

He kissed me a week ago. Caleb's kissed me since, quiet moments as we explore the neighborhood on his board, jumping off when we're confident we won't be seen. I want to hop on the board and align my body with his. I fall asleep wanting to feel his breath on my neck, his hands around my waist.

Music consumes me. It always will. But until now, I've spent my days with Mom, sitting in the car or at the clinic rather than on the cool, polished wood of the piano bench. With Caleb, I have something to touch other than the keys.

I want to be alone with Caleb and I want to be alone to play. Something shifted with our kiss. I opened myself to him, and when I did, I saw things differently. There can be more than the house and the clinic. Maybe, just maybe, we could make the conservatories work. Our lives aren't as small as they were just last month. With her tender bossiness, Barb assumed custody of us all, putting food on the table, listening to Dad, and nursing Mom. I'm allowed to practice instead of cook. Barb, with all of her natural remedies and vegetarian cookbooks, makes our house feel like a home again.

Caleb liberates my heart—Barb liberates us all.

Except Mom. Nothing can free Mom, but Barb tends to her in a way none of us can. Not even Dad.

When I sit at the piano, I play with a newfound attention, as though I'm playing for my future, like everything depends on it.

Caleb doesn't understand that I'm not a performer, not in the way he assumes. Being in orchestra allows me to focus on music. Recitals and concerts are nothing more than requirements, transactions, a small price for hours alone with the piano. Come practice time, he sneaks into the room, which throws me off the clear constellation of notes. Too shy to ask him to leave, I fumble through new pieces, cringing at my crappy progress.

My compromise: Whenever he enters a nearby room, I switch to a mastered piece, one of the six I included in my conservatory applications. This works for a couple of days until Adrienne calls me out.

"You promised you'd never play that one again. *Ever.*" She turns to Caleb. "Holy crap, we had to listen to that for two months."

I slam the lid shut.

Mom defends me, telling Caleb about her favorites,

itemizing my solos, recitals, and awards. How she asks me to play the same piece over and over again, her "healing music," she calls it.

But even Mom's praise doesn't ease my nerves. Whenever Barb insists that I practice, excuses roll off my tongue and I find myself vacuuming under my parents' bed, cleaning Mom's vanity table, and tackling other intimate chores. There are windows of time, half an hour here and there, when the house empties for errands, and I stay behind to play without an audience. As long as I muffle the piano, I can practice while Mom sleeps, an increasing amount week by week.

Mrs. Albright assembled my summer homework with care. She organized the sheet music by level of difficulty, not in regards to skill, but emotion. She understood that I can't touch the keys without feeling, and some of the pieces paralyze me, especially Chopin, with his uncanny knack for leaving me breathless.

I may play by myself, but I don't play alone. Her spidery handwriting adorns the folder, her standing invitation to call or visit.

She wouldn't approve of how I break her carefully constructed order, but I can't squeeze in Liszt minutes at a time. He requires more—hours, even days.

After a few days of struggling with Liszt, I tell Caleb I need to skip the clinic sleepover. He studies the sheet music, reading the title, Piano Sonata in B minor, with an expression of bewildered jealousy. Even with cancer, he is unaccustomed to a rival.

They all leave without me. Dad comes home hours later, his arms filled with blueprints. "It's not like you to play hooky." He rests his oversize paper, building designs rolled like scrolls, on the dining room table.

"I've got to finish this," I say. "I'm not even close."

He wrestles off his tie and gives me a tired smile. "We'll work together. I think I can get this done by the end of the week. We're that close. Want anything from the kitchen, sweetie? I need a beer."

"No thanks. I'm good."

Even drinking a beer, Dad looks kind of elegant, handsome in an old movie sort of way. He pulls out a chair and taps a few keys, rapidly, like a player himself. "You need a better place to play. You shouldn't be cramped in here."

I release the piano from my sloppy soundproofing, covering the floor with blankets, a large pile that takes up too much space. I play a small part of the sonata, the few proficient notes. The sound can't compete with school's grand piano, despite its age and overuse.

"It's fine," I say.

He glances around the house. "We'll figure out something better after—"

Our eyes meet, both of us startled by the acknowledgement that she'll be gone soon, that we could consider rearranging furniture without protest, without negotiation. Without her.

I feel slapped by the brutality of the truth, something implied every day. She will die before long, a plain fact, but for how much we deal with the daily details, we never speak of our lives without her, not beyond the abstract. He covers his face with his hands. "I didn't mean it like that."

I close the piano, hoping that by hiding away the keys, I'll erase the betrayal.

"Yes, you did."

"I didn't mean for it to sound like that, Vanessa."

His eyes possess a pleading quality, and I understand that only I can assuage his guilt. Her death will destroy us, but it also will free us of small burdens, of the constraints of her fatigue and nausea and strong opinions. He is speaking of more than redecorating our house. They are horrible thoughts, thoughts that I have too, and I regret each and every one.

We had a dog once, a border collie, Smiling Joe. I don't remember, but apparently I begged for a puppy, and after a solid year of asking, I woke to bundle of black-and-white fur licking my face. Dad said that he liked having another male in the house, even if it was just a dog. My seven-year-old legs were too short to keep up with his bounding pace. He was built to run and herd sheep. I was twelve when he bolted out the gaping front door in order to chase a trespassing cat. Our neighbor tried to swerve. I doubt she could have missed him. Afterward, he howled and then let out a sound that was so close to human that I still remember it. I crouched next to him, avoiding the sight of his crushed hind legs, and stroked his ears. I didn't want to add to his pain by putting any weight on him. Just an hour earlier, I'd rested my head on the scruff of his neck. So, I hovered above him and whispered any reassuring thought that came to mind. Mostly a mantra of *I'm right here; it will be okay.*

Even in that moment, guilt was paramount, almost as powerful as grief. I should have shut the door. I should have taken him for a walk. I should have put him in our fenced backyard.

He kept making that human sound. I wanted him to be out of pain. I wanted him not to suffer. I wanted Mom to come out and help, but she was somewhere inside doing something that involved planning a dinner party. I wanted him to be quiet. It only took a second for me to realize that meant I wanted him to die.

"It's okay, Dad. Really."

He kisses the top of my head. "I'd do anything for you, kiddo."

"I know."

He fiddles with the handle on his briefcase. "What's that smell?"

I scrunch up my nose. Barb instructed me to stir the stew simmering in the Crock-Pot, a thick blend of stringy eggplant and crushed tomatoes. "Dinner."

The front door swings open. He freezes. They're home early. Too early.

I follow Dad to the front of the house. Adrienne carries a large box, the month's supply of medication and supplements. Marie holds Mom's hand like she's coaxing her inside. Mom walks through the door cautiously, as though she forgot how to put one foot in front of the other. Her skin is the color of aged newsprint. It must be eighty degrees outside, but she wears a thick sweater and shivers. Her hair, once a shiny gold, hangs limply on her shoulders. Despite her morning bath, she looks like she hasn't showered in a week.

"She wouldn't stay the night," Adrienne says. "There's a new doctor and he wanted to do some tests."

"Why?" This time Dad directs the question to Mom.

She stands in the hallway and rests her weight against the wall. "That doctor was barely out of medical school."

"Why did you let her come home?" This time Dad looks at Adrienne.

Adrienne gives him a furious scowl. "Why haven't you started your leave of absence? I can't tell her what to do. You're the one who should be there. Barb moved in *five weeks* ago and you're still working."

He flinches. "Where was Barb?"

"Where do you think? Caleb's getting his own infusion. She's not *our* mother, you know."

He turns to Mom. "Iris, why didn't you stay?"

She sweeps her hair from her forehead. "I couldn't let someone that inexperienced take care of me. I need to lie down. Vanessa?"

I turn on the hallway light and guide Mom to her room, the only consistently orderly room in the house. She sits on the edge of the bed and I pull off her shoes. She is impossibly thin; her ankles almost as small as my wrists. I watch as she closes her eyes and takes a series of deep breaths.

"Would you please fetch my robe?" Her voice sounds low and gravelly.

I open the closet and look at the long row of neglected dresses: the gown she wore to the museum's gala tucked next to her Christmas party cocktail dresses. We spent spring break placing them in clear garment bags, preserving Mom's favorites. I pluck the soft robe from its hook. I construct a cocoon of blankets and quilts. Even bundled, she still shivers. She tries several different positions—side, stomach, back—before getting comfortable. The peonies resting on the nightstand bloomed days ago, and now their petals spill over the vase, wilted and brown at the edges.

"Do you want to go to sleep?" I ask. "I can get you a sleeping pill."

"No, it's a struggle to stay awake. Stay with me?" She reaches out her hand. "I want to keep you close."

I rest my head on Dad's pillow and try not to think about Smiling Joe as I listen to her labored breathing.

"I won't go back if I have to see him again," she whispers.

Is she dreaming? Is she talking to me? "Who?" I ask.

She takes a deep breath, and just when I think she fell asleep, she says, "That doctor. He's a sadist."

I watch her face, and even on the verge of sleep, she looks afraid. I realize that she must be fighting fear like a low-grade fever, a constant threat of spiking. I almost take her hand, but she uncurls her fingers, her muscles relaxing as sleep overpowers her. I stay until her face loses its worried expression, frown and furrowed brow, and she falls into a sleep too deep to dream.

She sleeps through the night, and when she wakes, Adrienne, Marie, and I take turns in her room, even after Barb returns with Caleb, even when Barb tells us to let Mom rest. Adrienne rolls her eyes at Bossy Barb and lounges on Mom's bed, sketching portraits of Mom, filling out her cheeks and brightening her eyes in the drawing. I serve Mom tea and toast. Eventually she begins to improve; soon she's strong enough to help Marie organize her saint cards, their new project. Mom pulls out a photo album, a metallic gold one she'd been saving for Christmas pictures, and gives it to Marie. In elegant script, almost calligraphy, Mom copies Marie's favorite quotes, dying words of murdered virgins. A holy and morbid scrapbook.

She clings to us, though, telling us how much she loves us, how she is our mother, to never forget that, especially given how Barb has taken charge of the house. She doesn't mention the doctor again.

Adrienne, however, does. Dad makes her repeat every detail, but Adrienne and Marie spent the afternoon in the courtyard and never saw the doctor, much less met him. Lupe didn't mention a new doctor. Adrienne describes an ordinary afternoon at the clinic: heat and boredom and the smell of the ocean and blooming jasmine.

I feed Mom a sleeping pill so she can get some more rest. I'm desperate to see a hint of pink in her cheeks—anything to remind me that she is still alive. At least her breathing returns to normal, no longer low and rattling.

Caleb, stretched out on my bed, bolts upright as soon as he sees me. "Skate?"

After spending so much time staring at Mom, I can barely stand to look at the life in him: a slight sunburn, freckles, enough energy to stand, to walk, to hop onto his board. If I ignore the redness around his eyes, violet rings like Saturn's, he could be healthy. "Where are Adrienne and Marie?"

"Backyard. Adrienne's drawing and Marie is doing that catechism thing." Almost as a reminder, he takes a moment to get his footing, briefly closing his eyes, blinking them open.

I catch myself staring. He waves his hand. "Laetrile hangover. Let's go."

On the driveway, Caleb kneels down to bend my knees, moving my legs into position. Gently, he pushes the board. "Go. Now veer to the right. If you bend your front leg more, you'll go faster."

I glide down the sidewalk and then pause as I wait for Caleb to catch up. I watch him walk toward me, scrutinizing his face and his pink cheeks, fuller now than before, so unlike Mom's. The breeze presses his shirt against his body, emphasizing his broad shoulders. I want to run a hand across the width of them. He hops onto the board and places his hands on my hips.

We ride down the street, cupped against each other, venturing nine blocks, a record, before turning toward home. The sun dips in the sky, paling behind the clouds, the clouds pink and golden.

"You're quiet today," he says.

"I'm just thinking about my mom."

"That whole thing was crazy." He tightens his grip on me.

"You know what happened?"

"Yeah, I was there. My mom too."

I don't know how to brake. I drag my foot on the asphalt, but instead of slowing us down, I rock the board, tilting to the right, almost crashing. He brings us safely to a halt.

"What exactly did he do to her?" I ask.

Caleb shifts his weight from one foot to the other. "I thought she told you."

"Only that he's a sadist."

His eyes widen. "I don't know what the big deal was. He just wanted to take a blood sample. He said her medication is wrong and he wanted to check. She . . . I don't know how to describe it."

He stops talking and I resist the urge to shake him, restart him like a stalled battery. "And?"

He flips up the board and rests it against his knee. "It was nuts. She started screaming that he was going to hurt her and that he was stupid. She said he didn't know anything."

"But what did he *do* to her?"

He won't look at me. "Nothing. He didn't do anything but take a blood sample."

Finally, he looks up, and I wish he hadn't, because he looks at me with such pity, something I thought I'd never see from him. "I'm sorry, but she lost it. I mean, she went completely crazy. The nurses had to hold her down."

Mom, with brittle bones and sepia skin, disappearing right in front of us. Mom, who couldn't get out of bed. Restrained by nurses, not one, but plural, pinned down by firm hands.

"Why would they hold her down? What are you talking about?"

He shifts again, the sun hitting his face at a different angle, and in the change of light, he looks strange, backlit, two-dimensional.

"She was out of control. They were trying to calm her down and give her a sedative. Sorry, I shouldn't have said anything."

When he meets my eyes, something passes between us. I wonder if he's holding back, keeping details from me.

"Did you see anything else? Did the doctor say anything?"

He coughs. "No, that's it."

He looks at the ground.

"You know more, don't you? You're just not telling me."

"It's hard to understand what's going on down there."

"But you know something," I say.

"Not yet, but my mom is trying to make sure your mom's okay. She wants to figure out what happened so she can help."

"*Did* anything else happen?"

He nods. "Not to your mom, though."

"Then what?" I hate it when my heart picks up speed like it's doing now. "Tell me, Caleb. Please."

He must hear the desperation in my voice, because he meets my eyes and they don't contain any pity, or the devastated look they do when he talks about his dad or chemo. "I want to end treatment. I don't need Laetrile, and I'm beginning to think that it doesn't matter if I take it or not. I'm in remission. My mom's worried about my cancer coming back, but Laetrile can't stop that. It's a treatment, not a vaccine. I don't think it's good for me. Maybe they're right and Laetrile is dangerous. I told her when we drove back, but she shot me down. She's making me finish the cycle."

"It's your body. You can say no."

He shakes his head. "Not until October. I'm a minor until then."

"This is messed up. Tell the doctor. Pitch a fit like Adrienne. She'll teach you."

He smiles. "Believe me, I don't need Adrienne to teach me how to have a big argument with my parents."

This is the first time he mentions his dad—using "parents" rather than "parent"—and doesn't flinch.

"Then do it."

He waves his hand between us. "I want to end treatment, but what will happen with us? Mom and I are supposed to move out when I'm done."

"You're going to stop Laetrile no matter what. You're two-thirds done with your cycle." I look away. The thought of him going back to Seattle is unbearable. "Has she been looking at houses here? Are you moving here?"

"She circled some listings in the classifieds. She hasn't found anything yet. Is your dad still okay with us being here? Even though you're starting school so soon?"

God, school—I haven't even thought about it because it seems impossible that they'll actually make us go, especially now.

"Wasn't that the unspoken agreement?" Caleb asks. "That we'd be out by then?"

I shake my head. "We talked about seeing how things are going by the time school started, but don't worry about being here. It's so much easier, you know, with your mom cooking and everything. I think Dad's happy not having pizza every night. He likes talking to her. My mom does too."

He looks at a jagged crack in the sidewalk, the damage of a large oak tree's rebellious roots. "It's going to get harder with your mom."

"I know." I wipe tears off my cheeks. "I'm scared of you seeing it. Her getting worse."

"Six months ago, I was almost ready to give up. I couldn't

get out of bed because chemo made me so sick. I didn't have any energy. I threw up all of the time. I couldn't concentrate. I could barely think. I didn't think it was worth it if the rest of my life was going to be like that." He pauses, and I watch his face as he chooses his next words. When I reach for his hand, he weaves his fingers with mine.

"The crazy thing was that I was kind of okay with it. My dad was gone. Friends too. I couldn't skate or surf or swim or read. I couldn't do anything that made me *me*, you know? I felt like there wasn't anything left. I didn't feel like a person anymore. I wasn't who I used to be and I didn't think I'd ever become someone new, like a post-chemo person. A person who got through the worst part of life and then came out the other side. My body was dying and my head was so screwed up that nothing mattered but getting through the hour without puking. That wasn't living. Dying became a pretty appealing option."

He meets my eyes and I see the layers of emotion—hope and acceptance and resolve.

"I don't want my mom to die."

He pulls me close. "Me neither, but I'm trying to tell you that at some point she'll get some peace. You won't, because it isn't your body, but she will." He kisses my forehead.

I look up at him. "When did you get better?"

"A couple of months later. I finished chemo and then my tests came back. I couldn't believe it. Chemo was actually worth it. My mom used that to tell me that I need to finish Laetrile."

"How do you feel now? Not your health but what you said, as a person? You're not who you used to be."

He shakes his head. "That guy died during chemo."

"But you can skate again. You can read. I know it's not the same, but you'll be able to surf and maybe even play water polo. You're getting better every day."

"I'm not talking about sports and books. I know what it's like to be okay with dying. I lost a lot when I got sick. There's no way I'm going back to high school. I haven't told my mom, but I'm going to get my GED and then decide what I want to do after that. As soon as I turn eighteen, I'm going to make the decisions. I love her. She's an amazing mom. But now that I'm going to have a post-chemo life, I want to be the one who decides what I'm going to do next. My whole life was blown apart and I'm going to put the pieces back together. I'm not going to do it alone or anything, but I need to be the one who puts everything back." He taps his chest with his finger. "No one can do that for me. No one can tell me who I am going to be now that I'm better. I don't know what's going to happen—just that every decision matters."

"Which is why everything needs to be real."

"Yeah," he says. "And you're as real as it gets."

He shifts his attention to the skateboard. "Get back on."

Caleb pulls me toward him and adjusts my feet so they are between his, his left foot on the rear of the board and the right in front. He wraps his arms around my waist, pulling me so close that I feel his heart beat into my shoulder blade. "Just stand and lean next to me. Don't move your feet unless I tell you to."

He pumps his leg against the sidewalk, and we cruise, hopping over the grooves in the concrete, the board's even rhythm slow compared to the rapid beating in my chest. I don't want to think about the future, just the present, this moment. I concentrate on the movement, on his touch. He moves the board in a figure-eight pattern, slow loops up and down the street over and over again with me leaning against the length of his body. His hands inch down my waist, stopping right below my bellybutton, right at the top of my jeans. We ride until Barb bellows for us to come inside and eat dinner.

Seven

Marie and I judge the straightness of the lines as Dad and Adrienne hang enormous sheets of paper—Dad's sketches of the university arts and letters hall. His jackass of a boss tortured him for weeks, scrapping design after design. Columns versus skylights. Even a futuristic glass dome. Beneath each sketch, Adrienne tapes signs written in elegant script:

Neoclassical Columns per Richard the Dickwad
Glass Castle per Richard the Livestock Fornicator
Golden Rotunda per Richard the Asswipe

Eleven designs in all. Dad stands before the most recent and final one, just approved that day. It resembles his very first—a stately building, beautiful in a cathedral way, making the very act of learning sacred. Classes in epistemology and Shakespearean drama and the French Revolution. A wing devoted to music, a refuge of small practice rooms housing pianos and music stands.

This is it. After two months working on the building, he's done. He just has to finish out the week. Two more days before he starts his leave of absence.

Giddy, he points to one of Adrienne's labels. "That's not neoclassical." He taps another sketch. "This one is."

I can't remember the last time I've seen him smile like this, with such relief, unburdened. Pérez Prado, King of Mambo, plays on the turntable. Dad moves his hips like Desi Arnaz on *I Love Lucy*. A testament to his stories about courting Mom with his superior dancing skills. I think of the many photo albums filled with snapshots from trips to tropical places with spicy food and passionate music. Mom in one of her many party dresses. Dad grinning in every photo. Then came our slim baby books. They haven't been abroad since Adrienne was born.

"We should play a game," Adrienne says. "Like pin the tail on the donkey. Here." She hands Dad a sign, stiff with layers of scotch tape. "Close your eyes and spin around three times."

Mom emerges from her room, groggy from painkillers, which she consumes more than food since that horrible day at the clinic almost two weeks ago. Still, she dressed for the party in a sundress, turquoise, at least a size too big. More like two. A spaghetti strap slips off her shoulder, and I pull her shawl from the back of her favorite chair. I need to cover her, hide the sight of her bones, so visible under her translucent skin. She doesn't look like the woman in the vacation photos or in the snapshot from Sea World. More like a walking skeleton. She forces a smile. She put on lipstick for the celebration.

Marie bounds to Mom, arms open, eager for a hug. Small Marie, who now looks more substantial than Mom. "No!" I say too sharply. Marie isn't accustomed to being strong, to having enough physical force that she might squash Mom like a bug. I watch Marie's eyes widen and her smile vanish.

"I haven't seen Mom all day," she says with tears in her voice.

Mom's eyes, narrow with disapproval, land on me. "I'm perfectly capable of hugging your sister," she says.

"Sorry," I say. "I was worried you'd get hurt."

I can't read Mom's expression—the strangest combination of hard and soft. She opens her mouth and closes it again, clearly searching for words. For some reason, a shiver runs through me and my hands feel clammy. I haven't seen her like this for months. She doesn't look away. She wants something from me, I'm certain, but I can't figure out what. I've developed a talent for predicting her moods before she voices them: tired, nauseous, overwhelmed, in pain.

What could have happened? I wonder. But nothing's changed, our routine unwavering, with Mom and Barb spending even more time together, like this morning when they holed up in Mom's room with the door shut. Only then, Barb emerged lantern-jawed, almost scowling, walking down the hall with resolve.

"You shouldn't worry so much. I'm your mother. It's my job to worry. Not yours. And certainly not Barb's." Then, as an afterthought, "Sweetheart."

She doesn't sound reassuring.

"Iris!" Dad says. "Think you could manage a sip of something bubbly? Barb and Caleb are picking up sparkling cider and dinner. They'll be back any minute."

She smiles at him and her face fills with affection, almost normal. "What's that in your glass?" she asks.

Dad takes a sip. "Mediocre champagne. Nothing special. Found it in the pantry. It's perfect."

"I'll have some of that. Nessie, please pour me some."

Despite her softer tone, I want her to look at me, fill me with the same warmth she normally bestows, but she doesn't glance my way.

"Are you sure that's a good idea?" Dad asks.

"Absolutely." Mom cocks an eyebrow, catching me by surprise. Adrienne does the same thing all the time. Her punctuation. I'd forgotten she'd inherited it from Mom.

Adrienne turns her attention away from the sketches. "Jesus fucking Christ, if she wants some booze, why the hell not?"

Mom clears her throat and tightens the shawl around her body. Marie fills the chair next to her, resting her head on Mom's shoulder, holding hands. "I swear, Adrienne, it's like I never taught you any manners. I didn't intend to be so permissive. I should have done better, but you tired me out.

You pushed me all the time. Now, read those signs to me."

Adrienne does, losing confidence as she recites each one. *Fuckwit. Shithead. Penisbrain.*

Mom shakes her head. "My daddy would have slapped me in the mouth if I cursed like that. Once he gave me a fat lip because he overheard me say the word 'sex.' It's a good thing he died before you were born. Peter, you'll have to do a better job than me. It falls to you now."

Marie, startled by Mom's tone, inches away. I want to scoop her into my arms, but I don't dare cross Mom. It's been months since she acted like this, spontaneously cruel, with random moods that disappear as quickly as they come. Worse right before the diagnosis, but better until now.

Adrienne catches my eye, and I see the sting, but also her determination. She's tied her long hair into a high ponytail, making her look girlish and sweet, and as she turns to Mom, it swings in the air.

"You taught me to talk this way," she says.

"I did no such thing, Adrienne."

Adrienne smiles, the same smile she uses when she destroys someone at school, a bully or a rival. "If you'd paid more attention, you would have noticed that this is how I talk. You never *really* tried to stop me. This is who I am. I'm not a goddamn Southern belle. It's not like you named me Scarlett O'Hara."

"Adrienne!" Dad says. "That's enough."

"No, Peter, that's quite all right. Let's hear our eldest tell us how her dying mother didn't teach her proper manners. I know I failed you, Adrienne." Mom's voice loses its authority, its edge. She bends her head and cries, quietly, and if we all hadn't been staring at her, we may not have noticed. She's that quiet, that still. Marie squeezes Mom's hand.

Mom wipes her eyes and looks at me, her face now devoid of expression. She seems tired, only tired, not angry or icy or frustrated. "Take me back to my room, Vanessa. Please."

"No," Dad says. He reaches for Adrienne and kisses the top of her head. He does the same to Marie, and then me. "Vanessa, you stay here."

He helps Mom to her feet, and once she's steady, he looks at each one of us, stopping at Mom. "I want to make something clear. No one failed anyone. We're doing the best we can."

Mom, her eyes red-rimmed and enormous, looks almost extraterrestrial, with sunken cheeks and gray skin. "Adrienne," she says. "Come here."

Adrienne doesn't move. She doesn't say a word.

Mom shakes free of Dad and shuffles toward Adrienne. When she reaches her, Mom raises a hand to Adrienne's face. She never struck us, not once, not even a spanking. Still, I suck in my breath, a chill once again fills my body, and I wait for the sharp sound of a slap. It never comes. Instead, Mom strokes Adrienne's cheek and whispers, "Forgive me."

She turns and walks down the hallway alone, unassisted, and closes her bedroom door.

We celebrate without Mom, who doesn't leave her room for the rest of the night. Barb fills the vacant space, feeding us all, refilling Dad's glass of champagne. She came home with another bottle. Dad comes alive in Barb's company, gesturing with his hands and standing up as he describes the height of the building. Barb asks questions and keeps him talking. I notice that when he answers, he speaks in the future tense.

Later, after we polish off a bottle of sparkling cider, I volunteer to raid the kitchen for something else to drink. I'm the innocent one pining for soda. Adrienne schemes to sneak the last of the champagne.

I find Dad and Barb at the counter. With the precision of a sushi chef, she slices carrots and celery, fanning them around a bowl of hummus. They don't see me, and their words make me freeze midstep.

"The problem isn't the new doctor, Peter. The problem is Iris. There's no reason for her to react this way. She must've had these tests dozens of times. How else can you know she's terminal?"

Dad bows his head. "You don't understand. Her father was a physician and very strict. He died before I met her, but from what Iris has told me, he was abusive and brutal. She developed a fear of doctors, and it took her some time to find one with a gentle bedside manner. We have an appointment with him next week. I'm sure he can explain what's going on."

Barb sips her champagne and offers him a tender smile.

"Enough of this talk, my friend. We have more celebrating to do."

She picks up the vegetables, and just before she rounds the corner, I dart back to the living room and tuck my hand into Caleb's.

Will it be like this? After Mom's gone, after some time passes, will we spend evenings marking milestones, smiling and laughing despite the grief? She is with us, just down the hall, likely knocked out by a combination of sleeping pills and painkillers. Adrienne and I take turns shushing the room, fearing we'll wake her up, not knowing which version of Mom we would see.

We divide into pairs: Dad and Barb, Marie and Adrienne, Caleb and me. I cling to him for the rest of the night, and if I could get away with it, I'd slide into his bed, certain his heat would sedate me enough to sleep.

The next morning, Mom acts as though nothing happened. She has that pre-Laetrile infusion mania, talking fast and breathless, fidgeting constantly. She's worse today, fretting over the visit, still anxious about the last time, the "sadist." The only reason she agreed to go back was the promise that she would never have to see that doctor again. I can't bring myself to meet her eyes. She hasn't had a mood like that since right before the storm. The rain washed away her flashes of spite, or so I believed.

When it comes time to go to the clinic, I don't play hooky. I can't abandon them for the piano—not this time, our last sleepover at the clinic during Dad's final days at work. Adrienne and I help Barb pack the Suburban, and I squeeze in between Marie and Caleb, aligning our limbs, my thigh pressed against his. I spend the entire ride glancing at our legs, at the hems of his shorts and my skirt, at the inches of bare skin, his touching mine.

I reach for Caleb's hand and weave my fingers through his. Barb distributes peppermints, something that is supposed to settle the stomach. He inches even closer, and all I want is to taste his candy-cane mouth.

Caleb's body is growing familiar: the scar on his knee from an early skateboarding crash, the pale half-moons at the base of his fingernails, the way he takes a gulp of air before kissing me. He is a swimmer even if he doesn't play water polo any more.

Barb pulls into one of the parking spaces reserved for patients, and we walk up the entryway stairs, passing a large bed of blooming flowers. A man, someone I don't recognize, empties a trash can.

Caleb rests his skateboard on the ground, nudging me with his elbow. "Practice while I'm in hell, okay?"

I trace the inside of his arm while it's still smooth and intact. Barb pulls him away. "We're running late, Caleb. Let's get upstairs. Vanessa, I'll check on you girls later. You know where to find us."

I turn to follow Mom, but she raises her hand. "I'll be fine. Go play outside."

She must have noticed my skepticism, because she reaches for me, gently, but I still feel skittish. "I'm sorry, I wasn't myself last night, but I slept well and I'm ready for my infusion. Now go with your sisters."

She ascends the stairs slowly, gripping the handrail.

"You coming?" Adrienne hollers from the other end of the lobby.

We sling our backpacks over our shoulders and cut through the laundry room into the courtyard, settling in our usual places. Nothing seems to have changed. The landscape looks the same regardless of the season.

Adrienne spreads out her beach blanket on one of the old chaise lounge chairs. She reaches for her sketch book and colored pencils. She's determined to capture every view of the ocean. If she can't swim in it, she says, she'll at least document its beauty. Her art teacher loves her landscapes, and she flips to her latest drawing of the cliff adjacent to the clinic, which is storied to be an ancient site where humans were sacrificed to the gods.

She flips through her many portraits of Mom, younger, healthier portraits—memorials, really—and then the ones that capture the present. I can barely look at them.

"I don't know why you draw those," I say.

"They're honest and she likes them," Adrienne says as she stares at a particularly haunting sketch. "It doesn't really matter how they turn out. I just like sitting with her. Even if she's asleep."

I drop my backpack and push the skateboard back and forth, getting a feel for the wheels on the concrete path.

"I'm kinda hungry," Marie says.

"Let me check out the kitchen," I say as I park the board on the grass.

Roberto, one of the cooks, smiles when he sees me at the door. I'm so glad he's manning the stove. He is the generous cook, much more so than the woman who works on the weekends, when we went hungry for hours, sometimes the whole day. Roberto looks as old as Dad, and his two sons, about Marie's age, are among our clinic friends.

"Hola," I say. *"¿Cómo está?"*

"Bien. Very good. Hungry?" He slaps homemade tortillas onto the griddle, causing the butter to sizzle. "*Frijoles* again?"

"Por favor." I sit in the empty chair by the refrigerator.

"How's your mama?" Roberto asks with his back to me. He moves slowly between the large open pots on the stove and the counter covered with diced vegetables: carrots, onions, chilies, tomatoes, lettuce, and tomatillos. He rotates his broad body from counter to stove, tossing handfuls of vegetables into various pots. Soup, beans, rice, and stew.

"Worse. It's getting harder."

He pauses and turns around. "I see this."

Steam rises from the stove and Roberto flips the tortillas. He pulls three plates from the high shelves and scoops rice and beans onto them. Quickly, he moves the tortillas from the griddle, deposits them onto the plates, and piles onions and *pico de gallo* on top of *carnitas*. "I carry."

"Gracias."

"Almuerzo," he announces when he sees Adrienne and Marie.

Marie hops off of the chair and runs to Roberto. "Eat with us!"

"I make *sopa* for your mama. Next time. *Mañana*." He rests the plates on the metal patio table and produces forks and napkins from his apron pocket. "*Mis hijos* are coming soon."

Marie beams. "Soccer!" The game is the only thing that distracts her from her saints.

"Thanks, Roberto." Adrienne accepts a plate. "Come on, Marie. Eat."

I linger next to him. "Thanks again."

He looks down and smiles. He places a hand on my shoulder. *"De nada, mija."*

Roberto and Lupe bring such comfort. As I watch his heavy steps, I can't imagine life without either of them, two people I didn't know last year in a country I barely visited.

Marie quietly dips her tortilla in her beans. It's unclear if she understands the ritual of saying grace. Lately, she eats her meals in complete silence, explaining that she is praying.

I pick up my taco. The food tastes good, and who knows when we'll eat again. The kitchen is overwhelmed with patient lunches; then staff will get their break. Roberto's shift ends after supper. Later, we will fend for ourselves, piecemealing together leftovers. During our first weeks at the clinic, I read a good portion of the *Boxcar Children* series. Inspired by the multitude of survival techniques applied by the orphans in the books, I rummaged regularly through the closed kitchen. It was easy compared to hunting for berries in the woods while living in an abandoned train car. A welcome distraction.

When we finish eating, I stack the plates to return to Roberto. Marie kicks her soccer ball across the lawn. Leaving her sketchbook on the ground, Adrienne stretches out on her belly and absorbs the sun. I wander into the kitchen, but Roberto isn't there. It's too hot to go back outside, so I decide to check on Mom. Maybe I can even dodge the hovering nurses and sneak into Caleb's room.

The infusion rooms are on the third floor, dedicated to those who require the most nursing. I wander upstairs and look away from any room with a door ajar, passing the private rooms with beds full of cancer. I follow the noise down the hall, listening for Mom's voice. A scowling doctor rushes past me. I hear unexpected crying and am surprised when I turn the corner to find that it belongs to her.

Mom reclines in a gurney with Guadalupe next to her. Her hospital gown is wrapped around her in a style that looks more like a kimono. A needle pierces the inside of her elbow, linking to a full bag of clear liquid, which drips from the sack, through the tube, into Mom at the same speed that my heart is beating. The heat leaves my body. Goose bumps run up and down my skin, and I feel light-headed.

"*Mija*, you should go back downstairs," Lupe says.

"What's wrong, Mom?"

"Nothing for you to worry about." She wipes tears from her cheeks, but the IV tugs her skin, causing her to wince. "I just need to rest, sweetheart. Are you settled in?" I can see her veins through her cellophane skin. I imagine the Laetrile working its way through her blood, attacking the abnormal cells.

I shake my head. "Not yet."

Lupe stands and gestures toward the door. "Come, *mija*," she says. "Let your *mamasita* talk to the doctor. Let's find you a place to sleep."

I look back at Mom.

"You heard Lupe. Go now, Nessie. Scoot."

We walk down the tile stairs and stop at a door near the kitchen. The clinic must be close to capacity, because we rarely stay in staff quarters. The room is simple, a large white square with two sets of bunk beds, a painting of a dark blue dove against a pale blue sky, and a crucifix. Lupe gives me a tense smile before returning to Mom.

I sit down on one of the lower bunks and examine the underside of my arms, tracing my veins. I've seen Mom receive countless infusions, but each time is growing increasingly difficult to witness. I've never seen Mom cry from the pain, though.

I evaluate the room, relieved that we aren't placed in a

patient room filled with the odor of illness and rubbing alcohol, with steel trays and IV tubes.

Cheers and giggles come from outside, and when I return to the courtyard, I see Marie playing soccer with Roberto's boys. Two of the sick kids, a boy and a girl, join in, an easy game. Low impact. Nothing to tire them out. They run in slow motion, their legs moving cautiously. Marie is the fastest, but she doesn't show off her natural athletic abilities to the cancer kids. Marie understands disadvantage. She slows down and resists the opportunity to score over and over again.

Adrienne, who has resumed her sketching, looks up. "How is she?"

"Something's going on. She was crying."

"Why?"

"She wouldn't tell me. Lupe said Mom was talking to her doctor."

Adrienne's brow furrows. "Mom didn't say he'd be here today. I thought she had an appointment with him next week. Dad is taking her. He made a big deal about it."

I shrug. "All I know is that she's up there crying and I don't know what to do."

Adrienne meets my eyes. "There's nothing you can do. If she needs us, Lupe will come."

I nod and press my fingertips on Adrienne's arm, into her warm skin, and release my hand, leaving a white handprint. "You're getting burned."

"Whatever," Adrienne says. "It'll turn into a tan tomorrow."

I hop onto the board and follow the curving path around the courtyard, trying my best to take a sharp turn without falling. Finally, bending my knees and crouching down, I zigzag the board just like I've seen Caleb do dozens of times. I pump up the path, the wheels slowly thumping, calming me down.

It takes a second for me to figure out who is screaming, a familiar voice yelling, "No! You don't have my consent!"

A frantic wail.

Mom.

I don't remember falling off the board—the actual moment is completely erased from memory. My eyes fixate on my leg, which looks twisted and disgusting. Blood trickles down both knees, but my foot is bent in the most grotesque way. I can't breathe.

Adrienne hovers over me. I try to sit up, but she puts her hand on my chest. "Don't move," she says, her eyes on me for just a second before searching the courtyard. I spot the soccer ball in the flowers.

"Marie! You need to go get help. Get Barb or Lupe! GO! *NOW!*" Adrienne shouts.

Pain pulses up and down my leg. I want to move, to stand up, to straighten my bones into their natural position, but Adrienne holds me in place. "I mean it. Don't move. You'll make it worse."

Tears wet my cheeks and my whole body shakes from the pain. Marie rushes to me with Barb close behind.

"I'm here, dear one. The doctor is coming." Barb says. She looks up. "How'd she fall?"

"She crashed on the skateboard and went flying." Adrienne is more out of breath than Marie. "This is the perfect place to break a bone. There are what, three or four doctors on duty?"

A doctor, a man whom I've seen but doesn't treat Mom, appears and, without a word, touches my leg. I can't help but whimper. "Inside," he says.

They carry me into a large open room and ease me onto a gurney. My good leg dangles off the edge, and the other rests in a straight line, a miracle. I can't concentrate on their words, just the deep pain. Something is wrong, torn or broken, where the muscle meets the bone.

Barb clutches my hand. The doctor holds a syringe between his fingers like a cigar. A pile of gauze and a tub of white paste rest on a metal tray. I focus on breathing, inhaling through my nose and exhaling through my mouth, a calming trick Mom taught me.

I remember the screaming, not mine, but Mom's. "Where's my mom?" I ask Barb.

All of the muscles in her face tighten, and she frowns. "Don't worry, dear one."

"You're going to feel some burning," the doctor says in perfect English. His accent is as slight as his build. He is barely an inch taller than Adrienne, who stands in the background. He grasps my arm and inserts the needle into my skin. I gasp at the pain.

"That will help," the doctor says. He pulls a strip of gauze from the pile and unravels it like a rattlesnake unknots itself before an attack. He focuses on my leg. "I am Dr. Alvarez. I work with the children. The pain will be gone in a moment."

Dr. Alvarez is right. I feel my eyelids droop as I listen to Barb's reassuring voice. I know Adrienne and Marie are in the room, but I'm not sure where. It's hard to focus. The doctor dips the gauze into the cool plaster, wraps it around my ankle, and smoothes out each strip. I try to concentrate on his seamless motions and guess he is someone who can peel an orange in one long ribbon. Slowly, the pile disappears and he pours the remaining plaster up and down my shin.

"She will sleep now," I hear him say. "Stay with her and make sure she doesn't move her foot. She cannot walk on it. No weight. Understand?"

I hear footsteps and voices as people leave the room. Someone cradles my hand, someone smaller than me. Marie. When I wake up, she's gone.

Dad's voice fills my ear and I feel his sturdy hand on my shoulder. "Vanessa, Vanessa, wake up."

I try to adjust my eyes, to see if he is there or if I'm dreaming. There he is, still in his suit but without his tie. "Hey, kiddo, I'm going to take you home."

Pressure radiates up and down my leg, but I barely feel the pain—it still throbs, but from somewhere strange and distant. I barely feel my body. I look around the room. Kitten and rainbow posters line the walls. "Where's everyone?" I ask.

"Your sisters are waiting in the lobby." Carefully, he slides his arms under me. "I'm going to carry you now, okay?"

I nod. "She was screaming," I say. "Something's wrong with Mom."

"You were dreaming, honey. Let's get you into the car."

He lifts me off the gurney, holding me with great care, and I close my eyes again, wanting nothing more than to believe him.

Eight

I didn't begin with the piano. Vivaldi introduced me to classical music, with his urgent melodies and passionate arrangements. Everything deep inside me, everything I was scared to feel, much less express, exploded in his music. *The Four Seasons*. Winter. I'd never seen snow, but if a blizzard felt like his violin, I would have welcomed frostbite and exposure.

When I started violin lessons, the bow felt long and awkward in my hand, and when I moved it across the strings, I made a keening sound, high and screeching, the sound of something wild and close to death.

As the painkillers loosen their hold, my leg, from knee to ankle, embodies that sound. Long, taut, and completely dissonant. I clench my jaw and fists. Adrienne strokes my hair. We are in the backseat of the car. She senses pain—Mom taught us that.

"We're almost home," she says.

Dad talks over his shoulder. "I'm dropping off you and Marie. I'll take Vanessa to the emergency room before I go back to the clinic."

Marie snores in the front seat. She rests her head against the window, and her breath creates a circle of fog on the glass.

"But she has a cast," Adrienne says. "Why do you need to go to the hospital?"

"Did they take an X-ray?" Dad looks at her in the rear-view mirror.

Adrienne shakes her head.

"Did they even examine her?"

"I don't know," she says. "Kind of."

"That's why we're going to the emergency room."

I stay in the car as Dad carries in Marie, who can sleep through anything. I can't move from the backseat, can't block out the searing pain. I want to curl up, to hide from it, but I'm not that strong. Dad speeds through the neighborhood, taking shortcuts and blowing through stop signs.

The hospital seems quiet and organized, nothing like the clinic. Dad fills out a thick stack of forms and hands them to a woman sitting at the desk.

The nurse takes one look at me and says, "Let's bring you back."

Dad helps me through the giant double doors to an exam room with a bed. I notice the shiny equipment and realize how outdated the clinic's rooms are in comparison. Both share the same sterile odors, but this hospital has machines with blinking lights, an intercom paging doctors, and posters about poison and choking hazards.

A doctor enters, bald, grandfatherly, somewhat stern. He flips through the chart and assesses my cast. He extends his hand to Dad. "Dr. Sato."

"Tell him what happened," Dad says.

Complete sentences elude me. I do my best to describe the skateboard and the way my contortionist's leg bent in the wrong direction. I tell him about Dr. Alvarez and the shot as powerful as a horse tranquilizer.

"Where did this happen?"

"*Enfermería de Paz y Salud* in Ensenada," Dad says.

"You can't be serious. Are you sick?" The doctor examines our faces.

"No, my wife. Leukemia."

Dr. Sato turns away and reaches for tools lined on a tray. He selects a pair of pliers and a small saw. He looks at me. "I'm going to remove the cast. It'll be loud, but it won't hurt. Tell me if you need me to stop."

I nod and turn my head, attempting to ignore the high-pitched buzzing sound. The doctor cuts a straight line down the inside of my thigh, bisecting the cast. When he liberates my leg, it's swollen twice its normal size, and the skin is blue and purple. He squeezes my leg and instructs me to wiggle my toes, praising me when I do, as if this is an accomplishment.

"Now," he says, "move your ankle back and forth."

But I can't.

He turns to Dad. "We're going to get some film of that leg."

An older man with pale skin enters the room. I guess he's worked the graveyard shift for at least a decade.

"Are you ready for the X-ray?"

I nod and he pushes the gurney into a small room. After bashfully asking if there is a possibility I could be pregnant, he drapes a metal apron over my virgin body and instructs me to stay still.

He asks too many questions: *Does that hurt? Are you okay? Can you turn your leg to the left? Can you turn it more?* I wish he would stop talking. Just take the X-ray and let me rest. Please. I'm not sick like Mom.

If I squint and examine the wall closely, I suspect I'll see something disgusting. Some small fleck of something human. But the paint looks new and smells of disinfectant, a pungent scent of something pretending to be clean. I rest for a while, sometimes closing my eyes, sometimes examining the wall.

Just as I nod off, he returns me to Dad.

Not long after my hazy journey to the X-ray room, the doctor turns on the light box and places the X-rays on the surface, smoothing the edges like he's hanging new wallpaper. He traces the image of my leg, following the tibia bone. My leg is fine—not broken—a straightforward ankle sprain and a pulled ligament. The majority of the pain came from the irresponsible casting, which was compressing the nerve. *Entrapment neuropathy.* If Dad hadn't brought me in, I probably would have needed surgery. I may have had a limp for the rest of my life. Dr. Sato explains my simple recovery. I'll be spared a cast and crutches. Just a few days of ice packs and elevation. A thick Ace bandage. A blessing.

"I'd like to speak to you about your wife," he says to Dad. "I'm sure you're aware of the controversy surrounding Laetrile."

The doctor closes the curtain, shielding me from their conversation. I try to listen to their low and hushed voices, but I can't make out their words. The curtain gapes open, leaving a view of the other patients. A young boy, maybe five or six, cries as his skin is stitched. The nurse with the sewing kit coos at him, pausing to wipe away his tears. An older man, bloated from grease or alcohol, rubs his stomach. Careful of my ankle, I turn away from the door.

They take a few steps closer. I hear the rustle of paper and the quick sound of a pen.

"She said it was too late for chemo and now we're at the end," Dad says.

"It's a mistake to pursue this course," Dr. Sato says. "I can't emphasize that enough. Does she have nausea, vomiting, headaches, dizziness, difficulty walking?"

"Yes, everything."

"Those are the symptoms of cyanide poisoning," the doctor says. He enunciates each word, stressing the severity. "These people offer false hope, and they profit from patients and families when they're most vulnerable. There's a reason why it's illegal here. Here's the name of an oncologist. Tell him I referred you and you need an appointment immediately." I hear the rip of paper. "He'll be able to give you a realistic prognosis. They can't treat your wife at that clinic. Those are not legitimate hospitals. There are plenty of capable physicians in Mexico, but not the Laetrile peddlers."

"She's dying." I haven't heard that much anguish in Dad's voice since the diagnosis. "We're at the end. I'm going to get her as soon as we're done here."

"Let the oncologist run some tests," Dr. Sato says.

The doctor's words, clearer by the second, flood my mind. Dad said it is over—we are at the end.

Yet Mom can sit up and hold a conversation.

She isn't unconscious.

And she can scream.

I know some people think Laetrile is too experimental, but a hoax? This doctor has to be wrong.

They leave me cocooned until Dad signs the remaining forms. He wheels me to the car in silence. The morning air is crisp and clear; wisps of clouds streak the sky. It is five-thirty and the city is quiet, the freeway empty before the morning commute.

We drive west, away from the sun, which fills the sky by the time we reach home.

He clings to my hand the entire way.

Adrienne poaches extra pillows from Mom and Dad's bed to create a nest for me, "the cripple." I can't convince her otherwise, even when I hand her the discharge papers with my anticlimactic diagnosis.

She is stunned—not her usual self. She waited all night to tell me what happened at the clinic. After she tucked Marie in bed and Dad headed back to the clinic, she was alone with the news. Adrienne doesn't wear stillness well, and as she talks, I want her to gesture and tilt her head and grimace or smile. Anything to remind me that she is three-dimensional. That she isn't scared shitless.

While I was out cold from Dr. Alvarez's shot, Adrienne was busy learning about what happened to Mom. I *had* heard her scream. It wasn't a dream. Adrienne explains how the new doctor, the one Mom calls a sadist, insisted on examining her. Something happened with the IV and she was left punctured and bleeding. He said he needed more blood, another sample. Something was wrong with the other, the one he had forced from her before. He wouldn't leave, despite her injured arm and screams for help. The doctor removed Lupe from the room and brought in another nurse, also new to the clinic. They gave Mom a massive sedative. He threatened restraints, which he eventually used, tying her down to draw from her good arm.

Adrienne calls him a motherfucking vampire.

On the ride back from the hospital, Dad insisted that our clinic days are over. He is furious and talked of lawsuits and medical licenses. Of our limited time together. Quality of life. Family time. A countdown to life without her.

I tell Adrienne about Dr. Sato's damning words. When I finish, I look up, straight into her eyes, almost as familiar as my own.

"It could be true after all, right?" I ask. "Maybe Laetrile is killing her?"

A race between leukemia and cyanide.

She shakes her head back and forth. "All I know is that something bad is happening. When I got a chance to see her, she looked almost dead. Her head was slumped forward and her lips were gray. I couldn't believe it."

Exhausted and breathless, Adrienne and I curl up next to each other. When we were little, before my hair darkened to barely blond, we were confused for twins. An unlikely compliment made long ago, but there is some truth to it. Adrienne and I fit together. We make sense as a pair. Maybe that is why we rarely fight—it's absurd for anyone to consider us rivals.

Before Marie was born, my parents took us on epic road trips up the coast, stopping at lodges in Big Sur and Mendocino, beaches where forests met water. Adrienne and I loved our old station wagon, especially when Dad let us sleep in the back, curled up in sleeping bags, snuggled together as they drove in the dark.

Adrienne grabs my blanket and we share her bed, exhausted, twins again.

"You know what this means, don't you?" she asks.

We'd set an extra seat at the table for death. We know he is coming, about to blow us apart. Grenades and smithereens. Blitzed. Obliterated. Flattened. Our lives reduced to combat metaphors.

"Yeah," I say. "But I don't want to talk about it." I want to ask Adrienne to get me one of Mom's pills, it doesn't matter which.

She sits up in bed. "Someone's home."

I follow her down the hall, careful of my sore ankle. Caleb drops the skateboard. "Come on," he says as he takes me to his room—my room—and shuts the door, breaking Barb's rule.

I hear Barb's voice in the background. "Caleb, we don't have a lot of time. I know this is hard, but you need to be quick."

"Are you okay?" he asks, and when I nod, he kisses me, not just my mouth, but the side of my neck, and then my collarbone. A little rough. A little urgent.

"What?" I reach for his hand, pulling him to the bed. "What's the matter?" We sit side by side. I keep his hand in mine, holding it in my lap. I swear I can feel every nerve twitch in his body.

"I didn't know what to do when my mom told me you fell. You were gone by the time I was done with the infusion."

"It all happened so fast. I'm just glad you're here."

Just as I lean to rest my head on his shoulder, he pulls away. I stare at my empty hands and then at his face, at his watery eyes, puffy and swollen.

"What's going on?"

He curls and uncurls his fingers. He looks at the floor, not at me.

"Are you okay?" I ask. "Nothing's wrong with you, right? Your tests are normal?"

"Yeah, all of that's good. My mom is letting me stop Laetrile. I only have to go back for one last test."

He still won't meet my eyes. I touch my collarbone, the exact spot of his kiss, and then I reach for his face. "Why don't you sound happy, then? What's wrong?"

He won't let me touch him. He stands and takes a step back.

Can the body be crushed from the inside out? An unbearable weight fills my chest, like my lungs are turning into concrete. Layers and layers of panic wash over me. My mind jumps to dozens of worst-case scenarios. He isn't dying or kidnapped by drug smugglers or detained at the border. He is here, in front of me, but completely out of reach.

I try to steady my breathing, exhaling the last twelve hours: the pain and the shot and Mom. If I empty myself of some of that fear, maybe I can create room for courage.

Tears pool in his eyes. "My mom just told me to get my stuff together. We're leaving now. She found a hotel near the beach. I have to pack."

"What are you talking about?"

My heart beats hummingbird fast. I didn't hear him correctly. Mom and Caleb. One loss is staggering; two are unimaginable. How can this be happening?

"I don't understand," I say. "Why would you leave?"

"I don't have a choice. I don't want to leave. I want to be with you, but my mom said that with how things are with your mom, we can't stay any longer."

"But we need you," I say. "You can't leave. Not now. What about my mom?"

I've known Caleb for almost two months and I've lived with him for six weeks. I can't imagine him gone.

His eyes remain on the carpet, like he is counting the fibers one by one, like they are stars.

"Caleb, look at me. Please."

With his hair growing back, he looks younger, more his own age, and more helpless then I've ever seen him—even after an infusion, even after he'd collapsed on the beach. "My mom thinks something's up."

"Yeah, she's dying—*that's* what's up." I never expected I'd have to state the obvious to him.

"There's something else going on. My mom talked to that doctor. The one who took your mom's blood. She and your dad . . . things aren't adding up . . ."

"What?" I say. "Just stop. She's sick. Sicker than you. I don't know what the hell you think is going on, but you're wrong and Barb doesn't know what she's talking about."

"It's not just my mom."

"If things are *wrong*, if something's going on, why would you leave?"

I barely hear him when he speaks. "I don't have a choice."

He takes a deep breath, exhaling through his nose, just like they teach you when they give you a shot. Things are supposed to hurt less when you push air from your body.

"I don't want to leave you," he says, finally meeting my eyes, searching my face.

"Then don't leave," I say. "Stay."

It's what Adrienne would do. She wouldn't lose someone so important to her—not without a fight. "Let's go tell your mom. Just don't go."

"I can't stay, Vanessa." He turns away from me. "I need to pack." He drags a box over to the dresser.

Ignoring the pain in my ankle, I shove the box aside.

I can barely hear him when he speaks. "My mom said this is a toxic environment. We have to get out of here."

He might as well have kicked my legs out from under me. I stumble back to the bed, resisting the urge to burrow, to bury myself in anything dark and quiet.

I feel his body curl around my back like a shell on a snail, his arm sliding beneath my waist so he can hold me as tight as possible, so there isn't any space between us. His legs next to mine, his mouth on the back of my neck, his tears in my hair. "I'm sorry," he breathes.

I barely choke out the words. "I can't believe you're saying these things."

"I don't know what's happening, but it scares me. I've never seen my mom like this. Not even when my dad left."

"So you want to go? You want to leave?" I hide my face

and will my body still, but I can't stop shaking. Pain pulsates from my ankle. I don't want to cry, but my chest fills with tightness. Tears slip down my cheeks and I slap them away.

His voice fills my ear. "I don't want you to be alone."

"I have Adrienne. My dad. I'm not alone." A lie.

He pulls me closer. "I meant I wish I could bring you with me."

His hand moves up from my waist, stopping at the edge of my bra, feeling for the opening in my dress, the thin straps on my shoulder, tugging them off. I close my eyes when I feel his teeth on my bare skin, his hand under my bra. He holds me in that position, not moving a muscle, until the rhythm of our breath matches, a duet, violin and piano, alto and tenor.

"This isn't going to change anything," he says. "We can still be together."

"You don't know that," I whisper.

He pulls away, an abandonment I can't bear. I look around the room, at his books on my nightstand and his discarded clothes on my floor. This isn't my room anymore. It's his now. Ours. "This changes everything," I say. "I don't even know when I'm going to see you again. *If* I'm going to see you again."

I shoot him a look, daring him to make a promise he can't keep. I'm crying and furious, and everything is happening all at once and way too fast. Ignoring the pain in my ankle, I stand with shaking legs and clenched fists.

He steps toward me and wipes the tears from my cheeks. "I'm not letting you go. I swear, Vanessa."

I squeeze my eyes shut. "Do you even know the name of the hotel?"

His shaky breath warms my neck. "The Sandpiper Inn."

I feel young and foolish next to him, like suddenly I am the sick one. He leans down to kiss me, but I turn my head away. He doesn't withdraw. Instead, he puts his arms around me until my face meets his.

A knock at the door. Barb. "Hurry up, Caleb."

Four boxes. That's all it takes to erase him from my room.

I turn to Caleb, but his back is to me. He is changing his shirt, removing the one with a drawing of the Space Needle. I stare at his spine, visible through his pale skin, the perfect shape of each bone. I take a few painful steps and run my palm down the perfect line of vertebrae. He smells like the clinic, the lingering scent of rubbing alcohol, sterile and sick at the same time.

He hands me the shirt. "Here," he says. "I was wearing this when I heard you play for the first time."

He grabs a new shirt from a crate and moves to slip it over his head. I step forward to stop his hands and pull it down myself, running my hands over his skin, his belly, that line of muscle just below his hip.

He closes his eyes and lets me touch him. When he opens them, I see the tears stockpiled behind his lashes. We take a step back from each other. I pull his Space Needle shirt over my dress.

"I need to do something," I say.

When we come out into the dining room, I sweep the blankets from the top of the piano and expose the keys. Caleb puts his hands on my shoulders when I sit on the bench, pressing a little too hard, and I lean against him. This is what I want to remember, him standing with me while I play. I choose the one piece that makes me feel like I might survive all of this, the one that runs through my mind whenever I need to push the hurt away. Chopin's Nocturne No. 1 in F, "Andante Cantabile." I consider the piece a beginning, not an ending. I focus on the sound of my fingers on the keys and Caleb's breathing.

When I reach the final note, I want to keep going, seamlessly transition to Nocturne No. 2 in E-flat, but I haven't mastered that one. Mrs. Albright had me move onto Schumann.

He pulls me up. My body tenses. "I'll call you every day," he says.

I see him, truly see him, inside his heart and mind and very being. Everything that is Caleb, every quirk and passion and vulnerability. *Him.* I can survive with him. Without him, there is only doubt. No one and nothing, not even the piano, can cushion this loss.

He stares into my face, holds both of my hands, and leans close. "I have a post-chemo life because of you."

Limping, I lead him down the hall, through the front door

to his car, clinging to him as he climbs into the passenger seat.

Barb looks right at me and I see that she, too, is crying.

Anger swells in my chest. I borrow Adrienne's profanity. "I don't know how the hell you can do this to us."

Despite my fury, I want to hurl myself into the Suburban. I can't imagine living without them. In that moment, I despise Barb, loathe her very existence, but would donate a kidney, would swallow nails, for her to unpack the car and stay.

"Oh, dear one." She blows her nose. She cries that hard. "I would stay if it was possible. Truly." Her eyes hold mine and I know she means it. She looks like she has something else to say. She opens her mouth but changes her mind and rubs her temples like I've seen her do when she waits for Caleb's test results. "I'm so sorry, Vanessa. If you don't have anyone, call me," Barb says. "I'll do what I can."

"I need you now," I say.

"I wish things could be different. I've come to love you like my own. Please remember that."

Caleb grabs my hand, clutching tightly, only letting go when Barb turns the ignition. I watch as she reverses down the driveway. I endure the pain in my ankle and stand in the same spot long after their taillights disappear.

"Come inside," Adrienne says.

Caleb's skateboard rests on my bed. I pick it up and notice he wrote a note on the underside. Directly on the wood with a thick marker, he tells me to practice riding it. Then it will be just him, the board, and me.

I hold it to my chest until the wheels form creases in my skin. I squeeze tighter, absorbing the physical pain, hoping for bruises, a lasting mark, more than the memory of his touch.

Even when I fall asleep, I don't let go.

I wake bruised: purple and blue and a hint of green darkening my chest, ankle, and foot. Such minor pain, a nuisance, compared to the cannonball that blew right through my middle.

When I open my eyes, I don't mistake it for a cruel dream.

He is gone.

His skateboard fell to the floor, resting on its side as though sleeping, as though Caleb somehow inhabited it, napping beside me. My hand flies to my bra, to the spot he touched just hours ago.

The streetlight illuminates the window. It could be dinnertime, midnight, or four o'clock in the morning.

The phone rings.

He promised to call every day. I imagine him sitting on the edge of a bed covered with an ocean-blue comforter and cheesy hotel beach art on the walls.

I jump off the mattress, completely forgetting about my injury, cringing in pain. *Ring ring.* As fast as possible, I hobble into the living room, only pausing to pick up a piece of paper covered in Adrienne's handwriting. Something about getting pizza. *Ring ring.*

I nearly knock the phone off the table.

"Caleb?"

"No," Dad says. "It's me, honey. I'll be home in an hour."

"Is everything okay?" I ask, panting. "How's Mom?"

Dad takes a breath, pausing a moment too long.

"She's not coming home, Vanessa. She's never coming home." His voice is low and thick, almost slurred. He isn't drunk—he's crying.

If I had food in my stomach, I would throw it up.

My eyes sweep the room, pausing at her cherished things: a giant conch shell from their trip to Bermuda, honeymoon souvenirs like the Venetian glass vase and a framed photograph of Venice, things she would save in a fire. I see her in everything—not sick, but healthy, the mother I knew for most of my life.

I feel her with me, a quiet presence, a phantom limb.

PART TWO: *Diagnosis*

Nine

Dad isn't home, not yesterday, not the day after, and not today. Seventy-two hours since he returned from the clinic without her. Three full days.

He spends his time with Mom and doctors. He spares us details, even when we beg for information. No matter how horrible, we want a picture of the hospice, of how she is hour by hour, a terrible sense of her actively dying. It is the only way to be with her, tethered in some way, since kids aren't allowed to visit.

Marie joins Adrienne and me in our nest. Triplets.

We ask each other hypothetical questions, the same ones we desperately ask Dad. We guess how much longer she'll be alive. The first day of school, a reckoning day, approaches at the speed of light. Just two more weeks of summer. We use that as a marker, wondering if she'll be gone by then. A merciless guessing game. We'll never see her again, that much we know, but she is out there, lying in a hospital bed, barely alive.

I want to sit next to her, even for a minute, just to say good-bye.

I think of the last day of school, our afternoon at the theater and pier. I keep remembering Mom's pleading face and her words: *Wait for me*.

Then I replay the morning at the clinic when she ascended the stairs alone, insisting I go play outside. I wish I could go back to that moment, to when Mom said she could do the infusion alone. I should have taken her to Lupe, walked next to her, said something meaningful—something enduring.

Her last word to me was "scoot."

I wait for Caleb.

Sleep is an impossibility. Without him, my small bed feels vast, endless, larger than the Pacific.

Adrienne has a full-size bed, something she lords over me, given that she and Zach have been having sex for more than a year. She keeps the details vague. I pitched a fit when Mom and Dad bestowed her hand-me-down twin as a gift. Brand-new lavender bedding with violet flowers blooming across the quilt. I was supposed to feel grateful. Adrienne calls it her lucky bed, the deflowering bed. When they moved it into my room, I looked at the mattress with disgust, storming out, slamming the door behind me, leaving my parents hurt and confused.

But all summer long, I cherished that bed, the way it held Caleb and me so snugly, containing us within its petite dimensions. I was too self-conscious to christen the bed, to continue its lucky streak. We were rarely alone, and when we were, there always was the threat of someone walking in. Plus, I was too nervous about my body and doubtful of its abilities. Too naive to understand that our time was limited from the start. Too stupid to know that I'd lose him sooner or later.

And now he is gone.

I wander around the house searching for relief, but there isn't an antidote to grief.

Caleb is more than a buffer, more than a human painkiller. He helps me walk into the pain—not around it.

The phone doesn't ring.

His silence hurts. Not just the rejection, but the way he'd told me that something was wrong with Mom and then just vanished.

I wish it made me want him less.

So I do the only thing I know how to do—I grope my way toward the piano, where I work through all the questions. I rely on the physical aspect of playing, sitting on the bench and pounding the keys, wishing for his hands on my shoulders.

I blow through piece after piece.

Mrs. Albright will be proud.

I think I hear her laugh.

Then I open my eyes.

Of course. A dream.

I stumble into her empty room, frantic to feel something tangible. I spray myself with her perfume, choking on the earthy scent of cypress and rose.

Dad hasn't made the bed. I pull up the sheets and smooth the quilt. I place my palm on Mom's pillow, shocked to feel a few strands of hair. I hold them to the light, that deep shade of blond, that golden hue.

It is the last part of her I'll ever touch.

Five days.

She's been away for one hundred and twenty hours.

If I can't see her, if I can't hold her hand, maybe I can talk to her. Just one more time.

Craning to reach, I pull the phonebook off the shelf, flipping through the pages until I find the shattering word: "Hospice." Only two listed.

Mission Bay Hospice. I pick up the kitchen phone and dial the number. They answer on the first ring.

"I need to speak to a patient. Iris Babcock."

"I'm sorry," the receptionist says, a compassionate female voice. "Our patients aren't able to receive calls."

"She's my mother. It's urgent. An emergency."

"I'm sorry, but it isn't possible. Take care."

The phone goes dead.

Seaside Hospice. Maybe I sound too young. I'll speak with authority. I'll mimic Adrienne, but will refrain from anger and profanity.

A similar voice answers the phone, with the same

compassion as the other hospice receptionist, but older and male. I'm determined to be more assertive. To at least confirm whether or not Mom is there.

I make the same introduction, "I need to speak to a patient. Iris Babcock."

The receptionist repeats the same policy, explaining, "Our patients aren't able to receive calls."

"Why?" I ask.

"They're too ill," the man explains.

"But I'm immediate family and this is an emergency. It's urgent and I *must* speak with her."

"I'm sorry, but that's the policy."

"Wait, don't you have visiting hours?"

"What's the patient's name again?"

"Iris Babcock."

The silence lasts for a moment before the man returns. "We don't have a patient by that name."

"Thank you," I say. "Very much."

I return the phone to its cradle and rush to Dad's study, opening the top drawer and counting out four twenty-dollar bills. That will be more than enough.

Mission Bay Hospice is somewhere unfamiliar, past Sea World and near the port.

Half an hour later, the taxi cab deposits me in front of an institutional green building surrounded by shady pepper trees. I ask the driver to wait, certain I can't find my way back home on my own.

I climb the steps and try to push open the door, but it's locked. I buzz and hear the crackle of the intercom, static and a voice competing through the system. "Patient visit," is all I say. The door buzzes open.

A woman sits behind the desk, probably the same one who answered the phone. She is pretty in a bookish way. I smile and walked forward, doing my best impersonation of a charming Adrienne.

"Hello," I say. "I'm here to see Iris Babcock. My father arranged my visit with her doctor."

The receptionist, probably in her thirties, looks me up and down, frowning while doing so. "I'm sorry, but minors must be accompanied by an adult."

I prepared for this. I offer her a patient smile. "I'm a freshman at the University of San Diego. I'm eighteen."

She looks at me again, and I can't tell if I'm being successful or foolish. She raises a single eyebrow. "What's your major?"

"Music. Piano. You should come to my recital next month. The orchestra is playing at the Shiley Theatre in Camino Hall." This is true, an annual event.

Skeptically, she pulls a file from her desk, opens it, and asks, "You said Babcock?"

"Yes." Until now, I hadn't considered if Mom could even carry on a conversation. I just need to see her, be in the same room, tell her I love her.

She gives me a puzzled look. "I don't have a patient with that name. Are you sure she's here?"

I feel every part of my body deflate. I shift my weight from one foot to the other just to feel solid ground beneath me. I meet the receptionist's eyes, kind and bewildered, and ask, "Do you know if she died here? Is that in your book?"

She looks at me with such tenderness. She must see through my lie. Clearly I'm too young, too lost. "She didn't die here. She was never here. She must be at another facility or a hospital. Why don't you have a seat? Can I call anyone for you?"

The taxi idles outside. I shake my head, grateful for her offer.

"I don't have anyone to call."

"Where the hell have you been?"

Adrienne doesn't look mad, and with an impressive hickey tingeing her neck, she is hardly in a position to judge.

"Hey, Zach," I say.

He fills the couch, tall and lanky, his longish hair an indistinguishable shade between blond and brown. Zach tends to start a sentence several times before settling on a course, which I find oddly adorable. He does so now, saying first my name and then forming a question, "Are you . . . ?" "You hanging in . . . ?" "How are you?"

I regard him as the gentlest boy on the planet, not that anyone else would ever describe him—the hot surfer dude—that way.

"I'm okay. Thanks."

I brush past Adrienne, not wanting to say anything with Zach there. Someone left an orange juice carton on the counter and I drain it, crumple it up, and toss it in the bulging trash. My movements are quick and decisive—the exact opposite of how I feel.

No one kisses as loud as Adrienne and Zach. I practically cover my ears. A few seconds later, she walks into the kitchen flushed and smiling.

"You're scandalous," I say.

"You only wish you were."

She must have read the pain on my face.

"You didn't see the mail?"

I shake my head.

"Kitchen table."

A postcard rests atop a precarious stack of bills, growing taller by the day. My fingers smudge the glossy photo of a sandpiper, with long, slender legs and beak. I trace the script at the bottom, the Sandpiper Inn's name and address.

Hey Vanessa,

We're getting ready to leave for Seattle. My mom bought some camping gear and we'll stop in the Redwoods on the way. I promise I'll call as soon as we're home. I think about you all the time and I'm sorry I'm not there. I don't know what to say about your mom. My mom says I need to give you time. Everything is so out of control and surreal. We're going back to the clinic one last time to pick up some stuff, and I can't imagine being there without you. My mom doesn't want me to call right now. I promise I will when I can.

Love,
Caleb

Adrienne allows me to read it twice before speaking. "Bossy Barb is just getting in the way. I knew he would never leave you like that."

I scan the card again. "I really thought he had. He doesn't say anything about coming back. I don't know when I'll see him again." I look up. "What if he doesn't come back?"

"He said he'll call. Waiting sucks, but you're going to have to. Want to go to the beach with us?" She wears a batik dress that Mom gave her just a few weeks ago and fingers one of the many tassels adorning the hem. She hasn't seen Zach since Dad told us about Mom, and I know an afternoon at the beach will bring Adrienne as much comfort as Caleb would bring me.

"That's okay. I'll stay here and get stuff ready for dinner. Dad's picking up Marie?"

She nods and before I can respond, she grabs me in a tight hug. A sudden movement, surprising in its certainty. "I'll be back by dinner. I'll clean up. Don't worry about the dishes."

I hug her back. "They're just dishes. Go. It's fine. Really."

"Thanks," she whispers.

Right before she leaves the room, she turns around and gives me a leveling look. I swear she knows I'm losing my mind, going on dream-induced wild goose chases.

"He's not gone forever. You know that, right? You'll see him again."

I look at the overflowing trash can and overturned cereal box before finally meeting her eyes.

"We thought we'd see Mom again too."

There's no comforting Marie, so after dinner, Adrienne and I take her to the only place we can think of: church. Dad is gone again, taking care of Mom, he says. But when I ask him questions, when I push for details about the hospice, he's vague and preoccupied.

We walk into the sanctuary of Our Lady of the Immaculate Conception and take a seat in the back pew. Marie pulls out her pocket book of saints and flips through the dog-eared pages, pausing to read the ones with turned corners, her new favorites: Joan of Arc, Saint Ursula, Saint Barbara, and Saint Catherine. Young, innocent girls. Pure in the faith that pain was the cost of truth. I notice that Marie doesn't look at the sculpted Jesus hanging on the enormous wooden cross, but she does cross herself on multiple occasions. She pulls a saint card from the book, the Blessed Virgin Mary named in gilded script, and flips it over to pray the rosary. In her other hand, she fingers the beads.

I wish something would bring me the same peace.

Adrienne rests against me as Marie immerses herself in makeshift worship. She prays so hard that I expect her to speak in tongues.

I appreciate the sanctuary's quiet darkness in my own way, not stirred by the idea of anything holy, but accepting the fact that I may never get to say good-bye. I won't sit next to Mom, holding her hand, when she dies. I didn't realize it before, but that's what I expected—to be together until the very end.

The votive candles flicker, each one aflame in memory and prayer. I can't bring myself to light one for Mom. Not now. Not until I know she is truly gone.

All of the shock from visiting the hospice shakes loose. It's still there, but I don't wear it like a second skin. I trade it in for determination.

I need to know what happened at the clinic and what drove Barb and Caleb from the house. I don't need time. I don't need space. I need answers, and if I can't get them from Mom, I'll get them from Barb. There is more to the story, more than Mom vanishing so suddenly, and Barb was the one who talked to the doctors. Maybe they haven't left yet. Maybe I'll catch them before they head north.

The bus is full, but I squeeze on, my backpack padding me like a football player. I'm surrounded by accents:

the familiar Spanish and Vietnamese, the less-familiar Mandarin, and something Eastern European, a language I can't identify. Flanked by bodies, I keep my eyes on the floor to ease my sudden case of claustrophobia. Two stops past downtown, the crowd thins out and I slide into an empty seat and try to stop shaking.

The man sitting next to me shifts his heavy body. I glance his way and note his old age, something Mom will never reach. He clutches several sheer plastic grocery bags filled with fruit and non-perishables. He mutters to himself in what I guess is Russian or Czech, a Cold War dialect, a language from an action movie. I try not to stare at his thick facial features, his bushy sideburns and eyebrows that blend together like a lion's mane.

By the time I reach the stop, the bus has emptied of most of its passengers. I wander down the sidewalk, looking up, searching for the Sandpiper Inn. The lobby is just as I imagined. Beach art and a giant mermaid mural. I drop my backpack and smile at the man, his face like weathered driftwood, standing behind the counter like he's never been anyplace else.

I ask for Barb, spelling D-U-N-N-E.

He runs his finger back and forth across the page, touching each name as though they are written in braille. "Here she is. Checked out yesterday. See?"

He flips around the registry and I recognize her handwriting immediately, only instead of recipes and grocery lists, she wrote their address.

My mind skips back to Caleb's pictures, the house I remember from his Polaroids. Dove gray paint. Giant porch. A magical-sounding neighborhood: Queen Anne. "Do you have a phone number?"

He flips the page. "Afraid not. I was going to mail this, but do you think you can return it when you see them again?"

He places a book in my hand, a well-loved paperback. Jack Kerouac's collected poems. I hug it to my chest. "Yes," I say. "Thanks for your help."

This time, I ignore the others on the bus, too caught up in his notes. In the margin of "Bowery Blues," he wrote, *Vanessa gets it.*

He filled every page with me, the skateboard, and the beach. I look out the bus window, shielding my face from the other passengers, wanting to keep my tears to myself.

In the back of the book, just below Kerouac's brief biography, Caleb's handwriting fills the page, his penmanship much smaller, like he was writing a secret.

VANESSA BY JACK KEROUAC

"We agreed to love each other madly."—On the Road

"Her little shoulders drove me mad; I hugged her and
hugged her. And she loved it.
'I love, love' she said, closing her eyes. . . . Our stories were

> *told, we subsided into silence and sweet anticipatory thoughts. It was as simple as that."*—On the Road

> *"'It'll take you eternities to get rid of me,' she adds sadly, which makes me jealous, I want her to say I'll never get rid of her—I wanta be chased till eternity till I catch her."*—Big Sur

The ink bled through the paper, which was thin and cheap, barely stronger than newsprint. I read the quotations again, stopping at the words "love" and "eternity" before turning the page. The title sears like a branding iron, deep and burning, words that never can heal.

IRIS BY JACK KEROUAC

> *"You have absolutely no regard for anybody but yourself and your damned kicks."*—On the Road

> *". . . with the visage of a gruesome grieving ghost you go shuddering through nightmare life."*—On the Road

> *". . . there was nothing to talk about anymore. The only thing to do was go."*—On the Road

My eyes scan the lines, taking in each horrible phrase. How could he think these things about Mom?

I feel cold, the same chill as when I saw Mom get an IV, and overwhelmed with a combination of confusion and surprise and sadness and fury. My heart fills with a sense of deep betrayal, only I don't know the source: Mom or Caleb?

I can't bring myself to read the pages again. I slam the book shut.

Still, I clutch it in my hands, unable to tuck it away, unable to let it go.

I expect to walk into an empty house. Adrienne took Marie to her final summer game. Soccer camp turned out to be a bust with Marie, listless from grief, oblivious to competition. She didn't care about the ball, a shock to the coach, given Marie's status as a star goalie. She spent practices and games with her hand in her pocket, worrying her hidden rosary, tiny stainless-steel beads. She couldn't bring herself to care about the ball, which whizzed past her, caught in the billowing net. Her coach reassigned her to defense, where she could do little damage to the score.

Dad stands in the doorway, jingling his keys, his nervous habit. He seems both surprised and relieved when he sees me. I didn't think it was possible, but his eyes look more bloodshot than mine.

"She's dead," I say, a question masked as a statement.

He closes his eyes for a moment as though he's in pain or trying to remember something.

"Dad?"

His eyes pop open, and for the first time since I walked through the door, I feel like he's really looking at me. I watch as he takes in my face.

He shakes his head back and forth, slowly, like a shark. "No, kiddo. She's not. I haven't eaten all day. How about you?"

"Not really. Just cereal."

"Come on. You won't need that." He points to my backpack.

"I want to bring it." I'm not sure I'll show him the book, but I can't imagine leaving it unattended.

We drive to the boardwalk, parking as the sun slips into the water. When I join him on the sidewalk, he points to the enormous moon filling the sky. It's gorgeous, but my eyes return to him. Moments like this sustained me when I was little. Dad would take me aside and point out something as though he and I were the only people on Earth who could see it. A lunar eclipse. A procession of tall ships sailing the bay. The hummingbird that occasionally visits our mimosa tree. But tonight as I stand next to him, all I see are the other people strolling past. I wonder who else is suffering a loss. It used to be so easy thinking that I was the only one hurting. Now I realize how we all carry pain, how our lives can be turned inside out in an instant—a diagnosis, a break-up, a death.

He takes my hand, long enough for me to feel he's shaking. I'm about to ask what's wrong, when he releases me.

"Dad?"

He points to a familiar face, a guy selling small portraits

of dolphins and starfish. I used to beg for one. A couple haggles prices with him.

"I think it's time," he says.

His smile looks forced, his eyes tired, his jaw tense.

"You always said they were overpriced and cheesy."

He gives me a hard stare and my palms fill with sweat, something that only happens when I'm unprepared for a solo. I wipe them on my skirt.

"I see it differently now. Look at the seahorse painting. That's beautiful."

He gestures to a small canvas. I remember reading that the seahorse is the symbol of fatherhood in Greek mythology. I wonder if he knows.

The painting isn't bigger than eight square inches. The artist painted the background a deep blue and the small sea creature with its tendril tail a tangerine orange.

"I know it doesn't match your room," he says, "but I'd like to get it for you."

"Adrienne's the one who cares about how stuff matches. Not me. I love it."

Dad withdraws his wallet from his briefcase while the artist wraps one of the larger canvases for the haggling couple. I hope they paid a fair price. I always expected the artist, a middle-aged guy with long dreads, to be charming and chatty. Up close, I see that he's shy, maybe more introverted than me. I want to know why he parks himself on the boardwalk, displaying his work to tourists and jaded locals.

But he wraps my painting with such care, like it's glass, without a word. I don't want to intrude. His silence feels intentional, not in a rude way, but a meditation.

"Thank you," I say to Dad as I gently slip the painting into my backpack.

"I'm glad you like it," he says, but he doesn't look my way.

The mood changes and we walk in silence, but not the contemplative kind I sensed from the artist. Dad seems far away. I pull his arm around me, hoping the weight will make me feel less alone.

He pulls me closer and wraps both arms around me, kissing my forehead. In this position, I could be four, seven, eleven years old. Young enough to believe my father will always be there to protect me. "Hungry?" he asks.

I stand still for a minute, allowing my body to rest next to his. When I adjust my backpack, he steps away and I'm on my own again.

He points to a new seafood restaurant decorated with a sign flapping in the wind: GRAND OPENING. A restaurant without memories.

He turns to me. "Want to try it?"

I nod. We cross the street and scan the menu. Pub food. Fish and chips, battered shrimp, casual and easy.

I want to keep walking, to have a few more minutes with Dad without a hovering waitress, but my stomach growls and Dad is halfway through the door.

"Coming?" he asks.

Something about his voice, about the way he holds his mouth, makes me swallow hard. I follow him inside.

The hostess escorts us to a quiet corner booth. I look out the window, at the tide coming in, the waves covering greater lengths of the shore. I can't help but think of Mom, of the rickety pier and clams, of something only she and I enjoyed.

When the waiter comes, Dad orders a salad and fish and chips, his favorite. I order the same because Dad makes it sound so good. Not the wine though. He smiles when I ask for my first latte, something Caleb mentioned loving, a Seattle treat.

After three packets of sugar and a few sips, I feel the heat in my cheeks and neck. I'm as warm as if we were sitting in front of a fire.

"Vanessa," Dad says.

When I meet his eyes, he looks different, beaten and despondent in a way I never imagined. Like the light went out of his eyes. Now they seem as flat and worn as old pennies.

"I need to explain something to you. It's going to be very difficult to understand. I barely do. Your sisters don't know yet."

I'm scared and open my mouth, unable to say anything. "What?" I finally ask.

"I need to talk to you about what's really wrong with your mother. Where she is."

It doesn't matter that I spent the last couple of days

crisscrossing the city, searching for answers. Now that I'm about to learn the truth, all I want to do is cover my ears and bolt. I reach for my backpack and pull out the book.

"Look at the second-to-last page," I say.

After reading it, he places the book back in my hand. "This has been hard on Caleb."

"Is that why Barb isn't letting him call me?"

"We both agreed that we need some time to sort out our situations. They've been through the wringer too. I couldn't have done this without Barb."

I sip my latte, hoping to return some warmth to my skin. "Barb helped you with what?"

I wait, watching Dad stare at his wine glass, looking at everything at the table but me. Finally, he says, "Your mother isn't dying. She never was."

I gasp so loud that he looks startled. My fingernails dig in to my arm, hard enough to leave a mark. I need to redirect the pain. Words ricochet around my head, but I'm not able to pull together a phrase. Finally, I ask, "What do you mean?"

"Your mother never had leukemia. She was never sick. Not even in college—that small tumor. It was nothing. Probably just a piece of bone or a cyst."

I don't know how long we stare at each other, but the waiter delivers our salads. I gaze at the lettuce; the baby leaves of fancy greens mixed with figs and blue cheese dressing.

"What are you talking about?" I ask, shaking, looking at the food and wanting to puke all over the table.

He's quiet, and I glance around the restaurant, wondering if I just screamed at him. I don't think I did, because the handful of other customers keep chatting and eating their food like nothing happened.

He doesn't say anything, so I lean closer and ask, "What are you saying? If she's not sick, then where is she?"

"I don't know how to explain this, so just stay with me, okay?" His eyes are red and wet. Drops of sweat line his forehead. They cover his upper lip and collect in that soft spot between his neck and collarbone.

"I don't understand what you're trying to say." I struggle to get out each word.

"I know," he says. "Do you remember when I said she'd never come home again?"

"How could I forget that?" After months of illness, it's hard to believe that there's an end. Terminal means final, but leukemia is like death row: You get the sentence but know you'll be sitting in prison for months, maybe a year, maybe longer. "She's been so sick," I say. "She lost so much weight. She couldn't fake that."

Dad doesn't say anything. He seems to choke every time he opens his mouth.

I blink a few times so I won't cry. "You're telling me that isn't real?"

He struggles with his words. "Your mother is ill, but mentally ill," he says. "There's a psychiatric disorder called Munchausen syndrome."

"That sounds like something from the Nazis."

"I think it's a German name. People who suffer from Munchausen's deliberately act like they have a terminal disease. They lie and make everyone believe they're sick. They're desperate for the attention. A lot of people go to great lengths to convince everyone they're sick. Some even have surgery. Your mom was poisoning herself with Laetrile."

I try to listen, but I feel just as I did that last day when Caleb left, when Dad came home from the clinic alone, like everything was pulling away from me, like I was caught in a riptide. "So you're saying she's just some sort of hypochondriac?"

"Not quite," he says.

"But Mom had doctors. I went to the clinic with her. I saw all of those sick people and Mom looked just like them. She couldn't get out of bed for days, Dad. She was sick. She was really, really sick. I was there. We all were there. There's no way she made that up."

Now I know I'm yelling because the restaurant is still and people are staring. I look at my untouched salad. I want the food to go away. I want to be anywhere but here. My heart beats so fast, I wonder if *I* am the one who is actually dying now. Maybe I'm pretending that my heart is racing. Maybe I'm having chest pains and believe I'm having heart failure, but I'm really not. What was true? What wasn't true? The world collapses, or maybe just pretends to collapse.

"It helped that your mom's a nurse; she was especially convincing."

"What about the blood tests? Leukemia is a blood disease. They test your blood and know you have it. Mom had blood tests."

Dad pulls a thin folder from his satchel, sliding the top sheet across the table. "Here, read this. It will help you understand. It helped me."

The paper is filled with Dad's handwriting, notes written in tidy capital letters, not written in a rush.

> *MUNCHAUSEN SYNDROME:*
> *INTENTIONALLY FEIGNS PHYSICAL SYMPTOMS*
> *IN ORDER TO ASSUME THE PATIENT ROLE.*
> *WILL GO TO GREAT LENGTHS TO*
> *MANUFACTURE SYMPTOMS AND ILLNESS,*
> *INCLUDING SURGERY.*
>
> *MUNCHAUSEN SYNDROME BY PROXY:*
> *A PARENT INTENTIONALLY MANUFACTURES*
> *AN ILLNESS OR PERCEIVED ILLNESS IN A CHILD.*
> *PARENT IS MOTIVATED TO ASSUME THE*
> *PATIENT ROLE BY PROXY.*

My eyes scan the words, meaningless in the moment, they blur together. It might as well read *lies, lies, lies, lies, lies.* It's like my mind split in half, sliced like an apple, and my mother's lies are the seeds.

He hands me another sheet. "Now read this."

Treatment Plan: August 29, 1976

Administer 1,200 mg IV Laetrile weekly

Administer 300 mg tablets Valium twice daily w/ food

Limited activity recommended

Suspend bed rest

Patient's improvement indicative of remission

When I finish reading the sheet, I look up. I can't breathe. "August twenty-ninth is next week," I say, feeling sick to my stomach. "It says remission."

"I know. Read the name of the doctor," he says.

I feel like someone pushed me out of an open window. Jonathan Murray, M.D., signed the form. My grandfather.

"He died when your mom was a senior in high school. She must have his business stationery and prescription pad." Dad flips through the folder and pulls out various prescriptions for the medications that still cover our kitchen counter.

"Look at this one." He hands me a nearly identical sheet of paper.

Treatment Plan: August 8, 1976

Administer 1,800 mg IV Laetrile daily

Administer 500 mg tablets Valium twice daily w/ food

Mandatory bed rest

Patient's decline indicative of late-stage leukemia

I look up. "So she was dying two weeks ago and is in remission next week?"

"Do you understand what this means?" Dad asks. "She made it all up. She told the doctors at the clinic that *Dr. Murray* was her primary oncologist and he was unable to administer Laetrile because of the FDA ban. She told them that he managed everything—including her blood work. She's the only one of us who speaks Spanish. She controlled all of the information. She had paperwork for different scenarios: remission, bed rest, hospice. I never would have thought of questioning her. I wouldn't have, except that doctor got suspicious, the one who insisted on taking blood samples. Dr. Flores."

"How did you find out?" My voice sounds young, the same tone I used when I figured out Santa wasn't real. I feel as young and foolish for believing something so obviously make-believe.

"Barb. She knew something wasn't right. She found the folder when she was cleaning. She spoke with Dr. Flores and insisted he meet with me immediately. It happened very fast."

I try to assemble memories of that day just a week ago, but I was in so much pain from falling off the skateboard. Then the shot.

"Then what?"

"I confronted her. I found the prescription pad in her purse. She said she needed to go to a hospice. She said she picked one out, but when I called them they didn't have a record of her. She started screaming, hitting herself, pulling out her hair. Dr. Flores had to sedate her. Barb said that was how she acted the last time he took a blood sample. Hysterical. That was the day I told you she wasn't coming home."

"What do you mean? I don't get it. You knew she wasn't dying when you said she was going into hospice?"

I put my hands in my lap, holding them tightly, and try to stay upright. I want to sweep the dishes aside and rest my head on the table. All I can see is the kind woman at the hospice, her eyes full of tender pity. It's like a balloon pops inside my chest and I want to rest right here, in the booth. I close my eyes and squeeze my hands tighter.

"I was trying to protect you."

He stops talking and takes a sip of wine.

I speak carefully, choosing every word. "How could you do that? How could you think it was better for you to tell us she was on her deathbed than that she was crazy?"

His eyes stay on his glass. He picks at a fig, disarticulating the seeds, peeling the fruit from the skin. He places his fork on his plate and looks at me.

In that moment, I think what Dad has done is worse. He had the chance to stop things and he didn't. He had the full story. He is the dad, the adult.

He finally meets my eyes. "This week has been devastating. We spent hours talking. She told me everything, all the lies. She almost looked relieved. A psychiatrist insisted that I check her into an inpatient psychiatric hospital, but your mother refused to go. I got a lawyer who helped me commit her. I did everything they told me to do. Absolutely everything."

"Why didn't you just tell us the truth?" I hiss out the words like an anaconda. I welcome the flash of anger—anything to make me feel the least bit strong. I can barely speak above a whisper.

"I had to see a judge. The lawyer said I needed a restraining order. It's the only way I can protect you. With Munchausen syndrome, it's more common for the mother to say her child is sick. Marie could have been next. She could have said that Marie had leukemia too. She could have poisoned Marie with Laetrile. Killed her like she was killing herself. I did everything I could, Vanessa. I did my best. I'm so sorry. The judge denied our request today. The judge won't grant a restraining order because your mother didn't harm you physically."

"She didn't *harm* us?" I whisper. "That's where you were today? With a judge?" I'm a bird trapped indoors, flying around, crashing into windows.

I barely hear his answer. "Yes, in court."

Noise fills the restaurant. A waiter clears a table. Customers open the door. Someone coughs. I wish I could lose every sense, all at once, gone in an instant. Whoever said feelings couldn't kill you was lying. I breathe, in and out, one, two, three, until I feel like I can speak. I can't control the tears. My chin rests against my chest and I cover my face. I wish he'd told me at home or in the car. I try to be quiet. Dad squeezes my hand so hard it hurts. I worry my finger bones will snap like twigs. I get dizzy and all I see is the swirling face of my mother. I know I'm in some kind of shock because the harder I cry, the more I feel like I'm floating away from my body. The pain in my hand diminishes, as does my labored breathing.

The tears stream down my cheeks, too many to wipe away. "You just disappeared, Dad," I say, barely choking out the words. "You wouldn't talk to us or tell us anything. You should have told us the truth."

"Vanessa, I didn't mean to disappear. I should have been with you girls, but I had to take care of your mother. An involuntary committal lasts for ninety days. They're going to try to treat her. She could get phone privileges. She might be released in ninety days," he says.

I laugh despite myself, and I sound angry and hopeless. Like Adrienne, but drained of power. "I don't get this. I don't believe it." I try to free my hand, but I pull too hard from Dad's grasp and knock over his glass of wine. It breaks, sending shards into our salads. Wine seeps into the white tablecloth. The waiter hurries over.

"I'm sorry," I say.

"That's okay. Don't worry about it." The server stacks our plates and carries them to the kitchen before returning for the ruined tablecloth.

The wood is exposed, the deep red of the wine darkening the center of the table. Dad wipes up the liquid with his napkin and runs his hand across the smooth surface. His fingers stop at the knot in the wood.

"Your mother's like this," he says as he touches the dark circles of wood. "Most trees have knots, though not deep enough to break a branch. But sometimes the knot is so severe it destroys the tree. That's the case with your mom. I didn't want her to destroy you."

"I can't talk to her, Dad."

He nods. "I'll do whatever I can to protect you."

I feel the tears return and I take more deep breaths.

"Are you ready to leave?" he asks.

I nod several times, first in agreement and then to soothe myself. Dad tosses a generous amount of cash onto the table.

Once we're driving home, I rest my head against the window, feeling its coolness, knowing the closeness we felt on the beach is gone. Our secret isn't like the moon. It is too big for me to see, too blinding.

I want to grab his hand and hold on, hoping he will anchor me, will guide me through this.

But we both know it's too late for that.

We sit on the sofa, Marie nestled between us, with Dad in the opposite chair. Adrienne and Marie were waiting for us, with the kitchen table set for dinner, mac and cheese steaming on the stove. As soon as they saw Dad and me, they assumed the worst, just as I had—that Mom was dead.

I almost wish that was the truth. Almost.

The damning file folder rests on the coffee table, each sheet of paper confirming Mom's lies. Adrienne reads and rereads the pages as Dad explains the same details he just told me.

Most victims who survive shark attacks describe a similar experience: When the monster's powerful jaws, filled with rows of razor-sharp teeth, clamp down on a leg, an arm, even a torso, they don't feel pain. The shock is that unimaginable, that overpowering, that the body blocks out the sensation of being eaten alive. As I listen to Dad repeat the story, I understand that depth of shock, the sensation of being torn in half, yet too numb to feel it.

Marie sits silent and still. I wait for Adrienne to cry or scream, to storm out and slam a door, but she remains in her spot, crammed next to Marie and me.

"What about Lupe?" Adrienne asks. "Didn't she suspect something? She always talked to the doctors."

I know what Adrienne is asking: Didn't Lupe love us enough to protect us? Unlike Dad, she was there every day, monitoring Mom's health, every infusion, every pill. She always called us *mijas* with such affection. We were in her care as much as Mom. She doted on us more than any other patient.

Dad runs a hand through his hair and struggles with his words. "Lupe never worked for the clinic. She worked for your mother."

"That's bullshit," Adrienne says. "She worked harder than anyone else there."

Dad looks at her softly. "That's because she was there to take care of you and your mother. That's all she did. She was a private nurse."

"I don't believe you," Adrienne says.

Dad reaches into his briefcase and withdraws a book of traveler's checks. "Flip through this."

Months of checks made out to Guadalupe Ortiz. Five hundred pesos a month to perpetuate Mom's lies.

Marie, curled up between us, puts her head in my lap. I stroke her hair and wipe the tears from her cheeks. She lifts her head when she speaks. "Lupe lied too?"

Dad rises from the chair and kisses Marie on the forehead, whispering something only she can hear, before taking a seat on the floor. When we were younger, we sat in the same positions as he read us books, bedtime stories, and, later, chapters from his own childhood favorites, *The Hobbit* and *The Lion, the Witch and the Wardrobe*.

"Your mother had . . . how should I say this? . . . had an unusual arrangement with the clinic. Apparently, this happens a lot with Americans. We pay a lot to be there and that gives us more power. Americans come with their own staff and ideas, and the clinic accommodates them. The doctors supervise treatment in a different way. They're not accountable to insurance companies, and the Laetrile ban makes it difficult for American doctors to work with the clinics. And then there's the language barrier. I never would have guessed that your mom would exploit that to her benefit."

"What benefit? Mom poisoning herself? That's a hell of a benefit," Adrienne says.

Dad doesn't look up; he stares at the file, his eyes on the prescription pad and traveler's checks. He straightens his spine. "I keep trying to figure out when things changed. There must have been a trigger. Something must have made her do this. She was happy in college. She was so good at nursing that she talked about doing something more, even medical school. She threw parties. She had friends. She wasn't moody like she was with us."

I raise my fingers to my face, feeling my puffy eyes. "You never said anything about her moods."

"She could be hard on you girls. She could be hard on me. After she lost the baby—"

He snaps his head up, suddenly hyperalert. Before Adrienne, Mom miscarried. It wasn't a secret. She always spent the anniversary alone. Dad took the day off work, shepherding us to and from school, taking us to dinner at our favorite Old Town restaurant, La Sirenita. Mom's heartache was what Adrienne called our "hooky day."

"Oh my God," he says, covering his face with his hands. "Maybe it never happened. The miscarriage. Maybe she lied about the pregnancy." He cries until his nose runs, drying his tears with his sleeve. As I listen, it feels like time is moving more slowly, as though my mind knows this conversation will be one I replay again and again.

"I wasn't at the hospital when she miscarried," Dad says

at last. "I was at work. I never talked to a doctor. Your mom told me about it. Just her. I think this has been going on for twenty years."

"And you never noticed? I can't fucking believe this." Adrienne is so angry that she sounds calm.

He shakes his head. "I don't know what to say. I can't believe this either. I'm so sorry."

Adrienne stares at him, ignoring his tears and explanations and apologies. "You should have gone to the clinic with her—not us. You should have bought a Spanish dictionary. You never stood up to her."

He taps his fingers on the table. "You mother has never done anything she didn't want to do. This was on her terms. All of it. I wish I'd known—" He stops midsentence and rubs his eyes. "But you're right, Adrienne. Things could have been different. I should have taken control of her treatment, but you know your mom. She always had an explanation for everything. I relied on her for information. I shouldn't have. I know I should have been more involved."

"You never stand up to anything, Dad. Not to your fucking boss. Not to Mom. You could have stopped all of this if you'd tried."

Dad gives her a flabbergasted look, wincing at her words. Slowly, he shakes his head. "I don't think anything could have stopped her." Before Adrienne answers, he flips through the folder until he finds what he's looking for. He traces the words with his finger, following each sentence before he hands it to Adrienne.

It is in English, written in Mom's elegant cursive, a list of medications and combinations. She calculated the side effects, how much the drugs would make her sick. She wrote it all out. If she took a certain amount, she'd vomit. Another amount, she'd pass out. And the last damning line: the combination that would kill her. Her suicide. She was prepared to die for her lie.

My mind pictures the scene. Mom in bed. Me coming in to check on her, cupping pills or a glass of milk—whatever she needed. I would have discovered her body, rigid and cold and blue. I would have screamed. I would have called Dad or Barb. I would have shielded Marie, and even Adrienne. She would have done this to all of us, but I feel the betrayal the most deeply. She would have done this to *me*.

Adrienne bolts off the couch and walks over to the shelves lining the wall. Mom's altar, her photos and vacation souvenirs. She's going to hurl something fragile across the room, something made of crystal or porcelain, something precious and breakable. She lifts the giant conch shell and raises it to her ear before setting it down with too much force. Her hand travels to the Venetian glass, sunbursts of color, and grabs a vase. When it hits the wall, I feel like the whole world shatters. Marie screams.

"Shhh," I coo, pulling her closer. I don't tell her everything will be okay. No more lies.

Dad stands. "Adrienne, don't you dare do that again."

"Or what? What are you going to do, Dad?"

"Please sit down, honey."

Marie climbs into my lap. I wrap my arms around her, holding her as tight as possible, wishing away the pain, absorbing her tears.

"I'm here," I say. "I'm right here."

Marie hides her face and chants something about Mom and God, over and over again, half sob, half song.

"Adrienne," Dad says, his voice strained and hoarse, "we're in this together. I'm your father. I promise I'll take care of you."

She looks at him with such venom. "Oh sure, because you've done such a spectacular job so far. Let's see, you let your crazy wife fake cancer. You let her drag us down to that hellhole so-called 'clinic,' and then you tell us she's dying. Father-of-the-year award. Great job, Dad. You should be proud."

"I spent the day in court, Adrienne. I didn't want to hurt you any more than she already had. I had to make arrangements. I had to listen to the psychiatrist and the lawyer." He looks each of us in the eye. "I never meant to lie to you. I didn't mean to hurt you. I was trying to protect you."

"Well, you sure as hell failed," Adrienne says.

"That's enough," he says. "I know your mom isn't here to explain herself. You have every right to be angry with her and with me. But you have to calm down and listen. This is terrible, but you must believe me that I did everything I could. I did all of this for you."

"Bullshit!" Adrienne yells.

A shadow of anger passes over Dad's face before his eyes fill with tears. "I hope you'll come to see my side of things."

Marie squeezes me tightly, her face against my shoulder, whispering, "Mom, I want Mom."

"No, you don't," Adrienne snaps.

But Marie nods fiercely. "She's not going to die. She's still with us."

"You don't understand, Marie." Adrienne sits next to us and runs her fingers through Marie's hair.

"Yes, I do. I understand all of this." Marie points to Dad, who looks too hurt to speak. "And Dad really didn't mean to hurt us," she says, with tears streaming down her face.

I can't sit on the couch any longer, so I ease Marie into Adrienne's lap and charge into the dining room. Like a dog, I circle the room before sitting at the piano. I pick up a framed photo, a snapshot, taken at the clinic. In the picture, Adrienne, Marie, and I lean against a wall, standing in birth order. Adrienne has bougainvillea in her hair. Her hair is almost white in the sun. I am wearing my favorite sundress. Marie looks tiny and hopeful.

Suddenly, I feel as though I'm there again. Sitting in the backseat of Mom's car, resting against the door. I remember the wind and the view of the ocean. I shake away the memory and flip over the frame to pull the photo free. I place it on top of my sheet music and begin to play. The thump of the keys calms my nerves. I allow my body to absorb the sound, every cell filling with the music. The piano buries my heart deeper into my chest. It relaxes my muscles, but can't erase my pain and grief.

I try to focus on the music. The Chopin nocturne I hadn't mastered when I said good-bye to Caleb. Since then, I've played it dozens of times. The notes are delicate, climbing and descending the scales. Just when the melody sounds too sweet, the music takes a turn toward the dark and complex. Sometimes when I'm this close to the music, I feel as though I become the instrument. Skin and blood and muscle are exchanged for wood and metal. My bones become as fine as the keys, my teeth rattle with every note.

I have nothing left but the music, the cool keys. My fingertips grace the ivory, reminding me that my body was made for this. Not for illness and lies and betrayal. But for touch.

PART THREE: *Prognosis*

Ten

Tears flow as soon as my head hits the pillow. My fourth night in a row without solid sleep. I've taken to waking Dad in the middle of the night, asking questions that I can't bear to ask in daylight. I feel entitled to share my insomnia.

I sneak into their room. Dad sleeps in the center of the bed, alone, like he never shared it with Mom. He wakes in a snap. I sit on the edge of the mattress and swing my restless feet, forcing him to stay awake. The clock reads 3:57 a.m. "Tell me again," I say, as insistent as a three-year-old demanding another bedtime story. "Tell me how you found out."

He repeats the details, always the same. I hurl questions like an amateur darts player, some far-flung, some bull's-eye. At first, I can't shake the mechanics of the lies. I learned from the master, Agatha Christie, and make lists on inconsequential scraps of paper, the backs of receipts and junk mail envelopes:

Why didn't anyone notice that there weren't records from the clinic?
How could Dad go all that time without meeting her doctor?
Why did the pharmacy allow her to fill prescriptions of a dangerous combination of medications?
How could any of the clinic doctors let her take such high dosages of Laetrile?

His answers don't sound forced or scripted, and his helpless smile is just that—helpless. He looks like a man who barely survives the day, and yet I wake him night after night, not to be cruel, but to survive the darkness.

I want to look into Dad's face and believe him. I never doubt his love, but I doubt his words, the pauses in between. I hold my breath when he speaks, waiting for some terrible news, another brutal discovery.

"Did you suspect?" I ask. "How long did you know?"

He rolls over and lifts his head. "You know I didn't. If Barb hadn't found out, I think we'd still be living in that hell."

We're still living in hell, just a different kind. Cancer attacks white blood cells. Lies attack everything. Wreckage all the same.

After a silent moment, he asks, "Did you? You spent more time at the clinic. I know that wasn't fair—I should have been there. Did you ever see something that didn't feel right?"

Right or wrong, I feel like it always comes back to me.

"A natural caretaker," she used to say, implying that I'm the obvious choice, with Marie too young and Adrienne too volatile. My mind flashes back to her dosage list, that sheet of paper with lethal numbers scattered across the page, her suicide note. I gather the quilt in my hand and squeeze as hard as I can.

I shrug. "I don't know."

"Think," he says.

"I thought it was her moods. Sometimes I'd check on her in the infusion room and she would be with Lupe . . ." I still can't get over Lupe, whose deceit came with a price tag. I close my eyes for a second. "Sometimes they'd be laughing. Mom would have the IV, but she seemed almost happy. It was so weird to hear her laugh because she didn't laugh at home anymore. Not like she used to. But she did with Lupe. Do you think she was laughing at us?" I swallow hard.

"Oh God, no. Vanessa, it's not like that. What she did was horrible. It's the worst thing she could do to us, but she didn't do it to hurt you. I'm sure of that. Maybe she did it because of me. She wanted my attention. She wanted everyone's attention. You were the casualty—*not* the reason."

"We weren't enough for her." I want to scream like Adrienne, but all I do is whisper in the damn dark.

Dad tosses the quilt aside and climbs across the bed. With him right next to me, I can see the lines across his forehead, deepening by the day. I don't look away, even when furious tears fill my eyes.

He covers his face with his hands, quick, like he doesn't want me to see his expression. But I do. The same expression he wore when he first told me about Mom. He looks like someone pushed him from the top of a high rise, forty stories up, the last step before a deadly freefall. "Nothing was enough for her. She's mentally ill. There's something wrong with her. Not you. Not your sisters." Dad drops his hands. His face is a portrait of uncensored pain.

My head fills with memories of her protruding cheekbones, her raspy voice. "When you see her, does she say why she did it?"

He shakes his head. "She's still sick from the Laetrile, and they have her on a few new drugs. She's not very coherent right now. I want answers too. I'm going to keep visiting until I get them."

"But we could have done something, right?" I ask. "Couldn't *you* have done something to stop her?"

He looks surprised by my tone, sharp and blaming, yet not venomous like Adrienne's. Without hesitation, he nods. "I'm going to do everything in my power now. Absolutely everything. I won't let her do more damage."

"Where are you going in the morning?" I ask.

"To see the lawyer. There might be some other legal avenues to take. Since we couldn't get a restraining order, we may have to be more aggressive."

My back stiffens. "What do you mean by 'aggressive'?"

"We're looking at other hospitals. This isn't something

you need to worry about. I'll let you know if anything changes."

I try my best to meet his eyes in the dark. "We don't know what you do all day. You're just gone. I want to come with you."

He lets out an exasperated sigh, and when he speaks, he sounds exhausted. "You can't come. I've told you what I do. I talk to her doctors. I talk to the lawyer. I see your mother. That's all. I'm not keeping anything from you, Vanessa. The reality is that nothing about our situation is simple. Your mom did a hell of a job turning our lives upside down. There's a lot to manage."

"There was a lot to manage before, but we were the ones stuck doing it."

When he drapes his arm across my shoulder, I shake it off. I don't know what I want. I need him, but everything hurts so much, and no matter how hard I try, I can't find comfort in anything. Maybe I never will.

"I know your mother isn't here and you're angry. You have every right to be. I screwed up, but I am not the one who did this. I'm not your mom. I'm on your side, and I'm doing the best I can."

The plea in his voice sounds like minor keys, the piano notes that catch in my chest, the ones that bring emotion to a piece. Quiet and powerful.

"I know," I say.

The curtains gape open, just enough for the moonlight

to illuminate his profile. It's strange how I always searched for a resemblance to Mom, a trace of her beauty, but never to him. I inherited a feminine version of his nose. How come I never noticed before?

He says my name when I slide off the bed. "I love you girls more than anything."

"I know. Go back to sleep," I say before closing the door.

He's gone when I wake up.

Grief fills every corner of the house. The dining room holds too many memories. When I sit at the bench, fingers poised on the keys, all I think of is Mom in her usual seat at the table, pushing her plate away, complaining of a lack of appetite. Throwing our labor, cooking and grocery shopping, into the trash. My chest tightens with anger. I abandon Handel, the last piece in Mrs. Albright's folder.

I never thought I'd wish for Mom's death, but it would be so much more straightforward. Clearly defined. True/false rather than multiple choice.

Dad mentioned an appointment with the lawyer, and then visiting Mom, something I can't imagine. It is one thing to pace the house, as I do now, but another to picture her somewhere else, alive, going about her day. Rising from bed, drinking coffee, maybe reading the newspaper or watching television. *Existing* while we carry on, pretending she doesn't breathe the same air.

I walk from room to room, wondering when Dad will

come home, aimlessly waiting. Her face is everywhere, in almost every room, smiling from photos. We are a family obsessed with documentation. I haven't noticed before, the volume of framed photos hanging from the walls and gracing tabletops and bookshelves. School pictures and family portraits and an abundance of vacation snapshots. Dad has a good eye for composition, and he arranges the photos with the same skill as designing a building. Balanced and beautiful, deceptively so.

Adrienne's room functions as our new base camp—free of family photos—where we unearth memory after memory, marveling at the betrayal. It is too much to understand, or accept, so we ground ourselves in the practical details of buying school supplies, distracted by backpacks, notebooks, and calculators. School starts on Monday, just three days away. I can't bear to make another list, anticipating if we'll need wide-ruled or college-lined binder paper.

Caleb's absence leaves a gaping hole. I spend more and more time on the porch, waiting, sitting in the exact spot where we traded secrets and fears. Just like Mom, he feels like a ghost. I'm haunted by the living. I open the front door, only to close it. Restless and unsure of what to do with myself, I have that strung-out feeling I get whenever Adrienne convinces me to drink too much coffee when we cram for finals. Back when grades mattered. Back when anything mattered.

Caleb's skateboard peeks from under my bed. The picture

must have been there all along, the Polaroid trapped between the bed frame and the wall. I slither under the bed, reaching for the photo. Caleb, around ten, decked out in snow gear, his giant green eyes barely visible beneath his hat. I trace the curve of his lips. I used to wonder if I'd ever see him smile in such a pure way, liberated from cancer and uncertainty. Now I wonder if I'll see his face again.

I hop on the board and fly across the room, crashing into my desk. My ankle, still tender, throbs when my leg rams into the wood. Adrienne storms in just as I step back on.

"What the fuck are you doing?" She's taken to wearing her hair in a bun on the top of her head like a Hare Krishna. Ever since Dad told us the truth, Adrienne seems electric, like her simple touch will emit a deadly bolt of energy. She narrows her bloodshot eyes. "Didn't you hear the phone? It's him."

The receiver feels cold to my cheek. When I hear Caleb's voice, my muscles tighten, a surprise, the opposite of what I expect. "Hi," is all I can manage.

"Hi. We're home."

I don't want Seattle to be his home. I want him back here, within city limits, preferably within a five-foot radius. "How is it?"

"It's okay. Feels weird being back. I like having all of my stuff, but it's like I was someone else when I lived here. I miss you. A lot."

I'm not prepared for my reaction, to hear his disembodied voice, picture him, but, at the same time, also Mom.

My memories stack like a layer cake: Caleb, Mom, Caleb, Mom. At the clinic and at the house, monitoring both of them, their rest, their energy, their medication schedule. Their overlapping clinic appointments. Suddenly inseparable in my mind.

"Vanessa? You still there?"

"Yeah," I say. "I miss you, too."

"How are you doing? I wish I could be there with you. I'm sorry I left like that. My mom—"

"I know. My dad told me everything."

"Are you okay? I didn't want the first thing out of my mouth to be something terrible about your mom."

I shake my head, quiet until I remember he can't see me. "No. I don't know who I can trust right now and I really need to trust you. If you're keeping anything from me, you need to tell me right now."

"Listen, I knew something was up, but I didn't know what exactly, and my mom wouldn't tell me anything. I knew she was talking to your dad. But I didn't know the whole story until we checked into the hotel. I swear. You have to believe me."

I twirl the cord around my finger until the tip turns red. I tug harder. "That's what my dad says."

"Well, that's the truth. The only one who is lying is your mom."

"He let us believe she was dying. He didn't tell us right away and you . . ." I press my forehead against the wall a little too hard. "And you were just *gone*. When are you coming back?"

"I need to talk to you about that. My dad is here right now. He was waiting for us when we got back last night. It was one in the morning and he was sitting in the living room watching TV just like he used to. He told me he wants to spend time together. He's talking to my mom now. Closed-door meeting. I don't know what's going to happen."

I had cataloged my fears: Caleb knowing something, Caleb keeping Mom's secret, Caleb not coming back. But until now, they couldn't compete with Mom's betrayal. My heart isn't big enough, my stomach strong enough. Worry is one thing, but grief another. Anguish morphs into a new species of desperation, carnivorous. My tears come from so deep inside me that I think I'll cough up organs, essential parts of my body that I need to survive. I've held it all in, not just the tears, but the down-in-my-stomach vomit-inducing pain. I've been saving it for him, the one person I can count on to truly understand.

"Vanessa," he says once and then again. "Talk to me."

"So you're not coming back."

"I want to, but I don't know what's going to happen with my dad. He said he'd like to check out California. I'll be back. I promise. I just don't know when, exactly. I'm going to call you every day, okay? I'll keep you posted."

"I'm hearing that a lot right now," I say. "My dad just said that about my mom."

"I miss you, Vanessa. I'm coming back."

Caleb wants his dad more than anything, and now he has him. I should be happy, but I'm too selfish to be that generous. I'm not enough for Mom, and now I'm not enough for him.

Our house perches on a hill, the height deceptive until you look out the kitchen window at the blur of lavender bushes at least a story below. I balance the phone between my jaw and shoulder, freeing my hands to wrestle the window open, something Barb used to do every morning.

A trio of ceramic birds, souvenirs Mom picked up in Ensenada, line the sill. One by one, I poke them in the chest, directly in the center of their painted blue feathers. I'm too high up to hear them break. Maybe they don't. Maybe they land in the bushes, cradled by the flowers, hovering just above the ground, intact.

I back away from the breeze. The late-morning light floods the room, illuminating the wall. Mom smiles from a triptych, framed above the table. Mom holding each of us as newborns. I need to get out of this room. I need to leave the house. Caleb's voice isn't enough to anchor me. Not now.

"I miss you, too. Marie is calling for me," I lie. "I'll talk to you tomorrow."

"Wait."

"I've got to go." I hang up before he can say another word.

I grab the board and head outside without telling Adrienne and Marie. I want Caleb, just Caleb, separate and distinct from Mom. Riding the board might help. My movements lack grace, but I don't crash. Snaking through the neighborhood, I rely on muscle memory for balance.

Maybe, in the back of my mind, I intend to go there, to Mariposa Street, to Mrs. Albright's house. It's an easy ride, smooth and flat. She kneels in her garden, the wide brim of her straw hat blocking the view of her face.

My feet carry me across the lawn. She looks up with a surprised smile.

"Vanessa," she says, seeming truly happy to see me.

I can't hold back the tears. "I'm out of music."

She rises and tugs off her gardening gloves. "Let's go inside for a cup of tea."

I wince when I catch a glimpse of myself in the mirror. I look like hell in wrinkled clothes and tangled hair. Feral once again.

Abstract art and family photos line the walls. Two college-age boys, one in uniform and one in a cowboy shirt, smile in a formal portrait. Both have her eyes.

"My sons," she says, pointing from left to right. "Jackson and Philip." She taps Jackson. "He was drafted the first year of the war. He died after a few weeks in Vietnam."

That would have been in 1970. He's been dead for six years, since before I met Mrs. Albright. I can't imagine my own pain, so all-consuming, easing over time. How can she carry grief with her, just below the surface, every day, surrounded by kids not much younger than her dead son?

Tears stream down my cheeks. "I didn't know," I say. "I'm sorry."

"I told you that I knew grief. Did playing help?"

I nod. "I couldn't have gotten through the summer without the music. I didn't finish, though. My mom . . . she . . . I just have one piece left."

Mrs. Albright raises two fingers to her lips, kisses them, and then touches her sons' faces, smudging the glass.

"I promised you tea," she says. "Follow me."

As soon as I sit at her kitchen table, I blurt out the truth. "My mom isn't dead. She lied. She was never sick."

Tall and willowy like a sunflower, Mrs. Albright stands over the stove with her back to me. I hear the *click-click-click* and *swoosh* of the gas flame. The tea kettle clanks on the element. She turns to me, her face a puzzled mask, ready to listen.

"This sounds like a long story."

I nod vigorously. "I'm sorry . . . if you're busy, I—"

"You're rescuing me from weeds. I don't have other plans. I'm all yours."

She slides a mug across the table, along with a plate of cookies. I take a deep breath, count to five, and exhale.

"That's a good start," Mrs. Albright says. "Just like when you play. Clear your head. Let everything come into focus."

"There's a disease, a mental illness, and people who have it pretend to be sick. My dad says they can't help it. I don't see how that can be true. But my mom has it."

"Munchausen syndrome," she says.

"You know it?"

"I've read about it. Newspaper stories. There was a woman in Fallbrook who killed her child. She told everyone he was sick. The medicine killed him. She went to prison. It was all over the news for a while."

I reach for a cookie, a thick shortbread square, and break it in half. "That's the thing I don't get. Doctors give people tests. You can't fake tests."

She shakes her head, never taking her eyes off me. "No, but this woman took her child from emergency room to emergency room. Never the same one twice. She told them he was sick and they believed her. We don't think of mothers as people who would intentionally hurt their own children. It's inconceivable."

"My dad said that she could've done it to my little sister. That she might try if she gets out of the hospital."

Steam rises from the teapot, and the scent of peppermint floods the room. I take another deep breath.

"This mint is from my garden." Mrs. Albright fills my mug and takes the seat across from me. "Vanessa, she could have done it to you, too. None of you were safe. And I believe she poisoned you in a different way, which is damaging too. Would you like to see those articles? I'm happy to go to the library. I think it would help."

"Yeah," I say. "Reading helps. It's like playing."

She smiles. "You and I are very much alike. When did you find out about your mother?"

"About a week ago. I don't know what to do." I look at my tea. Tears fall into the mug, creating ripples, like a stone tossed into a pond. "I don't get how this wasn't on purpose. Why didn't she stop? How could she do this to us? My dad keeps saying that she couldn't help it."

"I'm not a doctor, Vanessa, but I do know that mental illness is still an illness. If the doctors are saying that she has this disease, then they're probably right."

I don't bother wiping the tears from my cheeks. More will come, a steady stream. I pick at the cookie, eroding the edge, causing an avalanche of crumbs.

She cocks her head. "Have you seen her?"

My hands clench, knuckles instantly white. "I can't. She's dangerous. My dad went to court."

"It sounds like he's doing what he can under very difficult circumstances."

I don't know how I'm going to face school, especially when everyone finds out the truth. I won't be able to hide behind the piano all day. I rest my head on my folded arms, trying to be quiet as I cry.

"Shhh," she says, rubbing my back. "I know it hurts."

"Couldn't someone have stopped her?" I ask, half choking out the words. "How could she get away with this?"

Magically, a box of tissues appears. "Do you know those special pencils that I use when I mark up sheet music? They're hard to find. My husband, he's English, brings them home whenever he goes to London. Years ago, I had a student who stole them.

"What was remarkable was how he did it—right in front of me. After Jackson died, I saw things differently. The details, I guess. They seemed more important. One day, this student took a pencil and I saw him clear as day. He'd been doing it all year. Afterward, he said that he always stole in plain sight because people couldn't believe that anyone would ever be so bold. He was quite the shoplifter. Does it help to think of your mother in those terms?"

I say, "I think so," even though nothing truly can help me understand how she could do this to us.

"Just allow yourself to feel right now. You don't have to understand it. That will come later. It may never come, honestly. Just play the piano. It's the best thing you can do. Remind me, what was the last piece?"

"Handel."

"Well, he won't do. Come with me."

I follow her into the small living room, where an impressive baby grand takes up most of the space. She opens the bench and fingers through several books. She hands me a slim red volume. Stravinsky's *Firebird Suite*.

"You'll stumble over every note. Don't worry—that's the point. This is something that will demand your full attention. Give yourself over to it. Read through it before you start. I have something else for you."

It is sacrilege, but I have never been drawn to Stravinsky or Rachmaninoff and their frenetic passion. They are masters of control, but to me, they feel untamed and on the brink of something awful. I don't tell anyone my opinion. Mrs. Albright knows Chopin is my favorite composer, inspiring me in a way Stravinsky and Rachmaninoff never can.

She returns with a couple of envelopes in her hand.

"I had them sent to the school just as we agreed. You have your choice, Vanessa. You got into two of the conservatories and both awarded you scholarships. I explained your circumstances—that you have a family emergency—and they're willing to wait for you to decide. Take them home and think about what you want next. You need to make up your mind very soon, or you can defer for a year."

She places the two envelopes in my hand. The first letter, printed on a heavy textured paper, is from a conservatory we visited last year for their annual holiday concert. I remember sitting in the auditorium and dissecting the notes, amazed kids my age could play as well as the San Diego Symphony. I never thought I could be one of them. Especially now, music is so personal to me, an extension of my fingers, my breath. It hits me all at once: the complete yearning to go and the reality that I can't leave my family.

I remember when I graduated from scales and exercises to a song, a simple lullaby. My fingers barely spanned the keys. I practiced over and over again until a clear melody emerged. The music was simple and unremarkable, but it came from the deepest part of me. Everyone commented on the speed with which I picked up pieces. I am a quick study, with instinctive fingers, but that's not why the conservatory accepted me. It's the way I feel the notes travel through my diaphragm and sternum and limbs. I bring my whole body to the instrument, and playing music has always been what I wanted, has always been enough.

It's a fantasy, but I allow myself a few moments to dream of playing in that auditorium, of playing Chopin onstage surrounded by others who share the same passion.

I got in.

Months of mastering pieces, practicing the same ones over and over until I was good enough to record my audition tape, paid off. It was worth it.

My eyes feel swollen from tears and my heart feels tight with grief and pride. I can't help but grin even if I don't know what the future holds.

"Now, play," Mrs. Albright says, returning my smile. I smooth out the music, messing up over and over again as I play, but she's right: After a while, I don't think of anything but the notes.

Eleven

The first day of school, I walk the halls like a ghost, looking at the faces of my classmates, thinking, *I am not one of you or you or you or you . . .*

Last night, Caleb gave me instructions: Don't make eye contact with anyone; look at the ground and walk with purpose. This way, everyone will leave me alone. These were his survival techniques from his last months at school. I half expected him to tell me how to combat hypothermia and bear attacks, dangers of the wild.

He keeps his promise and calls every day, just after dinner so we won't be rushed. Quick to run out of words, I end the calls after a few minutes, then long for him all over again. He's become a spiritualist, a medium who summons Mom whenever he calls. I listen to his voice, his stories about outings with his dad, their ambiguous plans to return to San Diego, only to catch glimpses of Mom, nothing but memories, recollections of her sitting at the table or baking chicken pot pie. His calls raise the undead.

At school, I heed his advice. Mrs. Albright opens the music room early and I rush there, head down, to review my class schedule. No surprises—the same college-prep classes, the only difference from last year is chemistry instead of Earth sciences, precalc instead of trig.

Mrs. Albright takes the seat next to mine. "What did your dad say about the conservatories?" she asks.

"I haven't told him yet. I can't up and leave for boarding school. I wish that Point Loma and the San Diego Conservatory hadn't rejected me. Maybe I could go to the Coronado magnet arts school? I know it isn't a conservatory, but I could take more piano classes there."

I reach for one of Mrs. Albright's cherished pencils and doodle on my class schedule, spirals, tendrils, and waves. I want to transfer—no question—but I couldn't do that to my sisters. Or even to Dad. I find myself thinking about the conservatories at random times: in the shower or while I'm cleaning the house or braiding Marie's hair. How could I transfer when the guilt of leaving would strangle any joy and creativity I have? I wish I could escape to music camp for just a week. If I ever get the chance, maybe I'll move to Idyllwild, high in the mountains. I've always been happy there, safe and enveloped in music, surrounded by others who love it as much as I do.

Conservatories and camp and the mountains are meant for the future. Not now.

Gently, Mrs. Albright plucks the pencil from my hand. "They're not that far away," she says. "Both are in driving distance, just up the coast. You have a gift, Vanessa. Music is a part of you. Every few years, I have a student like you, except you're different. You've been through something none of them have. I want you to have the opportunity to play through your pain."

"It's too much to figure out," I say.

"Did I ever tell you what inspired me to learn the piano?"

I shake my head.

"When Beethoven started to lose his hearing, he sawed off the legs of his grand piano. Then he lay on the ground right next to it, and pressed his ear to the floor and played. Imagine going to such lengths to hear a single note of music. I couldn't believe someone had that much passion. I wanted to feel that way.

"I'm not saying transferring will be easy, but I see something in you. I worry that you'll lose it if you don't devote yourself to music."

When I gaze out the window, I see the boys' cross country team running around the field. They resemble Canada geese, flying in formation, migrating to their next destination. Some of the guys run without shirts. A few of them are as tall as Caleb, others runty. All skinny, but not skinny like Caleb, whose body shows hints of his past health, his broad and once muscular shoulders, his chest temporarily concave. I look away.

"Okay," I say. "I'll talk to my dad."

She nods her head, serious instead of smiling. "As your teacher, that's all I ask."

When I leave the music room, I hear Adrienne all the way down the hall. I rush past everyone, the entire junior class lining the lockers, trading summer vacation stories. Her shouting is urgent as a fire alarm. They all start turning their heads, craning their necks to see what's going on: my sister shoving her boyfriend against a locker.

"What the hell is wrong with you?" she screams. "How could you do this to me?"

I drop my backpack and run to her, functioning like a human shield so she won't hurt Zach. I stare straight into her eyes, absorbing her fury. She looks right through me.

"Let's go," I say. "We can go to the beach. Anywhere you want."

"I want to kill my stupid EX-boyfriend!" she screams. Her face contorts with rage.

I turn to Zach, who stands guppy-mouthed and shocked.

"What happened?" I ask.

"I told Tina and Kim that they shouldn't bring up your mom. I thought that would be easier on Adrienne, you know, if they knew what was going on." His voice shakes and I realize that I've never seen Zach upset. Bummed about beach closures and bad pop quiz scores, but not *upset*.

And I've never seen Adrienne this angry.

She pants, out of breath like she just finished running a

marathon. "You had no right to tell anyone anything about me. I can't believe I ever went out with you. Don't ever talk to me again. Don't call me. You can go fuck a donut for all I care!"

I yank her arm and drag her to the front entrance, past the reviled senior English teacher, Mrs. Hacker, who shouts for us to stop.

The door slams shut and I release Adrienne, leaving fingerprints on her skin from where I clutched her arm.

"Come on," she says. It's her turn to pull me along, and I'm never more grateful to go to a huge high school. I don't recognize half of the people we pass, blending in with thirty-five hundred other kids, a cover of anonymity.

We stop at the art classrooms, at a patch of grass protected by several giant eucalyptus trees. Adrienne pulls me to the ground. I hate the way she gasps for breath. She's never looked more like Mom.

"You know," she says, "the whole school will find out by lunch."

"Maybe it won't be that bad." I know she's right, though, and I already imagine all the eyes on me, the whispers, the pointed fingers. *She's the one with the crazy mother.*

"God, he had to tell Kim and Tina of all people? They're the ones who told everyone that Bethany Carson got knocked up. I love them, but they're shitty friends when it comes to stuff like this. He's so stupid. I can't believe he did this to me."

I lose some of my sympathy for Zach. Our lives are going to be a living hell. I don't know how I'm going to face everyone in class, not if they all know.

"Let's go," I say.

Adrienne surprises me by shaking her head. "Not yet. We can't let them scare us off that easily."

"Wait," I say. "No one did this on purpose. Zach was trying to help."

"You need to wake up, little sister. People are going to be assholes, and some of them will try to use this against us. Me, anyway, and I'm going to go all *West Side Story* on them when they do."

"Give me the car keys," I say.

"Are you going to go joy riding with your permit?"

"I need a place to go, Adrienne." Already, my chest feels boa constrictor tight. Mrs. Albright will let me stay in the music room as much as possible, but she won't permit me to miss all of my classes.

She tosses me the keys. "I'll meet you right here. Don't be late."

I've driven Dad's car, a cream-colored Mercedes, not at all a family car. Even after two years, it still smells new, barely used compared to Mom's Datsun, prematurely aged from our countless border crossings. Sticky from spilled soda and road trip snacks.

When I slip into the driver's seat, I place my hands in the same position that Mom does, just above the center, at ten and two o'clock. Always in the same spots, even when she drove through the storm. Precise, but then again, liars rely on precision.

I expect to feel like her, somehow, by occupying her car, her seat. I glance in the rearview mirror. She would have seen me in the reflection, always sitting behind her, always hoping she felt well enough for the trip. But I only feel nerves as I head north on the Pacific Coast Highway.

The empty stretch of sand never seemed so desolate. Not a single surfer dots the waves, nor a fisherman on the rickety pier. I don't bother locking the car. The man recognizes me and waves. After years of buying food from him, did Mom ever ask his name? I offer a polite hello, but otherwise wait for the clams in silence.

My feet freeze midstep. I intended to eat the clams at the end of the pier, something Mom and I used to do. But when I look at the ocean, at the endless expanse of blue, I can't will myself to walk. The planks creak beneath my weight, and in between the worn wood, I watch the water wash to the shore, covering the creatures burrowed under the sand. Gulls caw overhead, scavenging for scraps, and a hollowness fills me, something so deep and desperate that I think I'll never escape.

I toss the clams into the water.

I'm seized by the desire to drive her car off the pier, not to commit suicide, but to destroy her vehicle of deceit. It was a mistake to come back here, to think that I could take comfort in nostalgia, even something so commonplace as fried food on the beach. She robbed me of that.

Slamming the car door shut, I smack the center of the steering wheel with my open palm, a slap that sounds the horn. The glove compartment gapes open, sending paper to the floor. I reach for the clinic brochure, black-and-white, with photos of the courtyard, the welcoming fountain, and the grounds like it's a hotel. The text tells a different story.

> The Laetrile molecule chemically reacts with healthy enzymes of noncancerous cells before effectively destroying active cancer cells. This process produces results in a matter of months, but in some cases, a matter of years.
>
> To accompany the therapy, patients must adhere to a strict diet, including taking the following dietary supplements.
>
> Within weeks of Laetrile therapy, most patients show signs of increased energy and activity, pain relief, fall of blood pressure, and improved appetite.

Sitting in her seat, placing my hands on the faded traces of her fingerprints, won't help me understand. Just like tormenting Dad won't give me answers. Only Mom can tell me why she did this, how she decided her children are disposable, are nothing to her. I crumple up the brochure and toss it out the window, hoping the wind will carry it to the water for a sailor's burial.

The music comes slowly, an unconscious tapping on the steering wheel. I rush out of the car to chase the brochure, rolling down the cement sidewalk like a tumbleweed. I could pull my notebook from my backpack, but this paper, these words and images, are my accompaniment. I scrawl notes in the margins. I scribble over words of false hope with my first piece of music, writing until it's time to meet my sister.

Adrienne scrambles out of the car before I turn off the engine.

"I mean it, Zach. Get the hell away from my house. GO!"

She tosses her backpack at him, which he dodges with ease. He picks it up, doing his best to act like everything is normal. But I see the pain in his eyes, and it reminds me of why I like him. Zach is good and pure-hearted, a guy from a book, the goofy, cute sidekick. And in his case, in this moment, profoundly stupid.

"Okay, A, I'm going to let you calm down."

When she storms past him, I half expect to witness an act of violence. He steps aside, standing still even when she slams the door in his face. Through the window, I see his profile, the way he closes his eyes.

"Jackass," Adrienne says.

I turn away. I want to tell Adrienne everything, about the conservatories, about Mrs. Albright, but she needs space.

I wish she could put her anger aside long enough to really talk to me. I need her to listen without exploding. I want her to hear my dream of going—really hear me. But she can't do that now. She'll be fine if everyone leaves her alone for a little while. I just have to be patient, like Dad is doing with her. Adrienne turns on the radio, some rock song by Queen. I try to block out the sound, replacing it in my mind with the notes I conjured at the beach. No matter how painful, driving there unlocked something deep inside me, something that was missing all summer long. A certain quality of playing, a power almost beyond myself, when the music roots me completely.

"Mind if I practice?" I want to keep the music alive in my mind.

Adrienne turns off the radio. "Go for it. I want to sketch, and your music will make me feel better."

I tug her sleeve. "You know he didn't mean to hurt you, right?"

Adrienne stares at me with eyes full of fury. "It doesn't matter. He shouldn't have done it. I thought you had to practice."

"I do."

Adrienne joins me in the dining room, spreading out her sketchbook and evaluating her work, the dramatic Mexican landscapes and something new, a scary portrait of Mom, her face cadaver thin with Medusa hair full of writhing snakes.

Before I have a chance to sit down, the doorbell rings.

Adrienne looks up. "Can you get it? Can't deal."

"Sure." I open the door to Zach, who runs a hand through his hair.

"Has she cooled down?" he asks. "I heard music. Music relaxes her."

His face holds several expressions at once: confusion, concern, and sadness. I hear Adrienne's determined footsteps.

When she sees Zach, she says, "How many times do I have to tell you to leave me alone? Seriously, I don't want you here. Leave now. NOW!"

Zach, in his seemingly endless valor, doesn't descend the stairs, but takes a seat at the top, his long legs stretching out in the sun. "Nope."

Adrienne slams the door with such force that the floor shakes like an earthquake's aftershock.

I look at her. "Don't do this."

Adrienne peeks through the curtain. "He's still there," she fumes, and storms into the kitchen.

I hear the sound of the faucet and Adrienne returns with a pitcher full of water. I stare at her, knowing there's nothing I can do to stop her. So I take a seat at the kitchen table, putting aside my urgent need for music, and listen to Zach's shocked yelp.

She rushes back to the kitchen.

"Adrienne, please," I plead. "Stop."

"No. Don't make me cry. I can't fucking cry."

I try to hug her, but she holds up the pitcher to block

me. Mom's wedding crystal. Adrienne hurls it across the kitchen, barely missing the window, and the crystal splits into shards the way everything in our lives is shattering.

"Leave it," she says with tears streaming down her face. "I'll clean it up. Get out of the kitchen. You'll cut yourself. Okay?"

I stand there, dumbfounded.

"Vanessa! Did you hear me? Get out of the kitchen."

I nod, my eyes volleying between Adrienne and the broken glass. She might not get over this. We all might be broken—always. Collateral damage, the price for Mom's lies.

Dad carries Marie into the house like she's a toddler again. He lifts her up with ease, all seventy-five pounds of her, and holds her tenderly. She wraps her legs around his waist, crossing her bare feet, and rests her head on his shoulder.

"Down you go, baby," he says.

As soon as her feet touch the ground, Marie tugs at her new dress, the one Adrienne bought for her first day of school. She clutches her rosary and walks down the hall, humming to herself. I hear Adrienne open her door and the two of them talking.

"Did she have an okay day?" I ask.

"Come." He gestures to the door. "I picked up some groceries."

The afternoon sun evaporated the water, evidence of Adrienne's assault on Zach. I almost tell Dad, but the idea of

Adrienne turning her anger on me stops me cold. She swept up the crystal in silence, and we resumed our music and drawing for the rest of the afternoon.

Dad reaches into the trunk and hands me a gallon of cold milk, the handle wet with condensation.

"I didn't tell Marie's teacher or the principal," he says. Another omission, but this one feels right. He sees my flicker of support and smiles. I smile back. "I thought I'd give her some time to settle in."

If we can spare Marie from a few days of hovering teachers, that will be a blessing. I wish Adrienne and I could share that luxury, but Zach's carelessness destroyed that.

I transfer the milk from one hand to another. "Any news about Mom?"

He meets my eyes before shaking his head. "Nothing to report. How about you? How was your first day?"

"Exactly what you'd expect."

"I think our lives are beyond expectations, don't you?" He stands with resolve, and while I see his pain, it seems distant now, as though he stashed it in the back of a cupboard, safe from view, and only takes it out at night. On our way into the house, he squeezes my shoulder, his touch light and fleeting. My feet stop midstep and I half hope he'll pick me up like Marie.

In her room, I comb through Marie's drawers to find her something to wear. She says she hates the dress, the fabric feels like fire, like it's burning her skin. Only holy clothing from now on. Adrienne hides her disappointment, not a surprise, since she's always gentle with Marie. I unfold each of her saint shirts, displaying them on the floor for her to pick. Marie doesn't bother looking.

"I want my Joan of Arc one," she says, pointing to her most gruesome, her favorite.

I smooth out the green fabric and hand it to her.

"She's your favorite today?" I ask.

Marie smiles. "She'll be my favorite from now on. See?"

She displays the underside of her arms, covered with made-up prayers, haiku-short, that she's written on her skin.

Adrienne and I exchange a startled look.

"My teacher doesn't like them," she says. "I have to wash off the ink or she's sending home a note, so I'm writing where she can't see."

"What are you talking about?" Adrienne asks. "Where?"

Marie wiggles out of her dress so we can see her chest and belly, inscriptions written in permanent marker: *If I am not, may God put me there; and if I am, may God so keep me.*

"See, Joan rode into war for God. Just like Joan, I will do whatever God tells me."

I pick up her arms, reading the quotes she inscribed: *I am not afraid . . . I was born to do this. Act, and God will act.*

"You can't write on yourself," I say, shuddering. "Come on, we need to wash it off."

"No, please let me keep it," she pleads. "It's my protection."

"I have an idea," Adrienne says. "How about you take a

bath and I can make you a shirt instead? That way you can wear it without writing on your skin."

Marie sits on her bed, unsure, clearly carrying on an internal debate, closing her eyes, moving her lips in prayer. I wrap my arms around her, wanting her to talk to me rather than send her words up to Joan or God. I wonder if this is how she spent the day, at her desk and on the playground, reciting quotes and prayers in the hope that someone divine will hear, will consider her voice worthy.

But we aren't worthy, not to Mom. Of all her sins, this is the greatest.

Twelve

Adrienne ditches me as soon as we walk into school, but not before giving me a hug and slipping the car keys into my hand. Her backpack bulges with paper and art supplies. A glittered piece of construction paper, caught in the zipper, sparkles in the sunlight as she walks down the hall with determined steps.

Mrs. Albright gives me an encouraging nod as I climb the stairs to the piano. Annie Kilsgaard can't take her eyes off me, and as soon as Suzie Hendricks sits down, she whispers into her ear.

I imagine them murmuring through the winds, then the strings. A Greek chorus of gossip. I close the piano's lid and then my eyes. I imagined this in the halls, in science, and in math, but not in here, not in the same room as the instruments, as Mrs. Albright. I feel the comfort of the car keys, wrapping my fingers around the cold metal, as I rise from the bench and rush out the door.

I round the corner and find Adrienne taping a sign to the wall. In between posters announcing the first meetings of the debate team, yearbook, and drama, I spot her elaborate poster that reads, ZACH ROSSMAN GAVE ME GONORRHEA. She filled every inch of empty space with similar signs, some collaged, some painted, all profane, and all about Zach.

ZACH ROSSMAN CAN'T GET IT UP

ZACH ROSSMAN SODOMIZES LIVESTOCK

ZACH ROSSMAN COULDN'T GET LAID IN A WHOREHOUSE

I tug on her backpack. "Come on, take these down before you get caught."

"I don't care," she says, pointing to the door across the hall. "I want Zach to come out of biology and see my masterpieces. That should teach him to keep his mouth shut and leave me alone."

Before I respond, I hear footsteps.

"Both of you, go to Dr. Whelan's office. If you don't, I'll make sure you're suspended. Is that clear?"

I turn to find Mrs. Hacker, Adrienne's English teacher, standing behind us. Of all the teachers, she has to be the one to find us? She busts students for sport.

"*Now.*" She folds her arms across her modest chest.

Adrienne gives her a scathing look before turning to me. "Sorry," she whispers.

I'm glad she doesn't have to go alone. Maybe I can keep her calm, save her from suspension.

The guidance counselor's name is printed on a plaque,

one large capital letter followed by smaller capital letters, the same lettering as on Dad's business cards. DR. DONNA WHELAN.

Her door is open, but we sit in the corner. Adrienne slumps next to me and sketches another defaming sign. I see Dr. Whelan, but she doesn't see us. I don't know much about her. She started last year. She came from New Mexico, and I think she looks a little like a cactus. Plump, with enough water to survive a drought. I watch as she picks up her misting bottle and sprays water on ancient, distorted orchids, some beyond blooming, which line the sill of the blazing windows.

Adrienne mutters "bitch" when Mrs. Hacker appears. She is the self-proclaimed savior of our school. She fixates on a student, and then, once or twice a semester, she schedules urgent meetings with the school counselor and principal to discuss how the disturbed student is on the brink of some emotional break.

Everyone knows the story of how years earlier, Mrs. Hacker spotted warning signs in a reckless, introverted boy who wore a uniform of Toughskins jeans and Hanes T-shirts, each with a philosopher's name scrawled on the shirt with a permanent marker. It's school legend. When he wore his Nietzsche shirt all week, the English teacher phoned his parents and asked how things were at home. After a string of events, long altered by time and embellishment, the student was found ready to dive off the roof of his father's office building. Since then, Mrs. Hacker has had a deep, one-sided connection with the troubled youth of our school.

Clearly, Adrienne and I are the newly ordained problem students.

Mrs. Hacker huffs past us and twitches into the counselor's office, hands fluttering about her body, patting her hair, and smoothing her skirt. She looks like the nervous Chihuahua that lives on our block.

"Good morning, Dr. Whelan," she says.

"Hello."

"Mind if I close this?" Mrs. Hacker doesn't wait for an answer before swinging the door shut, but the door is new and thin, and I hear every word.

Dr. Whelan asks, "Who's the topic this morning?"

"The Babcock girls. Adrienne is the real problem."

I hear the thump and I know Mrs. Hacker collected Adrienne's signs.

"Shit," Adrienne breathes. "I used up all of Marie's construction paper for nothing."

I raise a finger to my lips. "Listen."

"Is she taking art?" I hear Dr. Whelan ask.

"How would I know?" Mrs. Hacker responds.

"I was under the impression that you monitor the emotional state of our students," Dr. Whelan says. "Excuse me for a moment."

I assumed she knew we'd been sent to her office, but when the door opens and Dr. Whelan sees us, she looks surprised.

"Adrienne, are you taking art?"

"Yeah, Mr. Klein's studio class. Since freshman year."

"Wait here. I'll be with you both in a moment."

She walks into another room and returns with two files. After she closes her flimsy door, Mrs. Hacker says, "Dr. Whelan, don't you find these at all disturbing?"

"Maureen, didn't her mother die over the summer? Of course she's disturbed. Thank you for bringing these to me."

"Don't you know? She wasn't sick. The mother is insane. They had her institutionalized. This family has a history of mental illness."

"Thank you. I'll take it from here."

Everything is quiet.

"Don't you need to get back to your class?" Dr. Whelan asks.

Mrs. Hacker opens the door. Glaring at us, she shakes her head, clucks her tongue, and warns, "I'll see you in class, Adrienne."

Dr. Whelan waves us in. "Come."

I stand first, aware that I obey her not because I feel obligated, but because I actually want to. By the time we make it into her office, she is standing behind her desk and flipping through the stack of Adrienne's signs.

"Impressive," she says.

Adrienne and I sit and wait for Dr. Whelan to say more, but she continues to look through the posters. I watch as Adrienne crosses her legs a couple of times and sweeps her hair away from her face.

It's like Adrienne can't stand the quiet. "I hate Hacker. Everyone does," she blurts.

"This isn't about Mrs. Hacker. This is about your behavior."

Dr. Whelan looks at me. "Tell me your name again?"

"Vanessa."

"And do you share your sister's artistic inclinations?"

Adrienne plants both of her feet on the floor. "She tried to stop me. She didn't have anything to do with this. She didn't even know."

Dr. Whelan raises a hand. "Despite the impression Mrs. Hacker gave, you are not in trouble. You're not going to get detention and I'm not going to call your father unless this emerges as a pattern. Clear?"

I nod, scared to say anything that will change her mind.

"I want to hear how your classes are going, how it is being back in school. I understand your mother has been struggling."

Adrienne scoffs. "Nice euphemism."

"Isn't it a struggle?" she says, without sounding condescending. "I understand you both are having a difficult time at home."

I break eye contact and look down. My hair falls into my face. Talking with Mrs. Albright is one thing, but I suddenly feel claustrophobic, like detention might be better after all.

"Adrienne, it looks like you're excelling in art." Dr. Whelan holds up a poster before opening a folder. "They're well done. You have talent. It looks like you do well in English and math, too.

"Art isn't enough, though. You're a senior. In two or three months, your college applications will be due. You have good PSAT scores. By December, you need to take the SATs and apply to schools. If you continue to behave this way, you'll alienate your teachers. You already have a problem with Mrs. Hacker. Most college applications require three letters of recommendation." Dr. Whelan pauses and looks at Adrienne, who taps her foot against the floor.

"I suspect college hasn't been on your—or your family's—mind."

Adrienne and I both shake our heads.

"That's understandable. But you need to think about it now. You'll regret it if you don't."

Adrienne glares at her. "You have no clue what I will or won't regret."

Dr. Whelan points to the diplomas and awards on the wall. "Let's say I can make an educated guess."

Adrienne exhales and shrugs. I lean over and whisper, "Listen to her. We don't want her to call Dad."

"Your sister is wise," Dr. Whelan says, looking at me.

She opens the other file on her desk and panic fills my chest. What if there is something about the conservatories in there? I haven't told Adrienne yet, not after what happened yesterday.

"Vanessa, it looks like you're working closely with Mrs. Albright. Your grades are strong. Stay focused on that."

I exhale loudly, causing Adrienne to give me a questioning look.

"In a year or two, you both may not want to be limited to attending a junior college here in San Diego. You'll want options."

"You have no idea what we're going through. And my top school is here. UC San Diego."

I wonder if Adrienne intends to sound so harsh, as if all adults are suspect.

"No, I don't know," Dr. Whelan says. "But you won't get into that school unless you do well now. Can I ask you something?"

"Do we have a choice?" Adrienne asks.

Dr. Whelan laughs. "Not really. Have either of you talked to anyone about your mother? A therapist?"

I want to tell Dr. Whelan about Caleb, about Barb, and how they know everything but vanished. How as I fall asleep, I have long conversations with Caleb in my head, ones I can't bring myself to have on the phone.

"No," Adrienne says. "No shrinks. And besides, we're sitting here because I told my idiot boyfriend and he told the school. Hence the signs."

"But you two talk to each other, correct?"

Adrienne turns to me and nods.

"Vanessa, have you talked to anyone?"

"Mrs. Albright."

Adrienne raises a curious eyebrow, with a frown that tells me she feels betrayed.

I look at the clock. Half past nine. My eyes return to the floor.

"Are we done yet?" Adrienne asks.

"No," Dr. Whelan says. "It's not acceptable to post these flyers. I know you're upset, but you can't launch a public campaign against Zach. You can still make posters. You can make the posters about anyone—Zach, your mother. Anyone. As many as you want. Just don't post them in public places, especially school."

"You want me to make more posters?" Adrienne asks.

"That's not what I said. But I think it's good for you to release your emotions. I'd like you to make an art project about how you're feeling, and then we'll meet to discuss your work. I'll invite Mr. Klein to join us. Vanessa, you too. I'll talk to Mrs. Albright."

"When am I supposed to make this magical healing artwork?" Adrienne asks.

"Due tomorrow. Come here after last period."

I look at the clock and stand.

"Do we have to go back to class?" Adrienne asks.

"Yes, you do. Vanessa, looks like you missed most of yesterday. Are you feeling okay, all things considered?"

I nod.

"Good. Check in with Mrs. Albright at lunch. And Adrienne, please watch your language."

"Yeah right," Adrienne says before we exit the office.

I haven't told Mrs. Albright about the piece, the notes written on the clinic brochure. I need to remove the knot in my stomach, the ache in my chest, and only finishing it will help. I embrace the assignment, to compose something—anything—that expresses emotion, regardless of length. I can't play at school, not now anyway, so she grants me permission to compose at home.

With the quilts returned to the linen closet, my spinet sits naked in the dining room, yet I hold on to the old worry that my playing will wake Mom. I'm not one to obsess about whether I locked the door or turned off the stove, but now I wander through the house worrying that Mom is still here, sick, needing me. There isn't enough room for two nightmares—leukemia and Munchausen's. We should only have to suffer through one, and I choose the former, the honest death.

An old medicine box sits in the corner of the garage. I don't bother with newspaper; I don't care if the glass breaks. I stack frame upon frame, any photo with Mom, starting with the triptych in the kitchen, leaving only two rooms untouched: Marie's bedroom and Dad's study.

Mom's room suffers the most. Not only do I remove her pictures, but her things as well, her most precious possessions arranged atop her dresser and bedside table. Jewelry, books, knickknacks. The engraved sterling hairbrush and mirror. Volumes of poetry with pressed flowers tucked within the pages. Artifacts no longer sacred. Rubbish. I'm not trespassing, I tell myself. I am ridding the house of bad spirits. Of menacing ghosts and memories. It's her or me—something I feel to the core. If I'm going to live in this house, if I'm going to feel a sliver of peace, just enough to make music, maybe even sleep, then she has to go.

Bare walls, with exposed nails and sun-bleached paint, darker where pictures once hung. Years of lies buried in a box. I hide them in my closet, in the same place I stored Caleb's things.

A test. I dial his number. Maybe I can hear his voice—just his—without evoking Mom. He answers on the first ring, sounding loud and angry.

"It's me," I say, knowing his tone is intended for someone else.

"I thought you were my dad." His voice barely softens. "He's leaving us for good."

"Leaving?"

"Yeah, the whole thing was bullshit. He made it sound like he wanted to move to San Diego too. They saw a realtor today and it turns out that all he cares about is the money from selling the house. He wants to stay in Seattle. He's divorcing my mom. He's such an asshole."

"Oh, Caleb. I'm so sorry."

"I kind of thought that if he saw me when I was better, he'd stick around."

"Did he tell you why he's doing this?" I ask.

He lets out a bitter laugh. "No, but there's a garbage can full of beer bottles that should have given us a clue. I missed him so much that I forgot how he always stayed out drinking with his friends. He wasn't around that much before I got sick. And now he acts like I'll go back to being the same guy I was before. Like none of this ever happened and we can be buddies. He doesn't know anything about me. He doesn't know who I am now. I don't think he wants to."

"Maybe he will," I say.

"You of all people know that's probably not going to happen."

At the clinic, the moment Caleb woke from an infusion, he was confused, asking where he was, looking tired and hopeful, almost smiling. A nanosecond of amnesia. Then, in a flash, he'd touch his arm, the puncture mark left from the IV, and run his hand over his head.

When it comes to my mother, I never have a moment of relief, not a fraction of a second. I suspect it will be the same for Caleb. There's something inescapable about abandonment, an ever-present feeling of dread, an edge. I want to take his hand, to walk side by side in our grief, but there's something else about being unwanted: It leaves you feeling completely alone.

My eyes rest on a stray photo, unframed, from Marie's first day of kindergarten, serving as a bookmark in a cookbook. Mom, smiling down, holds Marie's hand. I barely see her eyes, but her smile, wide and proud, dominates the picture. I shove it into my pocket, hiding her face. "So what now?"

"You know my mom. She's all business. She rented a U-Haul and we're leaving as soon as it's loaded."

"You're coming back."

"Yeah, this week."

As I walk across the kitchen, the telephone cord stretches into taut coils. I pull out a chair. My hands relax, spreading open on the kitchen table like jellyfish. He's coming back. "I didn't know if that was going to happen."

"I promised you I would. Hang on." I hear voices and a door open and close. "My mom just came home with boxes. I'll call and let you know what day we're getting there, okay? I have to go. Miss you."

The same sheets cover my bed, and as I bury my face into the blankets, I catch the faintest scent of him. My hand reaches for his Space Needle shirt tucked under my pillow, and I pull it over my head, feeling buoyed enough to finish my piece.

I haven't written much, but more than I remember as I copy the notes onto a fresh sheet of music paper. Unlike with the Stravinsky, my fingers don't struggle with the keys. My makeshift exorcism allows me to remember Mom on my own terms, as she really is. Not the woman in the photos, but the woman who prefers a hospital gown to a party dress. I think back to the day I met Caleb, before seeing him in the courtyard. I had walked up the stairs, delivering Mom to Lupe, who dressed her in a gown and helped her into bed. Mom had smiled as she extended her arm, offering her vein like a gift. The needle went in smooth and quick.

After running through the piece a few more times, I

retrieve the cassette recorder and play for keeps, filling one side of the tape and then the other. Just as I finish, Dad opens the door, home early with Marie.

There was an incident at recess. Scrapes and scabs cover her knees and shins, but she refuses to say what happened.

I kneel down to inspect her wounds, all minor, all clean. "Do you need a Band-Aid?" I ask.

"I'm okay. You should know that I forgive them." She says the same thing about Mom.

"Why don't you change, and I'll see if I can get the blood out of your skirt," I say.

I follow Dad to the living room, where he pulls a piece of paper from his pocket and hands it to me. In slanted cursive, Marie wrote, *Children say that people are hung sometimes for speaking the truth.* A drawing of a girl, wearing a peasant dress, dangling at the gallows.

"It's a quote from Joan of Arc."

"She left one of these notes in every desk. The teacher thinks it sounds threatening. The principal agrees."

"It's just a stupid quote," I say.

"Well, Marie's teacher thinks she needs professional help. She wants her evaluated. She doesn't think she can be in the class and recommended special ed."

I place the note on the table. I should have seen this coming. Marie isn't in any shape to go to school. I can't sit in a classroom. How can she? "They want her tested because of her crazy saint stuff?"

"That's part of it. She made up her own vocabulary list. Religious but hard ones, like 'transubstantiation.' I doubt her teacher could spell them, much less define them. Instead of doing math, Marie drew this."

He hands me another piece of paper, a horrifying drawing of a burning Joan, her melting face.

"They won't let her go back to school, Vanessa. Not until she's evaluated."

"What are we going to do, Dad?"

I'm surprised when he smiles. "My attorney does a lot of work with a family therapist specializing in situations like ours. Mental illness. Dr. Shepherd saw Marie today, and when she looked at the drawings, she suggested Catholic school, given how safe Marie feels at church."

I nod. "They know her there. They won't think she's a freak." I wave the drawing in the air. "They'd probably give her extra credit for this. You'll have to tell them about Mom, though. They need to know why she's acting weird."

"I've already put in the call. You'll like Dr. Shepherd. It will be good for all of us to see her. I'm glad your mother's psychiatrist recommended her."

My eyes remain on Marie's sketch. "Did you see Mom today too?"

"I did."

"I want to know what it's like," I say, thinking of my music, of the vivid memories that infect my brain. "It has to be better than what I picture in my head."

"It's an ordinary hospital. It looks like the hospital we went to for your ankle."

"And Mom?" I ask, raising my eyes to his. "What's she like?"

"More or less the same. She's still foggy from the medication."

"But she hasn't been in a coma for the past two weeks, right? Dad, I want to know. I need to know because she's all I think about. Please tell me."

He leans back in the chair and looks at everything in the room but me. "What did you do with the photos?"

"They're in a box. I had to do it."

He gives me a hard stare. "Do you really want to know?"

"I *need* to know."

He looks at the far wall, but for the life of me, I can't remember which picture used to hang there. "It was awful. For the first two days, she screamed for hours. They sedated her, but as soon as it wore off, she started screaming again. She was out of control, scratching herself, pulling her hair until it came out in fistfuls. They've been working on her medication ever since."

I smooth Marie's drawing with my palm. "You said she could get out. That you might need to be more aggressive."

He nods. The lines surrounding his eyes and mouth have deepened, making him look severe. I hadn't noticed and it shocks me. I'm used to him looking softer, open, even if he is half-consumed by work and fighting off his demanding asshole boss.

"Yes, she could. I am doing everything I can."

I want to stop crying, have my tear ducts sealed shut. My chest heaves and I want him to hold me, but when he does, even though it feels good, it just makes me cry harder. I can't find a safe place in the house, a corner of comfort, any place where I can rest and have a break from memories of Mom. Every nook and cranny is tainted by her lies.

"I don't know if I can stay here anymore," I say. "It hurts too much. It's like she's still here."

He leans back so he can look at my face. A memory flashes through my mind. I was six and went through a brief phase of being terrified of water. I couldn't go to the beach without screaming. He took me to the boardwalk, and when I started to panic at the sight of the giant waves, he told me that we weren't going to walk on the sand. We would stay on the concrete. He'd looked at me the same way he does now, telling me a promise that he kept.

We went there every night. Each time, he said we could walk on the sand if I wanted. That's it. He didn't pressure me. He must have planned it, because when they had the sand castle building contest, I wanted to go see them, excitement eclipsing fear. Too absorbed by turrets and moats, I let the water splash over my feet. I barely noticed. When we left, he hugged me.

"You're my brave girl," he said.

We went swimming the next day.

He was right. If I know anything about myself, it's that I have courage.

"I got into the conservatories. I want to go. I don't know what else to do," I say.

He shakes his head. "I'm sorry, honey. You can't. What would your sisters do without you? It will get easier. We'll see the therapist. We're going to go through this together."

After dinner, Dad sits in his study, on the phone, first speaking with the Catholic school, and then to Barb, reviewing rentals from the classifieds. Marie and I watch *The Muppet Show* as Adrienne paws through the box of freshly removed photos. The family room reeks of something sour and I crack a window to let in some air. We both ignore the unwashed dinner dishes. Adrienne raids the junk drawer and covers the floor with concentric circles of organized stacks—felt, glitter, plywood, and ancient copies of *Architectural Digest*. She disassembles the frames, removing the glass from the wood, taking out the pictures.

Adrienne holds up the photos: our trips to Catalina Island and Disneyland, and countless pictures of Mom pregnant or holding a newborn baby girl.

"Stop," I say. "I don't want to see any more."

"Fine." Adrienne is in her art zone. She chooses a photo, one of her with Mom, and glues it to a piece of felt. With a razor blade, she traces the outline of Mom's image. Once the image is free, she glues it to another piece of felt.

I can't watch. It's like surgery. The credits roll across the TV screen. I click it off. "Come on, Marie," I say. "Time for bed."

Adrienne keeps her eyes on her project. "Don't wait up. This is going to take me all night."

Teeth brushed, I pull a book from the shelf to read to Marie. Her arms appear free of ink, a relief. "Did you write anything new on your body?" I ask.

She shakes her head. "My favorite quote is too long. Wait, could you write it on my back? It goes like this: 'One life is all we have and we live it as we believe in living it. But to sacrifice what you are and to live without belief, that is a fate more terrible than dying.' That will fit, right?"

She sweeps her long hair over her shoulder so I can evaluate the length and width of her torso.

"What's this?" I ask, looking at a cropped spot at the base of her neck. I stroke her hair, holding it high like I'm going to pull it into a ponytail. She trimmed off several inches from the back of her head, cut so short that I can see her scalp, but unnoticeable when she wears it down.

"I need help with the rest. I don't want to cut myself."

I rub the nearly bald patch. Her hair is shorter there than Caleb's was when we first met.

"Why did you do this?" I ask.

She hops over to her shelves and removes a new book, a biography of Joan of Arc. She flips through the pages, full of vibrant illustrations, and points to two portraits. They look like one of those before and after makeover articles. In the first picture, Joan looks like an average girl with long hair and a peasant gown. She gazes at the sky with a radiant smile, a sign of her secret pact with the lord. In the other, perched on a white horse and brandishing an impressive sword, she wears a suit of armor. Her long hair now short, a pixie cut like Mia Farrow's in *Rosemary's Baby*. I don't turn the page, wanting to avoid the explicit drawings of the stake—smoke, chains, and flames.

"That's how I want my hair cut. Just like Joan's."

I wrap my arms around her, wondering when her fascination turned to obsession. She rests her head against me, and I smooth her hair to hide her shorn scalp.

"You don't have to cut your hair off to be like her," I say. "You're brave and strong. How about we make some new shirts this weekend? Adrienne can copy that picture." I point to the warrior painting.

"I still want to cut my hair," Marie says. "I need to be like her. I can help Mom if I'm like Joan."

I take a deep breath to ease the shaky feeling that never seems to go away. Dad is right—there's no way I can leave her. "Marie," I whisper. "You can't help Mom. Only doctors can. She's sick, just a different kind of sick."

Marie smiles, an eerie resemblance to the first portrait of Joan. "You're wrong," she says. "I prayed for her not to die and she didn't. She doesn't have cancer."

A chill climbs up my spine and I blink back tears. I won't cry in front of Marie.

"Hey, do you want to have a slumber party?" I ask.

She snaps out of her saint trance and jumps to her feet. "Yes! Yes!"

"Your room or mine?" I ask.

"Definitely yours," she says, giggling, almost like her old self.

I fill my arms with her favorite stuffed animals: a penguin from Sea World, a bear from Yosemite, and a bunny from Easter.

"Grab your pillow, okay?" I ask.

Marie does, and then reaches for her Joan of Arc saint card.

"You won't need that," I say. "You have me."

My body fills with relief when she rests the card against her lamp. She clasps my hand. "Will you make popcorn?"

"Of course. And Ovaltine. Just like we used to."

Before the diagnosis. Before the clinic. Before the saints.

Thirteen

It's six o'clock in the morning when I wake, the first one up. It takes me several minutes to feel my limbs, and when I do, it hurts—not the burning, prickling sensation of numbness, but the simple fact that they are there—and I feel a crushing weight on my chest. I fell asleep thinking about Marie's hacked hair and Caleb's return. With him back, maybe it will be endurable.

I start working on the dishes, quietly dipping them in soapy water, rinsing, and stacking in the drying rack. As I wipe off the counter, I find her note:

Not feeling well.
Sleeping in. Will go to school late.
Lunches made.
Don't wake me up or I'll kick your ass.
Love,
A

Peanut butter and jelly for Marie. Turkey and American cheese for Dad and me. Apples and granola bars. She prepared their picnic. Dad promised to take Marie on a holy outing to Mission San Juan Capistrano, which brought a grin to Marie's face. He hasn't told her about getting kicked out of school, not yet, not until the meeting with the Catholic school later in the afternoon.

I finally coaxed Marie into telling us what happened on the playground. Two girls were spinning on the monkey bars, apparently so fast that Marie worried they'd get hurt: skulls splitting on metal, spinal cords broken on the blacktop. The lord told her that they needed her protection, to keep them safe, so she pulled them to the ground. They taunted her, shoved her down on the blacktop, the asphalt digging into her skin. Marie didn't fight back.

I look at Adrienne's note again. If she skips the meeting with Dr. Whelan, she'll surely get detention or worse. Our family can't take a second school crisis.

At school, I don't see her all day, even at lunch, when I wait at her locker. After the final bell rings, Dr. Whelan, Mrs. Albright, and I sit before the portable tape player ready to listen to my piece. Mrs. Albright is pressuring me to give it a title, but I can't, not yet. Everything that comes to mind is too personal. I can say what Mom did, but it's something else to describe Mom as a person. Not just the lies and betrayal, but all of her. The intersection of memories. Sea

World and the clinic. Laetrile and Christmas cookies.

How can I name that?

Ten minutes pass and Adrienne still isn't here. I hope she hasn't done something stupid, like painted a mural of Zach in a compromising position, covering the wall facing the parking lot. A crazy but plausible stunt.

The second hand travels the circumference of the clock, and Dr. Whelan says, "Okay, let's go ahead and get started."

Mrs. Albright pats my shoulder before reaching to press play. As I listen to the recording, objectively, away from the piano, I realize my intent. I'm not processing what happened—what Mom did. I wrote it for Mom to hear. This is my good-bye, all of the words I want to say to her but can't. Maybe my song can get through to her, "my healing music," as she always called my playing. Mom might understand the meaning of the piece—or not. Six years of clarinet gave her a glimpse into my world, even if she never felt the same pull. Music can't compete with prescriptions and syringes, with exam rooms and doting nurses. Dr. Whelan and Mrs. Albright may be listening with me, but they're secondary. I have an audience of one in mind: my mother. It's a relief that Adrienne didn't hear it.

"I'm proud of you," Mrs. Albright says once the song ends. "You've done well with composition assignments, but you never produced anything like this."

"It helped that I didn't have time to overthink it," I say.

Dr. Whelan smiles. "That's a good point. How can you

express yourself more without 'overthinking,' as you put it?"

"I do in orchestra. I wish I could spend the whole day there." I hope they don't check my attendance and notice my complete avoidance of English class, where they're reading *A Separate Peace*, exploring themes of death, guilt, and grief.

"You could do that if you attended one of the conservatories," Mrs. Albright says.

I glance at the clock, losing faith that Adrienne will show, and listen to them discuss the benefits of my transferring. A moot point after talking to Dad.

"You're sure she's coming?" Dr. Whelan asks.

"I think so," I say.

Mr. Klein walks in as Mrs. Albright says good-bye. He looks nothing like an art teacher. His gray buzz cut is more suited for the ROTC recruiting officers stationed at the top of the concrete stairs in front of the school cafeteria. He wears an industrial apron over his neat slacks and polo shirt. Paintbrushes peek from the apron pocket.

"No Adrienne?" he asks. "She missed class today."

"I'm surprised," Dr. Whelan says. "Did you know that?" she asks me.

"No. She made something. She worked really hard on it. She'll be here."

Please come, Adrienne, please.

"I thought you'd like to see some more of her work." Mr. Klein lifts sheet after sheet of drawings, some in charcoal, others in pencil. "Here's what she made yesterday. She's discovered *Los Dias de Muertos.* Day of the Dead. It's her strongest work yet."

I can't stand to look at Mom in skeleton form, with protruding cheekbones and clavicle, jutting joints as pronounced as the Rocky Mountains, hills and valleys once occupied by muscle and flesh. In the sketch, a crown of bright flowers sits upon her head, and Adrienne's dressed Mom in a frock as festive as a piñata. Three dead babies, helpless skeletons, writhe on the ground. One sketch after another, all bare bones, violence parading as pageantry.

He collects Adrienne's sketches, rolls them closed, and secures the paper with a rubber band. Just like the photos, I can't look at them, at any version of Mom's face.

Adrienne appears in the room—finally. I recognize the glass panes and clipped pictures, which she assembled into a building, model scale, just like Dad's architectural work. Before I get a closer look, her elbow hits a bookshelf and her project crashes to the ground.

I rush to her and see blood dripping from a gash in her left palm. "You're hurt," I say.

"I don't care. I just care about my piece."

Shards of glass scatter across the floor, but the structure is still intact. Adrienne starts to cry. Mr. Klein first helps her up and then, with great care, he lifts the piece and puts it on the desk. Dr. Whelan retrieves a first aid kit and delivers it to Mr. Klein. While he bandages Adrienne's hand, I clear the glass from the floor. Adrienne doesn't stop crying.

I wonder what aches more: Adrienne's wounded hand or the disappointment of the broken project.

"How deep is the cut?" Dr. Whelan asks. "Do you need to go to the emergency room?"

"I don't think so," Adrienne says, her eyes still full of tears.

Mr. Klein nods in agreement. "It isn't deep. The hand bleeds a lot. Like the head."

"I'm sorry I was late. I've been working on this for hours. I didn't sleep. I got the idea from this office," Adrienne says as she points to the orchids. Blood seeps through the bandage.

"You're here. That's what matters," Dr. Whelan says.

Mr. Klein gestures at the piece. "Go on. Continue," Mr. Klein says.

"It's a greenhouse. See?" She runs her index finger over the roof.

So that's what she was doing with the glass. She assembled an A-frame structure with wood and metal, fusing picture frames together. Inside, flowerbeds shaped like coffins cover the floor. Felt flowers lie on the beds, resting like dead bodies rather than plants growing upright. Mom's face blooms on each flower. Marigold petals cover the floor.

"Your mother?" Dr. Whelan asks.

Adrienne nods.

"You look just like her," she says.

"I know."

Half of the glass panes are shattered or cracked, but the

interior is untouched. I didn't see it before, but I like the way it's cracked, like it survived a hurricane, like it's ancient but still standing.

"You did a magnificent job," Mr. Klein says. "Everything is the correct scale. The repetition is powerful. What glue did you use?"

"My dad's wood glue, mostly. Some crazy glue. After everything was stable, I ran a match up and down the sides to make it stick more. See that?" She points to the base of the structure, to the corners where the panes come together. "I melted candle wax over the glue. I like how it looks. It softens the glass too, takes away the sharpness. Makes it safer to handle."

We lean closer to the piece and note the different expressions and poses of Mom. In the far corner, two figures rest in a coffin bed. I squint to see Adrienne, grade-school age, curled against Mom.

I take my eyes away from the piece and look at Adrienne. She looks disheveled and exhausted. Paint and glue dirty her fingernails. A stray marigold petal clings to her hair. She wears the same ripped jeans and wrinkled T-shirt as yesterday. For the moment, there's an absence of anger. Just a bandaged hand and a broken memorial to Mom. Hothouse flowers exposed to the cold.

That afternoon we go to the Catholic school as a family, the three of us and Dad. I expect the classrooms to resemble a chapel with burning candles and biblical-themed stained-glass windows. While it has religious flourishes, portraits of Mary and ornate wooden crosses, the school is as institutional as mine. Smaller rooms, cleaner desks, and fewer students, all looking crisp in their ironed uniforms.

A circle of girls speak in hushed tones. I wander over to find out what they're talking about: a *Little House on the Prairie* episode. They all wear dainty sterling crosses, and one of the girls added a few saint medallions to her necklace. I want to ask if she emulates the saints, if this is some phase only obsessively religious nine-year-olds share.

Our Lady of the Immaculate Conception accepts Marie, along with Dad's generous check. The school principal, Sister Mary Margaret, a woman we recognize from Mass, isn't disturbed by Marie's behavior, not even surprised. Instead, she jots down notes and suggests books that will focus her piety and prayers. We don't go as far as to tell her about Marie's shorn hair, how she thinks her prayers somehow spared Mom's life.

We sit in the principal's small office, the only adornment a picture of the pope.

"What about clothes?" Adrienne asks. "Marie likes to wear these special shirts."

Sister Mary Margaret smiles, yet still manages to look stern. "Yes, I've seen them and they are quite impressive, but you can't wear them here. We have uniforms." She presents Marie with a folded bundle.

Marie accepts the plaid skirt as though it's a gift from the holy spirit. Who knew cheap polyester could be regarded as divine? She smoothes the fabric.

"I have something else for you, Marie," the sister says as she runs her finger along the spines of a full bookcase. "Here."

Butler's *Lives of the Saints*. "I think you'll enjoy this more than any of the other students. I've had that since high school."

"Thank you for loaning it to me. I'll take good care of it."

"It's for you, Marie. Think of it as a 'welcome to school' present."

My heart swells with gratitude for this woman, as nondescript as a Ford sedan, dressed in a simple khaki skirt and white blouse, who just saved my baby sister. A superhero without a cape. That guidance counselor was right. It's an obvious choice, the best one, to send Marie here, a place where she feels safe. She isn't the first to be rescued by myths and invisible friends. As we say good-bye and walk out the office door, Marie looks over her shoulder at the stained-glass windows.

Adrienne and Marie drop Dad and me at the house before setting off to buy knee-highs and Mary Janes—items Adrienne thinks will somehow complete Marie's new school wardrobe. A makeover: less tortured martyr and more studious school girl.

Dad and I sit in his study, a long and pale room the color of the sky on a breezy afternoon. His drafting table faces the window. Stacks of books and files cover the surface. More stacks, some on the floor, blanket the carpet. The piles obscure the framed photos, most of our family with a few scenic shots, the rest architectural. As I glance around, I notice that all of the pictures of Mom—wedding, honeymoon, island vacations—are flipped over, face down, completely hidden from view. But not packed away.

"Will it work for you and Adrienne to drop Marie off and pick her up like usual?" he asks. "We need to get back into a routine."

"You sound like Barb."

"I'm trying to be like Barb."

I'm not prepared for his voice to catch, for his knuckles to turn white, revealing a fresh scar. It's then that I notice the window, the pane cracked like a fault line, the point of impact the size of his fist.

I inspect his hand. "When did you do that?" I ask, searching my mind for a memory of Dad losing it. Not a single one. "What happened?"

He avoids my eyes. "I did it after I told you about your mom. When you were asleep."

I shake my head, too shocked to push him, too worried about what else he's broken, what parts of the house and his body. My father, so gentle he refuses to eat rabbit and lamb, punched his fist through glass.

"Are you okay now?"

"Better." He gives me a weak smile.

I glance at his calendar, spread open on his desk, the week filled with scattered appointments with names I don't recognize. He's due back at work in two weeks. Everything will change then. Maybe we'll be too busy to think about her every second, waking and sleeping. Maybe then my music will be about more than Mom. She is seeping into everything in my life, every molecule.

He follows my gaze and puts his finger on Friday, tomorrow, four o'clock in the afternoon. Dr. Shepherd.

"That's our family counseling appointment."

"I don't know if Adrienne will go," I say.

"Good thing Adrienne isn't the parent. She needs to give it a try. She might feel differently once she sees a counselor."

"She already has. We both have."

He leans back in his chair, waiting for me to continue, his mouth set in a straight line. I tell him about Zach and the crystal pitcher and the posters and Dr. Whelan.

"And you thought it was a good idea to handle this on your own? Your mother was the one who wanted you to take care of everything. Not me. You need to come to me with this. Do you understand?"

"We had to take care of Marie, and I wanted to give Adrienne a chance, you know, to have some time to figure this out. I'm telling you now."

He leans forward, his arms folded on the desk. "Do you see?"

"See what?"

"Sometimes we have to wait, especially when things are difficult and a lot is happening at once. This is why I needed time to tell you about your mom."

I'm not a runner, but it takes everything I have to keep my butt in the chair. I don't share Adrienne's constant fury, like the quiet hum of a wasp's nest. Mine flashes like a comet streaking through the sky, fast, appearing for a fleeting moment before burning out. Now my anger flares so brilliantly it could light up the night. "It's not the same thing. You let us think she was dying!"

"I didn't say it was, but I am hoping it gives you some perspective."

Only one thing will give me some perspective, what was born from my piece, unintentional but necessary. "I want to see her."

"Vanessa, this is not what I meant. You don't need to see her to understand where I'm coming from—"

I lean forward, pleading. "Yes I do."

"It won't help. She can't give you anything. She can barely speak a sentence. I'm not saying this to hide anything from you."

I place my palms on his desk, pressing hard. "Then show me."

"Maybe in a few days. I can take you after school, but I don't want Marie to know. She'll want to come and that would be devastating for her."

"Dad," I say. "I want to go now. Today."

"That's out of the question."

I smack the desk, startling us both. "No, it's not. We can get in the car right now and drive there. You want to help me, right? Then take me. Please, Dad. I need to see her."

He rounds the desk and pulls me into a bear hug, holding me hard like he did when I was little, like he does with Marie. "Let's talk to the therapist first, okay?"

I shake my head. "No, if I don't do it now, then I'll wimp out. I have to do this. Trust me, I know what I'm doing." I don't, though, not with my head; there's just something inside me propelling me forward, something I can't explain.

"You're absolutely sure?"

"Yes," I say, and I feel his embrace tighten protectively. Even when he lets me go, as I follow him to the car, he holds onto my hand.

He pushes open the heavy glass door and approaches the front desk. A stout woman emerges, smiling, saying his name. They talk like old friends. I watch her dark braid sway from side to side as she escorts us down the pistachio-colored hall, around a corner, and into a smaller lobby. The facility is painted in a sherbet palette: orange, strawberry, and pineapple. Colors of false cheer.

We reach a desk enclosed in safety glass. She rings the buzzer, waves at the nurse behind the glass. "Babcock," she says. Before she leaves, she turns to Dad and says casually, "See you tomorrow. Take care."

The nurse signals to a security guard and waves us through. I hear another buzz, and the guard opens the metal door and walks us into another room, small, white, windowless. Gone are the ice-cream colors. I'm reminded of the guards at the border crossing, the way they're both hyperaware and disinterested at the same time. I look around the room, bare as a prison cell. I imagined nurses and monitored walks through a garden, hedges masking fences. I know it is a psych hospital, but I hadn't pictured security guards and buzzing locks.

I would take a seat, but the room is empty. I turn to Dad with fear on my face.

"This is worse than I imagined," I say.

He steps toward me and wraps his arm around my shoulders. "I know."

Someone buzzes open the door and there is Mom, walking with a man wearing blue scrubs. She wears a bathrobe and pajamas I don't recognize. Someone cut her hair to her chin, and it looks nice. It frames her face. She gained back some weight. Not a ton, but enough to make her look human instead of like one of Adrienne's Day of the Dead portraits. It takes me a minute to notice her drooping eyelids, her open mouth. She shuffles forward. "Sweetheart," she slurs.

"What's wrong with her?" I ask.

The man, a nurse or an orderly, I can't tell, says, "They're still working on her meds. She comes and goes. I'll be right outside. Shout if you need anything."

The room feels ice cold. I flash back to pills, injections, and infusions. A prescription-fueled nightmare.

She says a garbled sentence twice before I understand her words. She speaks without enunciating. "I miss you," she says. She seems too tired to stand. She reaches out to hug me, and my first instinct is to step back before forcing myself to stop and greet her. I don't know if I'll see her again, if I can survive another encounter. This is good-bye, and I root myself in the moment.

She smells of rubbing alcohol and orange juice. She breathes through her mouth. Mom doesn't move, and after a few moments, I worry that she fell asleep, but then she says my name. Nothing else, just my name.

Mom can't explain herself. She doesn't have answers. This loss feels completely, univocally true. I start to cry, and then, almost immediately, try to stop. I'm there with a purpose: my music, my only language.

I lower myself to the floor, cradling the cassette player in my hands. "I want you to hear something, Mom. Can you listen?"

"Vanessa," she says again.

I pat the floor. "Sit."

Dad helps her down and they sit across from me, side by side, and stare at the tape player like it's from another world, evidence of extraterrestrial life. I press play.

Mom leans forward, and I think of Mrs. Albright's story about Beethoven, how he rested on the floor, next to his maimed piano, to absorb the vibrations. Anything to experience the music. I tell myself that Mom is doing the same, but she looks away and jiggles her leg. She strokes Dad's face.

He doesn't flinch. He doesn't move away. Tears stream down his cheeks as he meets my eyes. He understands the piece.

I was wrong—it is impossible to say good-bye in any language, words or music. She is out of reach, fingering a loose thread on her bathrobe, oblivious to any sound except for what is in her head. We will be here forever, suspended in this state of half truths and grief. We'll never know why she did this, or how we let her, all of us her witnesses. All of us her casualties.

Dad and I startle when she slaps the stop button. "I need to rest. I have chest pains. I need to see my doctor. I need to take something for this pain."

"But there is nothing you can take, Iris. You need to live with it."

"That's not what my doctor says. She says I shouldn't be in pain—"

The air leaves the room. I try to breathe, in through the nose, out through the mouth. Nothing's changed, but everything has. "I need to leave," I say, knocking on the door. "Dad, please. Now!"

The man opens the door. I turn to Mom, who stands in the middle of the room, and I see a flicker of recognition. She is just below the surface. I have months of practice seeing her like this, almost visible through the fog of drugs. We're back in her bedroom after an infusion. Peonies blooming on the nightstand. Mom struggling to get comfortable. Me feeding her pills.

Wait for me.

Scoot.

Before I can stop myself, I throw my arms around her, letting go as fast as possible. Catch and release.

"Bye, Mom."

She calls my name, several times, but I don't look back. Dad follows right behind.

I understand why Dad punched the window. I want to hurl the cassette player through the windshield, anything physical to mimic the shattering feeling inside me. To drown it out.

He unlocks the passenger door and I climb inside the car.

"You go every day?" I ask.

He nods. "For now."

"God, Dad. You still love her."

He takes me by both shoulders. "You do too. That music, Vanessa. It's extraordinary. I'll always love her, but that doesn't change or excuse what she did. She's safe here, and you and your sisters are safe from her. That is what really matters."

"You're torturing yourself by going. I can't go back. Ever. Why do you bother? She's not even Mom anymore."

He sighs. "The woman I married—the woman who had

you and your sisters—is somewhere inside her. That's why I go back. I want to see that woman again, but I'm beginning to think that will never happen." He rests his head against the steering wheel. "I didn't want you to see her like this. This is better than her screaming, though. I'm glad you didn't see that."

"I didn't understand, Dad. I really didn't."

"I know, and I didn't want to expose you to this."

I slap the tears from my cheeks. I wish I didn't have to live with the memory of today. There isn't any peace in this.

"It's not going to get easier," I say. "We'll always know she's here. I wish she was far away. I don't want her to be so close. I want to study music, Dad. I want to transfer. Please let me go. It's the only way I can get away from her."

He doesn't lie to me. He doesn't try to make me feel better by saying she'll improve. He looks me square in the eye and says, "This will never be easy, no matter where you are."

When Dad pulls me close, I finally feel a sense of relief, however slight. It's just like the moments when we saw the hummingbird and the harvest moon, only visible to the two of us. We need to protect Adrienne and Marie. This is something I never want to share with them, something I never want them to see.

Something else shifts inside me. I will transfer. No matter what, I will go. If I don't allow myself to play—really play—then I won't get through this. I need my family, I need Caleb, but I need music more. Mom can't be my future.

We drive toward the freeway. I turn on the radio. "Something" by the Beatles. My head fills with the song and Mom's voice singing along, so clear, like it's the only music I ever heard.

Fourteen

We strike a deal, Marie and me, that she'll leave her hair intact if we make a month's worth of saint shirts, one a night until we fill her drawers. We skim Sister Mary Margaret's gift, *Lives of the Saints*, a thick volume with few illustrations. Even though Marie dismisses the male saints, as well as females over the age of twenty-five, she has dozens of new discoveries. A bizarre sorority of virgin martyrs.

Joan still reigns supreme, but Ursula, the patron saint of school girls, catches Marie's interest. Adrienne, who agrees to illustrate the T-shirts, scans Ursula's descriptions, arching an eyebrow as she reads.

"I totally approve," Adrienne says. "She's badass. In order to avoid marrying some king, she took her ladies in waiting on a pilgrimage. She said she had to have ten girls come as companions, but each girl had to bring one thousand virgin maids with her. Eleven thousand girls went off in boats, but then some assholes killed them. Vanessa, with

Caleb coming back, I doubt you'd be eligible for the virgin voyage. Lucky you."

I toss Marie's first communion book at Adrienne, who dodges it like she's the soccer player in the family. I almost envy Marie, so clearly destined for the cloisters.

We spread out on the floor, carpet instead of beach towels, lamps instead of Mexican sunshine, and huddle close. Adrienne puts on a Blondie album, her new favorite, and sings along with Debbie Harry as she sketches the boats sailing across the sea, small dots in the waves, a Milky Way of vessels. Despite Marie's pleas, Adrienne refuses to draw saints in their final moments of torture and death. Marie picks Saint Agnes next, kneeling in prayer with steepled hands and a wry smile. The patron saint of chastity, yet Adrienne somehow makes her look slutty.

"It's crazy, but I miss the clinic," Adrienne says. "Not Mom's crazy fucking bullshit, but, you know, how we were together."

I wince at her words. After seeing Mom, I obsess about the details all over again, dwelling on Lupe. Still, I can parcel out my memories: Mom and Munchausen's, and then, separately, the courtyard and the ocean. I miss Roberto bringing us meals. I miss seeing Marie smile so freely, kicking the soccer ball with Roberto's sons. I doubt he knew about Mom. If he did, I believe he would have done something. Roberto is a father. He looked out for us—and I'm certain no one paid him extra to be a decent human being.

"I don't miss it. I missed Dad too much when we were there," Marie says without looking up from her book. "Now I miss Mom."

Every time I open my mouth to tell Adrienne about Mom or the conservatories, something stops me. Maybe it's the way she funnels her energy into art, with a pen or colored pencil tucked behind her ear. Or how she strokes Marie's hair, teasing the cropped strands at the base of her neck. Strong when occupied. But when she's alone, staring into the open fridge, her eyes narrowed in concentration, she looks young like Marie. Like she can't handle anything else, especially the reality of Mom in the psych hospital.

We make a list of the names, twenty-two saints in all, of the canonized girls. By bedtime, Marie commits their fates to memory. A holy savant. If she didn't seem so at peace, if she asked for Mom, I would be worried. But she doesn't. Wearing her new plaid uniform, she hums "Goodbye Yellow Brick Road" by Elton John, complete with dance moves. Adrienne puts on the record and they sing in unison, twirling around the room, giddy and dizzy.

Still, we don't take any chances. Adrienne collects all of the scissors and stashes them with her art supplies.

I remember Sister Mary Margaret's words: Marie needs structure and guidance. She will provide that at school and in the sanctuary. We're charged to provide that at home, with the help of Felicity, Perpetua, Justina, Solina, and the other girls who suffered the sword or the stake.

The final bell rings and I meet Adrienne at the car. I watch as she walks out the double doors. Last night, she chopped off her long denim skirt so it stops above her knees, such a different style than her ankle-length flowing gypsy skirts and scarves. She took a break from Marie's saints to adorn her own T-shirt with a portrait of Debbie Harry, who is eclipsing Stevie Nicks as her fashion icon. The heavy black eyeliner suits Adrienne.

Jeff, a painter, compact and muscular like a wrestler, calls her name. He's the one who introduced her to Blondie. She turns around and holds out her hand. He grabs it and laughs at something she says. He has the same easy smile as Zach, but intense eyes, observant, with the power to notice the smallest details in a painting, analyzing color and composition. In a black leather jacket, he seems tougher, like he can handle Adrienne's barbs. Not someone she can eviscerate with a phrase. He looks like he is falling in love on the spot.

She refuses to speak to Zach—and all of her old friends—trading them in for the art crowd. Both the ones who sneak cigarettes by the art classrooms, and also the serious museum-visiting ones who speak breathlessly of Rodin and Pollack and O'Keefe.

"Are you going to go out with him?" I ask, gesturing at Jeff as he unlocks an ancient Fiat.

"Probably," she says. "He's supertalented. He knows about Mom but hasn't made a big deal about it. Plus, look at him. He's gorgeous."

I wonder if he heard his name, because he turns and gives her a final wave.

When we arrive to pick up Marie, she stands off to the side, alone, fingering her rosary.

"How was your first day?" I ask.

"Okay," she says.

I inventory her limbs, not finding any hints of ink.

"You sure?" Adrienne asks, eyeing Marie in the rearview mirror.

"Stephanie is having a birthday party. All the other girls are going."

I turn around and smile. "That will change when you get to know them. Do you want to get a treat? We can go to Dairy Queen."

"Good plan," Adrienne says as she does a quick U-turn, setting off a chorus of blaring horns.

We drive along the beach, and it's hard not to think of crossing the border, of heading down to Ensenada. A breeze stirs the air. The hair around my face swirls and I absorb everything I love about the drive: the golden quality of light, blue jays and seagulls rivaling for food, and the scent of jasmine mixed with honeysuckle. Salt water. The wheels on the road. The destination doesn't matter. As long as I'm in motion. As long as I'm moving forward, away from the pain, away from the grief.

Cars flood the drive-thru. I point to a couple of empty picnic tables. "Let's sit outside."

With soft serve in hand, Marie perks right up. We choose the only table in the shade. I watch her eat, smiling, because even though this is hard, Marie is in a better school. I spare her the news that I saw Mom. It has to stay that way. All day, I couldn't stop thinking about those first few days without her. Back when I thought we were losing her forever, when I thought I wasn't going to be with her in her last moments, all I wanted was to see her. To talk to her. To say good-bye. I close my eyes and remember the taxi, the hospice, the feeling that my entire world had blown to bits. Then the reality of her in the mental hospital, shuffling like a zombie, but somewhere, deep inside, a glimmer of her true self—whoever that is.

There's no question that I need to transfer. The only question is which conservatory to choose. I can't be free while living in the house. Now that Marie is under the care of Sister Mary Margaret and Adrienne has found her new posse, they'll be okay. Fine, even. Dad will do everything for them, something I now understand deep inside. And he has to do this for me—let me go. He'll fight me, but I will win. I have to.

I push aside my malt, too nervous to take a sip.

I expected Adrienne to explode, but after I finish telling them about both schools, what I like about each one, she stares at her sundae, at the cherry sinking into the ice cream, with her mouth set in a grim line.

"I can't imagine you not playing, but I can't imagine you

gone," she says. "I wish you weren't so damn good. Then we wouldn't have to deal with this."

Marie wipes a smudge of chocolate from her chin. "You can go, but you have to come home whenever you can, because I can't lose you and Mom."

"Hey," I say, and poke her arm. "It's not like Mom at all. You're not losing me. I'll come home all the time."

Marie takes a bite of her cone, quickly catching the melting ice cream, staring at me, not saying a word. She used to eyeball Mom in the same way, like she was divining her fate. I peek under her sleeve, looking for more signs of markers and quotes. Nothing.

"What?" I ask.

"You're like Saint Bridget. It's kind of like going off to a convent. Just come home." She gives me a serious look. "Promise."

"I promise," I say.

My attention shifts to Adrienne, who shakes her head. "I think you should wait and go next year. It's pretty shitty timing if you think about it."

My chest tightens with urgency. Adrienne narrows her eyes. I can't wait—not even for Adrienne. I can't spend the rest of the year sitting through classes, especially English, where Jasmine stares at me with pity. I can't bear to spend every day in the house, dwelling on Mom's lies, analyzing every detail. I can't play at home, not like I need to, not like I do at school. Composing the song was an anomaly. It worked because Mom—not Liszt—was the focus.

"I'm sorry." I'm leapfrogging birth order, jumping ahead, leaving before my time. I know I'm asking for a lot—probably too much. "I don't know how to stay. I need to transfer this year. Now."

I can't read her expression, something between a smirk and a frown. "I can't believe you didn't tell me earlier, and now you want to bail."

She's right. I should have. But Dad is right too. I can't defend myself to Adrienne, because in order to do so, I'd have to tell her about visiting Mom—something I won't do. I'll never inflict that experience on my sisters, and if that means keeping a secret, I'll keep it.

She turns to Marie, who pops the remainder of her cone into her mouth. Adrienne brushes Marie's hair off her shoulders. There isn't a way to put it back without revealing the inches of cropped hair.

"Are you ready to go?" she asks without looking at me, only focusing on Marie. Like I'm already gone.

Dr. Suzanne Shepherd directs us to sit in a circle. She's an older woman, dark haired, elegant. I think this is how Mom would have looked when she approached her sixties. Well dressed, graceful, and a little formal, a little stiff.

Not now, though. Not ever.

I take the chair next to Adrienne, even though she refuses to look at me. She hasn't said a word, not driving back home, or riding with Dad to the therapy appointment. I spent years watching Adrienne's friends rotate in and out of favor, as she banished someone for sharing secrets or kissing someone else's boyfriend. Even now, with her new crowd, anyone can see that she's in charge. I just never thought I'd be on the outside.

"Tell me a little about yourselves," Dr. Shepherd says, pen and notepad ready. She gives encouraging nods, and, in Marie's case, a familiar smile as she jots down our hobbies and favorite school subjects, benign and boring questions leading up to a bombshell. I don't want to be here, but this woman saved Marie.

"Most families of Munchausen's patients suspected something was wrong. I want to hear from each of you, how long did you know?"

She doesn't ask us *if* we knew.

"I didn't know," Dad says. He looks at the three of us. "We've discussed this."

She puts down her pen. "Please know that I'm not accusing you of anything. I'm not saying you're complicit in any way. However, it will help all of you if you have a better understanding of how your mother's illness manifested. I'm not suggesting that you were helping her with her deceit, but identifying instances when you felt unease can be helpful."

"I felt that way every fucking day," Adrienne says. "What do you want us to say?" She turns to Dad. "This is bullshit.

I don't know why you won't let me meet with Dr. Whelan instead of coming here."

Dr. Shepherd looks over her reading glasses. "Adrienne, let's start with your father. Peter, when did you become uncomfortable with your wife's illness?"

"I was never comfortable with her being ill."

"How closely did you monitor her treatment?"

He inhales and holds his breath a moment before releasing it from his lungs. "Not closely enough."

"Until now?"

"Until a few weeks ago."

She asks him what changed, and he details Barb's suspicions, my injury, and the emergency room visit. "So," she says, "you first suspected something when Vanessa hurt her ankle."

"Yes," he says, and I wish I'd chosen the empty seat next to his. "It's true that I knew something was wrong—I just didn't know it was this. Our friend was suspicious, but even she didn't see Iris's duplicity. We thought she might be minimizing or exaggerating symptoms. Nothing like what was really happening."

"If I may." Dr. Shepherd pauses. "This is an extremely difficult situation, but I am curious why you allowed her to continue with Laetrile if she said it was hopeless. Why did you let her keep going? Why did you let her take your daughters down there?"

We all watch Dad, especially Adrienne, who assumes the posture of a cobra.

Dad hangs his head and I strain to hear him. "She said that it could give her more time. She was desperate about it. I didn't know how to say no to her."

"That's exactly right," Dr. Shepherd says. "Iris assumed all of the power. Do you all see that? Even if you suspected something was wrong, your mother was in control of the situation. Not you. This could have gone on indefinitely, but you stopped it."

"I think I could have done something," Marie says.

Adrienne scoots her chair closer to Marie's. "Don't be crazy. You couldn't have done anything. It was all Mom's fault. That bitch Lupe, too."

Marie shakes her head. "I saw Mom do things at the clinic. She would boss Lupe around and tell her how much medicine to give her. Lupe would say that it wasn't right, but Mom took the medicine anyway. She made Lupe hand her the shot and then Mom injected it herself. Even though they talked in Spanish, I knew Mom was lying about something. She made Lupe cry, especially when Lupe took my blood. That's why I don't think Lupe meant to hurt us. I forgive her."

No one says a word, not Adrienne, not Dad. When Marie meets my eyes, I remember the night of the storm, of the dining room filled with tea lights, and Marie's plain words: *You're going to die.* She looked at Mom in a similar way, almost a challenge, or a plea: *Tell me I'm wrong.*

Dad makes eye contact with Dr. Shepherd. His face is paler than Mom's was at her sickest.

"Marie, honey," he says. "Lupe drew your blood?"

Marie nods. She stares at her lap as though she is in trouble. Dad speaks gently, as reassuring as possible.

"That's why I knew that Lupe didn't want to hurt us. She cried a lot, but Mom screamed at her and forced her to do it. Mom just wanted to make sure that I don't have cancer."

Marie meets my eyes. "She did it to you too, didn't she? Mom said you were next."

It's as though the air in the room freezes. Goose bumps cover my skin, and my lungs feel frostbitten. Cold sweat runs down my back. I'm drowning in arctic water. It takes a minute before I can breathe or speak. Finally, I choke out, "No, she didn't."

I poke at the inside of my arm, at the shadow of veins beneath the skin. When I meet Dad's eyes, I understand that everything is different. Mom hurt Marie. Who knows what else she would have done if she'd had the opportunity?

"That means I knew, doesn't it?" Marie pulls her rosary—the one she made from the kit, the one lacking the mourning beads—from her pocket and fingers the beads.

Adrienne covers Marie's hand with her own. "That doesn't mean you understood what Mom was doing."

"Adrienne's right," Dr. Shepherd says in the kind of voice one would use when talking to an injured animal.

We could make a list, the four of us, Caleb and Barb, too, itemizing the small inconsistencies, the elements that felt strange, just a little off. Maybe then, looking at everything at once, compiled, we might have guessed. Marie couldn't have known what she saw—it's too inconceivable, too much to accept.

"Does this mean I helped her?" Marie asks. She tucks her feet under her body, curling up, looking half her nine years.

I shake my head, but it's Dr. Shepherd who speaks. "No. It means that the situation was too complicated to understand. Like Adrienne said, your mother is responsible."

Marie shifts her gaze to Adrienne.

"Why didn't you say anything?" Adrienne whispers.

I reach for Adrienne's other hand, but she yanks it away.

Marie slides off her chair and stands before Adrienne, tall, emulating Joan. "I didn't know what to do, and then I didn't want you to be mad at me."

"Girls," Dad says, ready to intervene if Adrienne loses it. But she doesn't. She scoops up Marie and holds her close. I want to share the same chair, at least move closer, but Adrienne won't even look at me.

Dr. Shepherd starts to explain the complexities of Munchausen's, deconstructing Mom's tactics, pathologizing her every move. My concentration remains on my sisters, but with each second that Adrienne refuses to look at me, I feel more disconnected. It's as though I don't share their grief. Maybe I don't, not the same brand anyway, considering I spent yesterday afternoon with Mom. Marie burrows her face into Adrienne's shoulder, and I look away.

Her words take their time reaching my ears. I look

out the window, at the sun dipping into the ocean, at the lapis-colored waves, until I hear my name. Everyone is looking at me. Even Adrienne. I don't know what they said or how long they've been talking.

"Vanessa," Dr. Shepherd repeats. "If you could have anything from your mother, what would that be?"

I don't hesitate. "I want her to disappear."

It's her or me.

Fifteen

In the beginning of the summer, back when they moved in, Dad presented Barb with a key. A new one fresh from the hardware store, the metal shiny and unblemished. But when they arrive, they ring the bell. Visitors now. Dinner guests. Nothing more.

Barb folds me in her sturdy arms. "Vanessa, I'm so glad to see you."

I hold on tight, overwhelmed by how much I missed her. I won't let Barb pull away, too gripped by my sudden neediness. She understands and squeezes tighter, cooing "dear one" until I can stand on my own.

"Sorry," I say.

"What on Earth for?" She gently pats my shoulder.

I feel like a scavenger, a young raccoon, rummaging for scraps of motherly affection. She steps inside and he fills the door. I waited so long that I began to forget the small details of his body. Has he always had so many freckles?

His forearms look almost tan. Curls sprout from his scalp.

"Hey," he says.

"Hey," I say back.

I pull him inside and feel that familiar rush when Caleb takes my arm. First, our hands touch, then our entire arms, shoulders, legs. This is the closest two people can get while standing side by side. Our legs should be bound together for a three-legged race.

"Caleb!" Marie yells. "We made something for you!"

Adrienne and Marie spent the morning in Adrienne's room. While the door remained open, I wasn't invited in, not even when I walked past, slowly, peering inside as they continued the assembly line of saint shirts.

At the sound of Caleb's voice, Marie bounds to the door, clasping a shirt in one hand and her saint book, fatter than a dictionary, in the other. "We made you a present!" She wears a proud grin as she holds up the shirt, adorned with a drawing of a teenage boy sporting a bowl haircut. He stands at the forefront of dozens of others. "In 1570, a bunch of Portuguese missionary boys fought off a band of pirates. San Juan was the only one who survived. You would totally fight pirates."

Adrienne emerges and drapes her arm over Marie's shoulder as though our little sister belongs only to her. "Welcome back, Cancer Boy. Hope it fits."

Marie leans into Adrienne, and I want to pry them apart like an oyster shell.

Caleb pulls the shirt over his head. "It's perfect. Thanks."

"We'll leave you to your make-out session," Adrienne says as she leads Marie back to her room. "Let's go finish Saint Agnes."

Familiar sounds of clanking pots and the whir of the blender come from the kitchen.

"My mom's making her own bread now. She's really into flax seed. Consider yourself warned. She's talking about becoming a nutritionist."

Barb could serve me cardboard and gravel—I'm that happy to have her back. "I thought maybe we could go for a ride? Since there's a full house," I say.

He follows me into my room, stopping as soon as he steps inside. "It looks so empty."

Except for the Kerouac, my bedside table remains cleared. It's not like I do anything but orchestra. Unlike the chaos of the rest of the house, the public space, I keep my room monastic neat. Purging Mom freed it of clutter.

"Here." I hand him the Kerouac.

"You had it?"

"You left it at the hotel. I went looking for you and the manager guy gave it to me."

He sits down on my bed and flips through the pages.

"Don't sit there," I say. "Let's get out of the house."

A flicker of hurt crosses his face, darkened eyes and a frown. "I never wanted you to read this. I'm sorry."

"It's not that," I say, meaning it. I found the book just

hours before Dad told me, and I can't separate the two. They speak the same truth, oral and written testimony, and I don't blame Caleb for recording it. I have too, now that I wrote the piano piece, now that I played it for Mom. If I learned anything, it's that we all are keepers of our own stories. Some too dangerous or too sacred to share in entirety or in fragments.

"I just hate being in the house, even with you," I say. "I want to go outside."

He drops the book onto my quilt. "Is it okay if I leave it here?"

I consider myself the book's rightful owner. He may have written the words on the newsprint-thin pages, but the revelation is about my mother. He's a witness—nothing more. "Yeah, that's fine," I say.

I pick up the board and accept his hand.

Stray bougainvillea flowers blow along the sidewalk, crepe paper petals dotting the concrete like breadcrumbs. We follow them down the driveway. I surprise him by taking the lead, by steering and braking, by showing him that I can own the board. I have more control than before, more confidence navigating the seams in the sidewalk, the rogue tree roots that bulge through the concrete.

"You're going fast," he says. "Careful. It's different riding with two people." He grabs my hips and my body responds like he never left. I need to concentrate on the curves of the road, not the way my muscles tighten. I pump my leg harder.

I want to soar off a cliff and glide through the clouds. I want to put distance between me and the house. I want to join the gulls in the sky.

He lowers his foot and drags his sneaker until we come to a halt. "You're going to make us wipe out, speed racer."

"Sorry," I say, sitting down on the curb. "I can't shake it. It's like she's still in the house. I don't know how to explain it."

I want to be plain happy to see him, not muddled with my feelings about Mom, not so wrecked. It isn't as bad as the phone calls, when everything felt intertwined. Now, Caleb is Caleb and Mom is Mom, and the painful absence of one isn't the same as the other. He stares down at me and I feel loved, belly-deep, and I wish it wasn't polluted by what happened at the clinic. I wish we met at school, where I would have admired him in class, sneaking glances at his profile. I want him to distract me from studies. I want him to eclipse everything else. No chance of that. We'll never have the luxury of being ordinary.

"You don't have to," he says. "I spent the week putting my dad's stuff into trash bags. We filled the whole garage. He wouldn't even help us load the U-Haul. When we were driving down the coast, I kept thinking about how even though it was really hard seeing him, I know where I stand now. He's not going to suddenly be a different person and show up tomorrow and act like he actually gives a shit. I kept thinking that there was a chance that things were going to change. But that's a bunch of crap. It sucks, but at least I know that now. There's something good about knowing. I'm not saying it's the same thing with you and your mom. I guess what I'm trying to say is that I know what it's like to feel like garbage."

"You're right. I saw her in the hospital—the mental one—and it is better knowing. It doesn't make it hurt less, though."

He looks at me like he did that first time we walked on the beach, when I recognized that he understood, that he totally got it. He lowers himself onto the curb and moves the board back and forth with his foot. "You make it hurt less."

I reach for his hand, and unlike Adrienne, unlike Mom, he holds on. Something has cracked inside me, something small and delicate and essential. I know I'm capable of repairing it on my own, but there's something devastating about being unloved, the most unique kind of pain. Mom volunteered for death, abandoned us with such brutal ease, like we're nothing, like medicine matters more than her kids. Like we're a nuisance.

She made a choice, conscious or not, to *not* love us. Not enough, anyway. Not in a way that is real and true.

I know she is wrong. I know I'm worthy, as is Adrienne, as is Marie, as is Dad. We deserve to be loved. In the haze of crazy lies, I don't doubt that.

And here is this boy, who acts like he spent his life with a map and I'm the buried treasure.

"You make it hurt less, too." I rest my head on his shoulder and he traces the indentation of my spine with his fingers, hopping over vertebrae like a car on speed bumps. I need him on a cellular level. When he kisses me, I swallow my grief. I speak with my body, the only language I truly understand.

He leans back so he can see my full face. "I'm never leaving you again. I swear."

A battered VW bus whizzes past, and I watch as it grows small in the distance. We are a couple of blocks from Mrs. Albright's house.

"I got into two of the conservatories," I say. "They need to know my decision by next week. I'm going."

He runs his hand through his short hair. "You know what Kerouac wrote," he says with a half smile.

"I don't have a clue what Kerouac wrote beyond what *you* wrote in your book."

"It's from *On the Road*. 'Nothing behind me. Everything ahead of me.'"

"Everything is behind me," I say. "Everything."

He inches closer and slips his hand around my waist, pressing his palm against the small of my back. The idea of restricting our time to the academic calendar, to only seeing each other on holidays, makes my stomach clench. We already lived in segments, time organized by Laetrile cycles and clinic trips. To recovering from infusions and seizing sudden bursts of energy. I rest my head on his shoulder, comforted by the knowledge that we can be together no matter what the circumstances. School isn't the clinic.

We don't have doctors and needles keeping us apart.

"So, your dad's okay with you going?"

Dad made it clear in so many words: *No. Sorry. You can't go. What would your sisters do without you?*

I stare at the asphalt, at the freshly painted yellow line in the middle of the street. "He told me I couldn't transfer, but I know he won't stop me. I just have to convince him," I say.

"How about Adrienne?" he asks.

I laugh. "I think she wants to kill me in my sleep."

"So that's why she's so icy. I thought it was me.

"Which ones did you get into? The San Francisco one?" he asks. "Kerouac used to live in San Francisco. I'll go with you. Remember, I turn eighteen next month."

"They didn't accept me. The famous one in LA did. Then there's one in San Clemente."

"We just drove through there and it's not even an hour away. You can come home every weekend. That sounds easy. Do you like it?"

I remember the holiday concert at the San Clemente Conservatory last year, the villa-style building, the bubbling fountain painted in the same hues as peacock feathers. Their orchestra blew me away, playing with fervor, each seat filled with a passionate student. It was on the bus ride home that Mrs. Albright told me I belonged at a conservatory, and when I picture going away, it's their auditorium I imagine, their music.

I nod. "Yeah, it's amazing."

He eliminates the space between us. "Remember what we talked about when I first stayed with you, how you were yourself when you played? That it was pure?"

I almost feel the keys beneath my fingers. "Of course."

"I'm not surprised you got in. I'm really happy for you. My mom promised me a car, a Remission Car. I'll drive you back and forth on weekends. Let's check it out tomorrow. We'll time it."

I kiss his shoulder, the knot of muscle left over from years of playing water polo. A swimmer's shoulder. "I forgot how bossy you are."

"So are we taking a road trip tomorrow? 'Cause you can't ditch me," he says, smiling, trying to get me to do the same. He climbs onto the board and holds out his hand.

"Move forward," I say. "I'm going to lead."

I circle his waist with my arms, holding tight as I steer us home.

Caleb and I follow the coastline north, whipping past the long stretches of sand, and when we approach the crab shack and pier, I look inland, away from the water and into the scattered scrub brush. I don't avert my eyes until the menacing double domes of the nuclear power plant come into view.

Last night, after dinner, we lounged on the couch and watched *The Six Million Dollar Man* and *The Bionic Woman*.

Two hours of mindless comfort with Caleb's hand in mine. We took up half the couch, with Adrienne and Marie claiming the other. Even if Adrienne embodied the Ice Queen, sitting as far away as possible, she occupied the same room without hurling wince-inducing one-liners.

As we drive, I lean against him and hear the steady beat of his heart. Just by listening to the basic functions of his body—his breath filling and leaving his lungs, his heart pumping blood through his veins, and his muscles constricting and contracting with movement—I know I'll push through the grief. I'll never get over it, but for the first time, I have an idea of what my life could be. I only wish that Adrienne could be happy for me despite my act of treason.

Quietly, we cruise up the highway until I spot the buildings nestled high on the hill.

"Fifty-one minutes," he says. "That's nothing."

We can't go inside, not on a Saturday. Dad, with his love of large picture windows, might as well have designed the campus. On the field trip, we were restricted to the orchestra hall, but now as we stroll around the grounds, I pause at the practice rooms, peering through the tinted glass into the closet-size spaces. Perfectly contained. The refuge I've been seeking. I turn around to check out the view of the ocean, something I would see every day.

"Isn't this what you want?" he asks.

I tug his shirt, bringing him closer. "Yes, and you."

"Fifty-one short minutes away. You realize that's half the time it took us to get to the clinic. And we won't have to deal with the border traffic."

Or guards. Or Mom.

"After you get your GED, you should go into real estate." Sound spills from the edge of campus—voices and music. "Must be the dorms," I say, suddenly feeling more like an intruder than a prospective student.

"Come on," Caleb says as he keeps walking. Then, looking back over his shoulder, "Don't you want to see? You don't have to talk to anyone."

Around the corner, a small circle of kids lounge on the lawn. A girl I recognize from music camp strums a guitar. Not someone I hung out with, but a familiar face, even though I can't remember her name. *D* something. Donna or Dorothy or Denise. She doesn't look up; it's a relief that I don't have to explain my presence.

The low two-story building lacks the large picture windows, but it looks comfortable enough. It hits me then—really hits me—how I'd spend nights away from home. I would escape the memories of Mom, but in doing so, I would leave my sisters behind. I would be away from Marie, who climbs into my bed after a nightmare. And Adrienne, who lets me do the same.

A new layer of grief washes over me. This is where I need to be. This school. These buildings. But in leaving, I'll lose them. Not completely. Not like Mom. But it will never be the same again. In letting Mom go, I'm letting them go too. It's the choice I have to make, but it splits me in two. This will be my new home, but now, this minute, I need to go back and be with my sisters. I need to look at them from head to toe, take them in, and know that even though I'll move away, we'll stay connected.

"Come on," I say to Caleb. A nearby kiosk displays brightly colored posters announcing concerts across the state and travel abroad opportunities. Summers in Florence. Semesters in London. He doesn't move, preferring to be a voyeur. "Caleb, I want to go home now."

Confused, he turns around. "But we just got here."

The Suburban hulks in the parking lot, so big it almost takes up two spaces. My eyes move from the car to him. "I've seen enough."

He joins me at the kiosk. "What's going on? Does this mean you don't want to go here? Look at this place."

I close my eyes and collect my thoughts, sort out all of my conflicting feelings, the excitement and the fear. Mostly the guilt. "No—I want to be here, but I don't know how to leave. What if I lose Adrienne by coming?"

He steps closer but stops shy of touching me. "You deserve a place like this, you know, for your music. I want this for you. Adrienne will too. She just can't see it now. I swear I'll be here every Friday to bring you back home."

"I know," I whisper. "But I'm so worried about my sisters."

He pulls me closer, my own private cocoon. "You dad can handle things. Adrienne will come around."

"You can't say that about Adrienne," I say. I take a final look at the campus, picturing myself as a student, sitting alone before the piano, practicing for hours while gazing at the ocean. Alone in so many ways, but maybe that is a necessity, a requirement. My price.

Sixteen

I flatten my feet against the floor in the hope of feeling some sort of foundation. My fingers curl inward, strong fists, and I bang them against my knees. I see the movement but don't feel the pressure on my skin, much less in my muscles. I want to turn everything off: the light, the sound, and the merry-go-round that has become my mind.

I play the message again.

You have a collect call from Buena Vista Hospital. Then, in the background, *Vanessa! Pick up the phone, sweetheart. Vanessa! Vanessa!* Click.

The front door opens and Dad rushes into the kitchen, the color draining from his face.

"Play it again," he says.

As soon as it ends, he walks to the wall and unplugs the machine.

"What are you doing?"

"She tried to contact you," he says, ears and cheeks scarlet.

"This is harassment. Between this and the fact that she took a blood sample from Marie, we might be able to extend her ninety-day commitment. This could be enough. Hopefully for a restraining order, too."

"Dad," I say. "You have to let me transfer. You have to let me go."

"This is about more than music," he says.

I nod. "You said you wanted to protect us. This is how you can protect me. I know she can't get out tomorrow, but she could get out in a couple of months." I can't jump whenever the phone rings, feeling like Mom is reaching for me through the telephone wires, from photos, from memories. He must understand that.

He places the answering machine on the kitchen table. "That's what I'm trying to prevent."

"I know, Dad, but even if you win in court, it's not like she's going to be locked up for years."

He waves to the empty chair across from him. "The lawyer says I have a good chance of keeping her committed until Marie is older. This is Munchausen by proxy now. There are criminal implications." He taps the machine. "This will make a difference. I'm sorry it happened, but it could change everything. She's a danger to herself. We need to prove she's a danger to others."

"She's a danger to me now," I whisper. "You promised you'd do anything for us."

I stare at his hand, at the faint white scar on his knuckle

from punching the window. When I look up, he nods.

"Do you remember when Marie said you were next to have a blood sample?"

"Yeah," I say. "That's not something I'll ever forget."

"I'm telling you this because I don't want to keep it from you, and it's the reason why I'm going to say yes to the conservatory. You've seen her now. You know what she's like. When I first admitted her and she spent days screaming, she was screaming for you. She said that you took care of her. She was fixated on you and Caleb. She said you understood illness. She said that you might have cancer. She tested Marie, but she was focused on you."

We lock eyes. "I worry about your sisters, but with your mother, I worry about you the most. She was attached to you in a way she wasn't attached to your sisters—even Marie. I thought if Caleb came back, things could get back to normal and you'd begin to have a sense of peace. I was wrong."

A combination of sickness and relief washes over me. My stomach seizes and my head clears. For once, Mom spoke the truth. Within the framework of cancer, I thought I knew what she needed: the right pillow, the right pill, the right song, the right food. Clairvoyant in so many ways, yet not in the way it mattered. I refuse to be her medicine now.

Adrienne's room is the opposite of mine, with piles of art supplies covering the floor and sketches of Mom tacked everywhere, chipping Dad's carefully painted walls. She covered the back of her door with a portrait of Mom, drawn on the wood with a Sharpie in the same style as Marie's tees. Bold, simple lines capturing doomed moments of fate.

I shake her awake just as I used to wake Dad.

"What the fuck, Vanessa. Get the hell out of my room."

She flips over and faces the wall, groggy and pissed.

I climb into her bed and rest my head on the edge of the pillow, close enough for her to hear me whisper. "You have to knock it off. I'm not Zach."

She refuses to turn over. "No shit. I'm sleeping, so if you won't leave, at least shut up."

I poke her shoulder with my finger, something Marie would do, hoping she'll remember that I'm her little sister too. "Adrienne, don't do this to me. Please."

She flips over, so angry I see her eyes flash in the dark. "Do this to *you*? *You're* doing this to *me*. You're the one who's bailing. Do you realize that I'm going to have to do all of this on my own? You're lucky that I want to go to college here. What if I really wanted to go to school in New York? Parsons or Pratt or Cooper Union? What the fuck would happen then? Did you even think about that? Fuck you. I'd never do this to you."

Years ago, back when I was terrified of water, back when Adrienne and I functioned more like conjoined twins than opposing soldiers in the Revolutionary War, back before Marie was born, we visited Crater Lake. Beautiful and clear and deadly, with tourists falling into the lake with disturbing frequency. Warning signs peppered the path, and I hung back, clinging to Dad's hand. Mom marveled at the view, at the staggering depth of water, at the clear blue below. Adrienne stood too close to the rim, telling stories about fresh water mermaids, flirting with legends, demonstrating fearlessness at eight years old. The remains of the volcano were no match for her, even then.

"You're an amazing girl, sweetheart," Mom had said to Adrienne. "I bet you could do anything you set your mind to."

Now, Mom's oppressive ghost fills the house. I've been too consumed by my own pain to recognize that I'm reacting to the present and not the future. I worry about my sisters, but in a day-to-day domestic sort of way. I haven't considered the future, however near. I look into Adrienne's eyes, filled with a desperate fury, and realize I'm sentencing her to house arrest.

"I'm sorry." When I hug her, she doesn't pull away like I expect. She feels rigor mortis stiff, but at least she remains right next to me. "You never talked about wanting to go to New York."

"That's because I don't really want to go there. Jeff does. Mr. Klein knows a bunch of people at UC San Diego and he's an alum. He says I'll definitely get in. He's going to show them my portfolio early. That's what I want, but I want you more. I can't believe you want to leave me," she says, her words catching in her throat.

"I don't want to leave you. But I don't know how to be

here anymore. It hurts too much. You draw her all of the time. Marie's walls are covered with pictures of her. How can you look at her? I can't stand it, and I'm not just saying that. I really don't know how to live here now. It's like she's following me around and I can't escape her." I wipe away my tears with the back of my hand. "It's her or me, and now it's me or you. I don't want to hurt you. I won't go if you're going to hate me for it."

"I could never hate you, but I don't know how to do this on my own. You're the only one I can talk to."

I hold her tighter, wishing she would hug me back. "I'll be home every weekend. Caleb said he'd drive me back and forth."

She pulls away and emptiness fills me. "How does Cancer Boy feel about you bailing on him?"

"He understands."

She squeezes her eyes shut, long enough for me to wonder if she's done talking, if she's going to boot me out of her room for the night. I reach for her again, and this time she is the one who wraps her arms around me. "I'm not okay with this," she says. "I won't hate you, but that doesn't mean I'm not really pissed at you. You suck."

"Does that mean I can go?"

She doesn't say yes, but she doesn't let me go, keeping me close for the rest of the night.

Adrienne, Marie, and I wander through Old Town, walking in and out of the shops, searching for a keepsake, something to remind me of home. We go into a little store, as narrow as an airplane, and scan the souvenirs on the shelves. I want something that will remind me of the good things about Mexico. I need a physical object to hold in my hand, to touch, to remind me of what I once had and what I'm leaving behind. Past the maracas and sombreros, I find it. My eyes rest on a tile, a perfect ceramic square, with a dark blue dove painted on a pale blue background. It looks just like the oil painting at the clinic, the one in the downstairs room near the kitchen, the room where we slept when the clinic was full.

I pay for it and watch the woman behind the counter wrap it in tissue. *"Gracias, mija,"* the woman says.

"De nada," I reply.

I return to Adrienne and Marie, who stand in front of a large glass case filled with Day of the Dead figurines, small wooden skeletons dressed in elaborate costumes. Haunting dioramas featuring a bride and groom, a boy riding a bike, even a dog with his cherished bone.

"Find it?" Adrienne asks. Her anger lingers, but more in an annoyed way, huffy and eye-rolling. She's coming to accept that I have to do this. Somehow, the fact that I'm leaving Caleb too—even just for weekdays—makes her feel better. Like it isn't complete abandonment. My penance.

"Look," I say as I unwrap the tile, exposing the bird.

"Let me see," says Marie. I hand it to her and Marie traces the outline of the wings. The image takes us all back to the clinic, to the courtyard, a reminder of how we'll always be together. We buy two more, one for each of our rooms.

Tourists and college students fill the dusty road. A crowd gathers on the expanse of lawn in front of the Mission San Diego de Acala, the bustling center of Old Town.

"Let's check it out," I say. "We have enough time before I have to meet Caleb."

We fight through herds of tourists wearing Sea World T-shirts.

"It's a feast day," Marie says. She starts guessing which saint, rattling off her list. When we reach the center of the festival, we see a banner celebrating the church's patron saint, Saint Didacus.

"Know him?" I ask.

Marie shakes her head. "No, must be one of the boring ones."

Each corner of the lawn features a different mariachi band. We mill through the crowd of families standing on the tree-lined lawn. Among the tall eucalyptuses stand two cherry trees, the only ones losing their leaves. The twin trees are turning for fall, and the remaining leaves are a stunning combination of color, some orange, some gold, some red, and some still green. I notice hints of white and indigo. It looks like the leaves turned into confetti.

"Let's go over there." I nod toward a group of people at a nearby table, right next to the trees, women, men, and children hunched over and writing on thick pieces of ribbon.

"What's this?" I ask the man sitting behind the table.

"For the wishing tree," he says. "Write down a wish and tie it to a branch." He gestures at the pile of satin.

We wait for our turn, and when a vacancy opens up at the table, we reach for our own colorful ribbons.

"Can we show each other our wishes, or will that make them not come true?" Marie asks.

"They'll still come true, right?" Adrienne looks at me.

"Absolutely."

Adrienne writes, *Keep us safe*. I know what she means—safe from Mom. She hands her pen to Marie. "Need help?"

"I've got it," Marie says. "You're not going to like it."

"Impossible," I say. "We'll like anything you wish for."

When she smoothes out the ribbon, I notice her arm, just above the inside of her elbow.

"I thought you weren't going to do this anymore," I say as I inch up her sleeve.

"But I love this one. Saint Lucy said it." *Those whose hearts are pure are the temples of the Holy Spirit.* She shakes off my hand and displays her ribbon: *Try to forgive*.

Adrienne rolls her eyes.

"See, told you that you wouldn't like it."

I try to glimpse what others are writing, strangers asking for everything from a new car to a healthy child. I consider everything I could ask for, but time travel isn't realistic, nor is asking for my past to be rewritten. I could ask for my sisters to be well, for Marie to grow up unscathed. But I know there are limits to desire, that some things can't change. I take a felt-tip pen from the pile and write: *Let us be free.* Adrienne and Marie wrap their arms around me. "Good wish," Adrienne says.

As I tie my ribbon to a slim branch, I wonder if my wish is far-fetched. Maybe it is unobtainable, but it's the one thing I allow myself to request, the only thing I want.

Acknowledgments

My deepest thanks to:

Faye Bender, my brilliant agent and champion, who believed in this story from the beginning and guided me with intelligence and patience. I am forever grateful.

My wise and wonderful editor, Reka Simonsen, whose thoughtful edits made this novel so much stronger. Thank you for understanding the Babcocks with such keen insight. I couldn't have asked for a better partner in bringing them to life. Endless appreciation to the all-star Atheneum and Simon and Schuster team, especially Wendy Sheanin.

I had the tremendous fortune of sharing writing with some amazing writers. In school: my comrade Julie Young-Ordeñana, and my teachers Neeli Cherkovski, Juvenal Acosta, Kim Addonizio, and Edie Meidav. Brenda Tucker and Renee Sedliar, you both are as generous as you are talented. The Kicking Muse gang, who saw the earliest drafts: Frank Dowling, Joe Franklin, Brian Boies, Diana Donovan, Katie

Antheil Boyd, and Caroline Chung-Wipff. I never would have finished this book (and so much more) without my Iowa writing group, our group's name too profane for even Adrienne: Jennifer Wilson, Catherine Knepper, and Kali VanBaale. Friends and writing partners for life. #hairtothechair

My family, the Rongerudes and the Yenters, who supported me with endless cheers and encouragement. My sister, Robyn, this book is for you. And most of all, my daughters, Lulu and Tillie, who are my inspiration and my heart.

A shout-out to the friends who shared the journey: Kelsey Crowe, who as my soul sister and fellow author shared every moment and every step. Pearl Piatt and Glen Price, for their decades of love, humor, and support. Andrea DeLara, whose friendship, wit, and heart know no bounds. Louis Lee, my human guide. Amy Tang, Gabe Jenkins, Stacey Murphy, Reena Krishna, Michelle Kuroda, and Hope Whitney (my fact checker).